BROKEN

ANNA LEGAT

Print ISBN: 978-1-917449-17-5

PART 1

ON A COLLISION COURSE

CAMILLA

My hand curls into a fist, and my long, calcium-enriched nails sink into the soft tissue of my palm. An unseemly thought enters my mind, *Don't you go breaking your nails, Mills. You only had them done last week.* Niggles like that swirl in my head and come to the surface at the most inappropriate moments. Will I be stressing about my nails on my deathbed? I wonder. And I answer myself without hesitation: Yes, I will. If they aren't perfect or, God forbid, the varnish has chipped, I will freak out. Even when I am dying and my whole life is flashing before my eyes at the speed of light, I will find the time to examine my nails.

This is worse than dying and yet I'm worried about my pesky nails.

They plough my skin until they meet with resistance on my fourth finger. It's my wedding band held down by the weight of my 24-carat diamond ring. Now, this is a nail-snapping accident waiting to happen. I don't care. I hook my nail under the ring and tug at it. I turn and twist it, trying to slide it off my finger. Though my skin is clammy and slippery, the ring won't go over my swollen joint. It's stuck. I catch Hugh staring at my hands. A frown tightens his face in disapproval, but he doesn't lift his eyes to meet mine and he doesn't say anything. I dare him to.

I gaze at his wide forehead with the receding hairline and a cluster of liver spots on his temple. The whites of his eyes are matt and yellowed like aged paper. Too much good living, I always tell him, isn't that good for you. Unlike my epicurean spouse, I do know how to rein myself in. Gone are my wild days. These days, I never leave home without my factor 30+ foundation on. I am a committed vegetarian and I drink in moderation. Hugh is a heavy drinker. He is overweight and he smokes. He always tells me, it's only a pipe, Mills; pipe is different. And I say to him, it may be different but not any less harmful than cigarettes. I permit him – under duress – to smoke the damned thing, but only in his study. It's like a gas chamber in there, especially when he is working on a case. Hugh is a criminal barrister. A very good one if his hourly rate is anything to go by. He is sought after. He can pick and choose his cases. He always goes for the high-profile ones, tricky as they may be. This strategy may be risky short-term, but it's a risk worth taking. Each such case bumps up Hugh's value in monetary terms, and when his fees go up so does his prestige. It's a win-win situation even when, infrequently, he loses a case. His job isn't about winning cases, he tells me, it's about making money, like any job.

Christopher has always looked up to his father and taken his teachings to heart. Look where that took him! I cringe at the thought.

This was the one and only case I begged Hugh to take on, but he said he couldn't. 'Not my own son.' He was adamant.

I pleaded.

He gave me that condescending, tight-lipped glare he does

over the top of his glasses when he means to tell people that they are wasting their breath, but that he won't waste his. Still, I insisted. I asked him if there was a law against it, because if there wasn't, he was the best man for the job. He told me not to venture into arguments I couldn't win. The matter was closed. As it happened, his pal James Conroy was available.

'James specialises in white-collar crime and he's the second-best silk that money can buy,' he assured me.

'Who is the first best?' I asked him. Only the best would do, we both knew that.

'That'd be me.' Hugh grimaced like it was a bad thing to be the best man to save his own son. I knew what he was trying to tell me – he was too emotionally invested to do a good job; he could make mistakes. But I didn't want to know. We were back to square one. He wouldn't touch this case and wouldn't listen to reason. He was wrong. I was right. Look where the second best has brought us!

'All rise!' The bailiff cries out.

I jump to my feet and momentarily lose balance. The courtroom spins before my eyes. The dark wood panelled walls warp and ripple. Bile comes up to the back of my throat. I clutch Hugh's arm to steady myself. He squeezes my hand, inclines his head towards me and mouths, 'Brace yourself, Mills. It won't be pretty.'

We promptly sit down again after His Honour settles in his throne and gives the room a curt nod. It is aimed at the two of us, and it hits us like a guided missile. In that moment, I know. He is apologising for what he is about to do. This is the only time he establishes eye contact with us. His expression takes away the last shred of hope from me. He looks at us with the eyes of an executioner about to pull the lever of the trap door beneath our feet. My throat feels constricted. I struggle to breathe. The noose, even if it is only in my mind, has tightened around my neck.

I avoid His Honour's eyes, but mine don't leave his lips. I need to be ahead of the game: to read his lips before he speaks the sentence. I'm so attuned that I can hear his breathing.

He looks different in his grey wig that fills the blank expanse of his bald scalp. His half-moon shaped glasses slide to the tip of his nose and sit there askew and misaligned with his face. I hardly recognise him. In his judge's attire, he looks like a badly painted vanity portrait, almost a caricature. His thin lips are taut with concentration. And now his eyes drill into Christopher.

'Christopher Bramley-Jones, you have been found guilty on two counts of fraud and conspiracy to defraud in common law and under section 1 of the Fraud Act 2006.' His Honour – Ricky, to Hugh and me – delivers his first punch to our son.

We knew this was coming after the guilty verdict. We prepared ourselves for it: tightened our stomach muscles and clenched our teeth. It doesn't hurt so much when our old family friend rams it into us. But Christopher looks wounded.

I watch my son, a man in his prime, standing meek and frightened as he is being assaulted by an old man wearing skewed glasses, a wig and theatrically red robes. Try to picture this. It's grotesque. It could be a jolly little joke to share at any of our soirees, and it would evoke a few chuckles, but right now no one is laughing. Christopher winces at every new punchline.

'You and your partner in crime abused your position of trust to unscrupulously plan and execute your scheme of greed and...'

I blank Ricky out.

I can see Christopher's chest rising and contracting under his expensive black suit. His silk tie reflects light and ripples like liquid silver. He shouldn't be wearing that mother-of-pearl tie pin or those cufflinks. People are quick to judge. They will say he stole them too.

Ricky's voice breaks through my barriers and I have to hear what he has to say, 'You deliberately targeted the vulnerable in society – the elderly...'

Christopher was a beautiful child. He had those angelic, golden curls right up to the age of six. He looked like a cherub. He is still beautiful in his thirties. He is tall, athletic and handsome like one of those male models from Givenchy TV ads. He could have any girl he wanted. I could not protect him from all of them. All I could do was to disapprove of his choices, but would he listen? He is so naïve, so trusting! He has been led astray by that woman.

'It does not speak in your favour that following the incapacitation of your accomplice, you attempted to dispose of the evidence against you and to divert suspicion solely against her. You attempted to interfere with the police investigation and to pervert the course of justice. You sabotaged or destroyed data on your bank's records and made every effort to manipulate your victims and prevent them from coming forward...'

The expression on Christopher's face is that of disbelief and pain, as is mine. It's not fair that he cannot say anything in his defence while Ricky showers him with wanton accusations. He has made a punch bag of my boy. And it's all lies. I don't recognise any of it. None of it applies to Christopher. Greedy? Unscrupulous? Manipulative? Christopher is the most upright young man under the sun – the epitome of the boy next door. He is funny. He is witty. He is the life and soul of the party. His charm is effortless. You can't be this charming if you are this evil! It is lies, lies, lies.

'Not only did you obstruct the police in their investigation, but you also lied and attempted to incriminate innocent work colleagues. You showed no remorse for what you had done and no empathy for people you'd robbed of their hard-earned life savings. You refused to return the misappropriated funds to your victims...'

It's not like he's killed anyone! I can just about hold back my frustration and not scream in Ricky's face. I don't want to be removed from the courtroom, not before he delivers the sentence. I will him to be lenient and sensible. Come on, Ricky, I urge him, be a decent man! You know Christopher is no criminal. He was led astray by that woman. He can just about manage community service.

'I therefore sentence you to five years in prison.'

The word *suspended* I crave to hear does not come. My beautiful baby boy is going to prison. I cover my mouth with my hand to push back a gasp. Christopher's face drops and I am sure I can see a lone tear rolling down his cheek. *Look what you've done! You made my boy cry!* I shout to Ricky, but my voice just like my gasp is trapped inside my mouth.

'You'll have to serve a minimum of half of your sentence before you're eligible for parole. You are disqualified from acting as a company director. Under section 13 of the Proceeds of Crime Act 2002 I impose a deprivation order on your assets, including your property at...'

Ricky has just made my son homeless. I stare at the old git. I wish him dead. He is no longer welcome in my house.

I take a long time in the courts washroom to sort myself out. After I throw up, I flush the toilet, push the seat down and sit on it. My head flops between my knees. I feel blood rush to my face. I give myself time. I can hear people come and go, doors banging, locks clicking, taps running, footsteps, paper rolls spinning. Smells waft by. It doesn't seem like the right time to leave the safety of my cubicle while people are about. I don't want anyone to see me like this. I am not ready for public consumption.

I cannot think straight. It's total chaos in my head. I look at the door and realise I haven't drawn the latch. Someone might have waltzed in here just like that. They would have found me slumped on the toilet with my trousers on. They could have challenged me: what the hell was I doing here, since I clearly wasn't doing my business? Was I doing drugs, for example? Maybe they would've asked me if I was alright. Should they call for help? Imagine the aggravation!

Just as I'm sitting and trying to picture it, someone tries to push the door in. I still haven't locked it, you see. I thought of doing it, and forgot. This happens more and more often of late. I forget things the moment I think of them. Then I have to start thinking again: I go back to the last thing I do remember and re-trace my steps from there. It is time-consuming. It annoys the living daylights out of Hugh. He keeps telling me I need to have my head checked. We are this age now, Mills, he tells me, it could be Alzheimer's. What on earth does he mean? I ask him. I am genuinely puzzled. What age? I'm fifty-five. He should speak for himself. The way he takes care of his health! At the ripe old age of sixty-seven years, he's on the fast route to an early grave. And that's what I tell him in reply.

I am quick to ram my foot into the door and force the intruder out.

'It's occupied!' I inform her. My voice hits my highest, shrill register.

'Sorry,' she responds, 'I didn't see...'

See what? I wonder.

I hear her steps recede. I hear her open another cubicle — right at the far end, as far away from me as possible. Good, I nod to myself.

As I pull back my foot, my door swings open. I kick it back

and slide the latch. I wait for the other woman to finish her ablutions before I finally leave my cubicle. I am alone. I wash my hands, on automatic pilot, because I don't have to, of course. I haven't used the toilet. I splash water on my face to cool it. Not too much water, so it isn't obvious. I don't want to wet my hair and come out of here looking like a plucked chicken. Peering into the mirror, I find myself surprisingly normal. Even if my face is flushed, it's not showing. I do wear decent quality foundation. 30+, remember? It's like wearing a fire blanket. I take out my compact and dab my cheeks with fluffy powder. It smells expensive. I brush my hair and re-apply lipstick. I force my lips into a smile. I stroll out of the bathroom refreshed and confident. No one will catch me off guard.

Aiden Turner is standing in my way. He has sprung from nowhere. He looks thinner than when I first met him, and even then he was a skinny man with a long, narrow face and a nose jutting out of it like a beak. His hair is white and his eyebrows jet black. How old is he? I try to calculate his age. He won't be much over forty. Why the grey hair?

I think he is blocking my way on purpose, but I can't be sure. Has he been waiting for me here while I was in the loo? Is he stalking me? I can't read his face. Is he angry? Is he gloating? Did he take pleasure in Christopher's plight – my plight? Why is he here? What is he hoping to gain by being here?

He doesn't budge and doesn't take his dead eyes off me. It's like he is haunting me. I know he blames me, but she is the author of her own fall. Sally Turner conceded her guilt when she did what she did. I didn't guide her hand. It was all her own doing. Alas she did it in a way that didn't benefit anyone, not even her. I wish she had done it differently. To be perfectly honest, I wish she could be here to tell the truth, to take the blame and to save my boy.

'Excuse me.' I brush by Aiden and hurry down to the lobby where Hugh is waiting for me.

'You're not excused! You will never be excused,' he shouts after me. Whatever he means by that? I refuse to answer that question.

My stilettoes tap away on the tiled floor, muffling Turner's steps. On top of the stairwell I look over my shoulder to check if he is following me, but he is gone. I inhale deeply to restore oxygen to my brain. I've been feeling lightheaded and unsteady on my high heels.

Downstairs Hugh rolls his eyes and flays his arms. 'What took you so long! I thought you died in there. I was about to call for help,' he mutters.

'Don't be daft,' I tell him.

JOSEPH

I have done enough for one day. A blister throbs on my index finger. Inside, the cabin smells of methylated spirit and the sealant I used on the windows. I feel lightheaded from the toxins I have been inhaling below deck. I take myself outside to the bench on the front-well deck and light a joint.

It's a biting night on the canal. I don't feel the cold at first. I have been physically active for hours and sweating like a pig. When the wind picks up, it chills my sweaty back and pinches my spine. I shiver, but I am too lazy to go inside to fetch my jacket. I listen to the water lapping against my boat. Gusts of wind rake the surface. After several days of rain, the water level is high. My boat, with me in it, wobbles from side to side. My eyes sink into the inky blackness of the thick foliage on the bank. A sequence of shrieks perforates the dark. A fox? A bird of some kind? It doesn't sound like an owl. My friendly companion, the heron, has departed to his lodgings for the night. His nest is somewhere there, somewhere high. I lift my gaze up the steep slope behind the line of trees. It rises and undulates into grazing paddocks. At the top of the hill, a silhouette of a cow cuts into the silver moon that has momentarily emerged from behind a cloud. What's that rhyme about a cow jumping over the moon? This cow is doing no such thing. It just stands there with its hooves firmly on the ground. Maybe it is admiring the view from the top as I myself do from the foot of the hill. Maybe it is sleeping, its head up in those sailing night-clouds, and dreaming of going to the moon. It is either an adventurous or a stupid cow to be standing on the hilltop in the gusty wind. I give it the benefit of the doubt and lean towards it being adventurous.

'Oi, vicar! Yo comin'?'

I tell them over and over again, I am a priest, not a vicar. They also know that my name is Joseph. Joe is fine, too. Still, they call me anything but Joseph or any of its variations. *Noah* seems to have gained some traction of late. It's to do with the pandemic. It was Loki who asked me the other day if my ark was ready for *the shitstorm*, and he referred to me as Noah. The name stuck. The others liked the biblical reference. My being a priest (or a vicar) probably played its part. So, I am Noah, the vicar, like it or lump it.

Loki is standing by my mooring, one foot on the rope. Loki isn't his Christian name, either. Come to think of it, I gave him this nickname. When I first saw him, he brought to mind a Viking god. He is six-foot-two and looks at you with those pale eyes, almost see-through, like ice. The straw of his blond hair is bunched into messy dreadlocks. He is often seen with his chiselling tools, and that includes a hefty hammer. His voice thunders and he is full of shit. So, I immediately thought of that mischievous Nordic deity – Loki. I know what you're going to say. I am supposed to be a catholic priest, not a blinking druid. I am only entitled to one God. I accept that. But Loki doesn't subscribe to Christianity. I can call him what I deem fit. *Loki* fits him best.

They have already started the fire. It is blazing in a recycled oil drum at the bottom of the slope where we normally gather for a nightcap. We clear the brambles every year because they tend to bounce back as weeds do if you don't keep an eye on them. Loki made benches from felled logs. Loki is a carpenter by trade and an artist by vocation. The benches are state of the art. He has sculpted battle scenes into them: rearing horses, firing cannons and battle standards. They are also very comfortable to sit on.

'Alright, Noah?' Jeremiah shuffles along the bench, making room for me. I greet him in return and ask how he's getting on. He flashes his canines at me and presents me with his regular answer, 'Same old, same old.' Jeremiah lives on an abandoned motorboat. He keeps it well camouflaged on the side of the woods which isn't accessible on foot, so that no one comes checking his papers. He doesn't have any. He is a failed asylum seeker. He sought it fifteen years ago and when he was refused he dived into the underworld. He supports himself from odd jobs, cash in hand. Don't bother asking him where he is from. He won't tell you. He says he is not telling because he *ain't going back there*. I think he had to leave wherever it is he comes from because he is homosexual. He made a pass at me once. I explained I was celibate but if I wasn't I would be fornicating with women. Men don't do it for me. He said, 'Fair enough. Each to his own,' and we never spoke of it again.

There is a whole crowd of us, boaties, here. Some are anchored here permanently, like Loki and Jeremiah. Others come and go. Travellers, peddlers, boating hairdressers, fortune tellers and even restaurateurs. Everyone is welcome to share in the warmth of the fire, and in the nightcap. We are a tight community, like the churchgoers of my parish. Probably tighter. We don't talk behind each other's backs.

The brew is making its rounds. It's a damn potent concoction. It winds you when you take your first swig. You literally cannot breathe. It burns your guts. By the third time round, you are used to it. You know what to expect, or maybe your insides have become fireproof.

'How ya gettin' on with the ark?' Ruthie asks. She is a Tarot card reader. If she was any good, she wouldn't have to ask. She also likes to read books. Her galley is lined with books leaning precariously over the cooker. It's a bit of a fire hazard, but it's not a subject I'm qualified to preach about, so I don't. She lives with her father, Ronnie. He no longer comes out at night time. He has mobility issues due to his advanced years. By day, you will find him sitting on the deck, his legs wrapped in a green blanket, people-watching. It could be a boring pastime in winter when there aren't many ramblers or dog walkers ambling by, but he seems to enjoy it. Apart from his mobility issues, he is also partially sighted. Most of the people watching is happening inside his head.

I tell Ruthie about my boat renovation progress. I am nearly there – just a few cosmetic touch-ups left to do. I have been building that boat for going on six years. What will you do with yourself when you're done, she always asks me this, and I always tell her that I don't think that far ahead. Except that now the works are nearly at an end. So tonight I say, 'Now, I'm just waiting for the Flood.' She erupts with snorts. That's how she laughs. Ruthie has a good sense of humour. I like her.

Loki and Jeremiah roll the drums over. Loki has made those by hollowing out tree trunks of different diameters and covering them with stretched goat skin. In his trademark fashion, he decorated them with battle scenes. These, for reasons known only to Loki, focus on the mythological militaria of Ancient Greeks: chariots, broad swords and plumed helmets, and half-naked warriors in the phalanx formation. He has painted them terracotta and black.

I clamp my drum between my knees. Loki and Jeremiah hold theirs their way. Loki has his in his lap and he dwarfs it with his size. We begin. It's out of this world! I am not musically trained, but it doesn't matter. The drumming takes you into the zone, and you just do it on autopilot, as if you have been doing this all your life. Jeremiah is in the same magic place as me. He throws his head from side to side. His eyes roll to the back of his head. His hands beat the goat-skin membrane like the wings of a big black bird. Loki is grinning. He looks possessed. If a stranger got stranded in the night and heard us, saw us here, he would think we were all possessed. I know a thing or two about possession and I can vouch to this notion. We are possessed.

Ruthie and two other ladies are dancing around the fire. They are swaying and stomping to the beat of the drums, thrusting their arms about their heads and shaking their tresses. They are like wild wood nymphs. We are like a pagan sect. I thank God Almighty that no one I know can see me.

I stagger back to my narrowboat an hour – two hours – five hours later. Time is lost on the canal. I am pissed as a newt and high as a kite. No way can I ride my motorcycle home. I'll have to sleep it off on my almost finished boat. I curl up in the hull with my jacket under my head. It's probably damn cold, but I still can't feel it. My arteries will be pumping fire for a good few hours to come.

I am not claustrophobic and am well accustomed to the confined space the confession box has to offer. It has been my second home for thirty-odd years. Sometimes I refer to it as my *holiday home* because I normally dwell here for hours on end in anticipation of holidays. Christmas and Easter are my high seasons. That's when the penitents come to unburden themselves. They whisper their transgressions into my ear – God's ear theoretically, but let's not split hairs. I grant them absolution so that they can go out into the world with their consciences clear. They will sin again and be back to recite their wrongdoings in the privacy of my wooden box. I will be here for them and we will go the whole hog all over again: confession, contrition, absolution and a few Hail Marys for their penance. I will mumble my chant of absolution in Latin, as you do when you are a catholic priest. I will sing to them the melodious incantation of *Et ego te absolvo a peccatis tuis in nomine Patris, et Filii, et Spiritus Sancti*. It's an uplifting moment – magical. It's like the beating of the drums in the night. The penitents' sins release their souls from darkness, and, so cleansed, my penitents walk away, light-hearted and hopeful, promising to be good, and meaning every word of it.

Except for that one man – the Prophet.

He doesn't mean any of it.

I can't absolve him without true remorse on his part, and he has none. He is proud of what he has done and what he will continue to do. He comes to me to brag about it. He knows I won't give him absolution, but he keeps coming back. It isn't absolution he is after. It's something else. I fear his purpose is to torture me: to taint me with his insanity and seduce me to the side of evil. He has made me into his accomplice – a silent partner in crime. That's because I cannot betray him. He knows he is protected by the seal of confession. I will sooner gag on what I know than speak of it to any living soul. It is between the monster and me. God is in on it too, I suppose. He is listening through me, and then He does nothing. I'd think it shouldn't be hard for God to strike the man dead on the spot. But no. God chooses to love the man and lets him perpetuate his evil. Does God love the man's victims less than He loves him? It's a blasphemous idea and I banish it from my thoughts. I hope God knows something I don't, and I submit to His will. We let the man walk away unscathed.

'I'm only a humble tool in God's hands, Father, doing His will.' The man's voice is no more than a low whisper, a tapping and hissing of consonants and only an intimation of vowels between them. He is careful not to raise his voice and give me an idea of his pitch and tone. He has bleached his speech free of accent. I may know him, but I wouldn't recognise his voice if we spoke outside the confessional. He has made sure of that. His breath is infused with mint. He always chews gum so that I can't smell his breath. He wears gloves and a beanie. It comes down to the bridge of his nose. I can't see his eyes. His beard veils his lips. I don't tell him this, but he doesn't really have to go to such lengths to conceal his identity. I don't want to know it. I am bound to secrecy and so I don't wish to discover who he is. My resolve would be tested beyond endurance if I did.

'I'll be back,' he says like he is the second coming of Arnold Schwarzenegger, an avenger of the innocent. He thinks he is. He definitely fancies himself a holy man. That is why I call him the Prophet. 'You can sleep in peace, Father. Happy Easter.' He crosses himself, pulls himself up to his feet and leaves.

The Prophet doesn't walk – he slithers. His steps are so soft that I hold my breath for a while, listening out and wondering whether he is really gone. A hot flush radiates through me. Beads of sweat blister my temples. I pant. It's a panic attack, I recognise the symptoms. The walls of the confessional close on me. Like I said earlier, I am not claustrophobic. But there is an exception: it's when I share space with the man. He suffocates me. He sucks the air out of my lungs. He is pure evil.

Mrs Keating bursts into the confessional. I can tell it's Mrs Keating even before she opens her mouth to utter her deeply-felt and profound greeting: *Bless me, Father, for I have sinned.* I know it's her because of the huffing. She enters the box on a huff. Then her whole body follows, and there is a lot of it. Mrs Keating is a massive presence in many ways. Like a distressed beached whale she fills the entire confessional. Her breath tells me she had an egg sandwich for lunch. I like egg sandwiches, but not second-hand. I am trapped with an egg-mayo dragon.

Mrs Keating is one of my most active parishioners, someone you might have once called a busybody. She has few sins of her own to confide. They are few and they aren't really her fault. It's her wayward husband testing her patience. He drinks too much, rarely gets off his lazy backside to help around the house and consistently fails to get the promotion so desperately desired for him by Mrs Keating.

Once her small personal transgressions are out of the way, she proceeds to list those of other people. That's why she is really here. That's what she excels at. Her gossip-mongering is legendary. She regularly updates me – within the sanctity of my confession box – on her neighbours' split-ups, affairs, unwanted pregnancies, job losses due to drunkenness and an assortment of other minor and major misfortunes, all of which she regards as offences against God. I listen with my eyes closed and I nod off from time to time, not that she notices. She is riding her high horse of indignation. Visibility is poor at such dizzy hights.

My night on the canal has caught up with me. I am knackered and probably still hung over. I am drifting away back to my narrowboat, to the heron – my old friend, to the moon and the cow, and to Loki and his battle scenes. The beat of the drums pummels inside my skull, as do Mrs Keating's words. Until something she says stirs me and I sit up to listen.

'I've seen men go in and out of there, Father. Married men, I know, some of them my Rory's friends... How long before he's tempted? You tell me, Father. I brought him up a decent, God-fearing Christian, but he's a red-blooded man, and I hope you don't mind me saying this, Father, but he has his needs and no wife to relieve him. He could stray. He's no saint, not like you, Father.'

'I'm no saint, Mrs Keating.' I realise she takes no notice of what I say, but I say it nonetheless, for the record.

'A whole bunch of strangers: in and out, in and out – like a train station. God knows where she finds them, you'll have to ask her yourself. But it isn't right, Father, it just isn't for such a woman to be putting her filthy hands on holy relics, and doing your bed, and such. And, if I'm honest, it rubs off on you, it does. She brings your name into disrepute. People are already talking. You don't want your name dragged through mud, Father. You're better than that. And I'll tell you this for nothing – there be decent, hard-working ladies aplenty what would do church duties and some light cleaning round the sacristy for half the money you pay her.'

I am blinking at her, venting my disbelief and discomfort. If she is right, and Mrs Keating is rarely wrong, I dare not contemplate the implications. I am like a stunned fish, belly up, unable to act. Words fail me.

Mrs Keating misinterprets my silence. 'She's a whore, Father. Take my word for it,' she clarifies more forcefully, 'Jane Cuthbert is a whore. I seen her get up to it with me own eyes. As God is my witness.'

I give Mrs Keating three rosaries as penitence and make the sign of the Cross over her head.

She says, *amen*, and then adds, 'You be best advised to get rid of her, Father, before she blackens your name. We wouldn't want that, would we.'

With all due respect and without meaning to sound rude, Jane tells me to mind my own business. She does so without taking her eyes off the mop. In fact, she grips it with renewed verve, slams it into the bucket and gives it a vigorous twist to wring out water. She then stabs my kitchen floor with it and begins to wash it, all over again. I have accosted her in the kitchen, which is big but not big enough to contain the raging Jane Cuthbert. She tells me to get out of her way; she is a busy woman, as it happens, and has two more jobs after this one. I river-dance around her rampant mop. Her face is flushed fire-engine red. I would wager that what rattled her is the shame that I know her dirty secret rather than the anger at me for meddling. I don't mean to put her in the spotlight, to name and shame her, but she takes my offer the wrong way.

'It isn't my intention to judge you,' I start my homily, but she won't let me finish.

'Why not? Everyone else does. You go right ahead, Father, judge away.'

'I won't judge you,' I insist. 'I am concerned about your safety. What you do, Jane – the *business* you've got yourself into – it's dangerous.'

'Not any more dangerous than crossing the road. You never know what's coming round the corner. A speeding car, or some such. So there, if it's all the same to you, Father, I'll take my chances with... what I do,' and she rams her mop into the bucket and prods inside it as if she was hunting for a sewer rat. The bucket rattles and slides against the stone tiles, emitting grinding noises that set my teeth on edge.

Jane is not finished. 'Thanks a million for your charity, anyways. Nice of you, and all. A Christian thing to care for your flock as well as you do.' In a gesture of finality, she rips the bucket from the floor, the mop erected like a sword in the other hand, and storms out, heading for the utility room.

I follow her, acting on the supposition of fools that one should never give up hope. I implore her to stop and listen to me for one minute. She won't spare me a second, never mind a whole minute. She is busy emptying the bucket and rinsing the mop. She has bent down, her back to me. Her tight jeans – they call them *skinny*, but there is nothing skinny about Jane – bulge with her curves. She has muscly thighs and a small waist. There is a rip in the jeans, just under her left buttock. The patch of flesh peeping out of there could raise the dead. I am not dead – on the contrary, I'm very much alive, and ablaze. I may be a priest, but I am a man too. That bit of flesh could easily lead me into temptation, though I'm too long in the tooth to let that happen. But other men don't have to censor their carnal needs. No wonder Jane's brand-new *business* thrives and gets noticed by the likes of Mrs Keating.

'You can pass my thanks to that trollop, Keating. Rather you than me 'cos God help me if I should get my hands on her!' Jane turns to face me and skewers me with the contempt I deserve for consorting with *the trollop*. 'She told you, didn't she?'

I hang my head on my chest and pull a contrite face.

'I knew it!' Jane shoves the bucket under the stairs, and pulls out a hoover, dragging it by the tubing. The cord trails behind her, and I follow the cord, still hopeful that she will come to her senses and listen to reason. I have to make her understand that this isn't about the damage Mrs Keating can inflict on Jane's reputation – this is about a far greater peril.

The chances of her listening, or even hearing me, diminish the moment she plugs in the hoover. I'd better save my breath until she is finished with this room. I sit in my chair and watch her. Admire her. Not her curves or her unblemished skin, but her resolve and the sacrifice she is prepared to make for her son. Because that's why she is doing it: running herself into the ground with several cleaning jobs by day, and selling her body by night. It's for her son, Matthew.

I remember when Jane Cuthbert became pregnant. It was twenty years ago. I had been the parish priest at The Sacred Heart for a couple of years by then, and I knew Jane's mother well. She had been devasted by Jane's pregnancy, but the question of termination had not entered any of our minds. A discussion about giving the baby up for adoption was squashed by Jane. She was going to keep her baby, and that was the end of it. She gave birth to a baby boy a few days short of her sixteenth birthday. Rumour had it that the child's father was her physics teacher, Dr Curry. He had left his post suddenly, in the middle of the spring term. Mrs Keating was quick to do the maths and successfully put two and two together. Jane was branded a floozy and a slut. Although she had earlier been hailed a child prodigy, with prospects no kid from Romley Estate before her had ever had, she did not complete her GCSEs. Instead, she devoted herself to bringing up Matthew and surviving on odd menial jobs.

Matthew grew up to be a fine young man and a gifted student, his particular talents lying in science subjects, especially physics. When he was accepted to study astrophysics at Southampton University, tongues began to wag all over again, Mrs Keating's wagging more vehemently than anybody else's. Her theory of Dr Curry having a hand – and more – in Matthew's conception had been positively verified, in her opinion, by Matthew's academic acumen. But to Jane that was ancient history and Mrs Keating, a relic of the past. Jane was glowing. She forgot the past and looked to the future. She had plans. She wouldn't be derailed a second time. She had promised herself that her son would achieve what she had not:

to climb out of the swamp of the Romley Estate and live his dreams. He was the first in the family to go to university. The first in the neighbourhood. Jane was determined that he would graduate. She took on extra work, slaving from dawn till dusk, cleaning, shelf-stacking at our local supermarket and manning the zebra crossing by Romley Primary School as a lollypop lady. But it wasn't enough. With all the student loans and grants Matthew managed to secure, it still wasn't enough, especially when last September he travelled to Boston, USA, on a research project at Harvard-Smithsonian Center for Astrophysics. That was when, I reckon, Jane began to prostitute herself.

I should have realised it sooner. She had been banging on for weeks about the eye-watering costs of living in America. Matthew needed regular cash injections to survive. He was deep in student debt. Up to his eyes, she would say, pinching her nose and pretending to be drowning. I explained to her how to set up a direct debit. We did it together. Since November she has been transferring five hundred pounds every month into Matthew's account. I never asked where she got the money from. It took Mrs Keating to open my eyes.

'It's a dangerous game you're playing,' I say as soon as she unplugs the hoover.

She responds with a weary sigh. She knows, she knows the risk, she tells me. It's only a year, less than a year now. She can manage, thank you very much for the kind offer, Father.

'A year!' I can't help but shout. 'It takes a few seconds to die, Jane!'

'I ain't dying, Father,' she laughs. Really laughs. Her laughter is a throwback to her happier, carefree childhood. Everything else about her is as tough as tanned leather. 'I'm just having sex with strangers, that's all.'

'Strangers who could harm you.' I know for a fact at least one of them is hellbent on doing just that. 'I'm offering you a way out, Jane. I need a full-time housekeeper, anyway.'

'No, you don't.'

'I can't pay you what those men pay you, but you'll be safe, you'll have a roof over your head with no rent to pay, full board, and every penny you earn will go to Matthew. It's a win-win.'

'And give that trollop Keating an excuse to call me a whore?'

'She's already doing it.' I resign myself to openly revealing my source.

'Ha! Nuff said!'

Jane is dragging the hoover to the sitting room. It's twice the size of my study. She will be busy here twice as long, buzzing and hissing, chucking cushions around, sticking the nozzle of the hoover in all the crevices where I keep my Pringles crumbs. I stay where I am – I have a sermon to write – but I give it one last go:

'It's a question of self-respect, Jane. You'll be a housekeeper, not a whore.'

She looks at me over her shoulder, cold contempt in her voice when she says, 'I'd rather be a whore on my own terms than a kept woman on yours.'

I give up. She has totally twisted my words. I know she has done it on purpose, to shut me up. She probably thinks she has done me a favour by declining my live-in job offer, and she is probably right.

CAMILLA

We drive to Christopher's to pick up Joshua. The weather is miserable – dull, chilly and sloppy. It has rained on and off for a week and now roadside ditches teem with dirt-green mud. Trees and hedgerows rise out of water like they are some gigantic rice fields. You don't expect any less from the month of March. If the muck wasn't enough misery to wallow in, the man on the radio intimates the possibility of lockdown. He is that unflappable politician they push to the front line to face the media when they have something bad to say. I forget his name. The cases are on the rise. Nowhere near as bad as in Italy and Spain where the virus is out of control. I detect a note of schadenfreude in the man's voice as he says that, but the nation has to prepare for the worst.

I sigh with relief. At least, we'll have Joshua staying with us. I can almost forgive Phillipa for abandoning my son and buggering off to Australia with her slimy lover-boy, who, lest we forget, used to call himself Christopher's best friend. Good luck and good riddance to the pair of them. I wish they'd stay there for longer than just a month. I wish I had more time with my grandson before they return and claim him back. And put ideas in his head.

I fancy it will be like going back in time to when Christopher was seven. We still live in the same house, in Middle Norton. Joshua will be able to play in the fresh country air in our big garden, just like Christopher used to when he came home for school holidays. He will have Christopher's room, and his playthings. I have kept most of Christopher's old toys. I stored them in the loft as if I knew they'd come in handy one day. His Lego blocks are in pristine condition. Christopher was brought up to look after his toys. We made sure to impress on him the importance of respecting one's possessions. Toys don't grow on trees, Hugh used to tell him, they cost money so don't you go thrashing them. All the superheroes, dinosaurs and Star Wars figurines are intact. I spent the whole of yesterday unwrapping them from tissue paper and giving them a thorough cleaning. I used Dettol to kill germs. One never knows where they're hiding. I'm particularly alert these days, what with the coronavirus rampant out there. Of course, I don't believe for one second that it's been hibernating in our loft, but there are other nasty microbes about. Mice flock to our attic every autumn, and mice carry disease. It's in their droppings and the fleas they carry. They have ravaged Christopher's rocking horse – nibbled through the material under its stomach. Sawdust spilled out of it. I will try to mend it if I can and if I have time later. My hands will be full with Joshua, I imagine.

Peter opens the door when we ring the bell. He is wearing casual, homely attire, including slippers. He invites us in. 'Pip will be down in a minute,' he informs us. As if we care to see Phillipa! We're here to pick up our grandson, that's all. Of course, I don't tell him that. I have promised Hugh that I wouldn't antagonise them. Apparently, I rub them up the wrong way. I say, thanks Peter, and take off my shoes before we go inside. Hugh keeps his on. I guess it doesn't matter how clean the house is now that it is about to be repossessed. Or should I say, *confiscated?*

The irony of it! Peter used to call himself my son's best friend. He doesn't do that anymore. Now that he has stolen Christopher's girlfriend and moved into his house, he has dropped all pretences. The sorry excuse for a best friend has the audacity to open the door to us, look us in the eye and still act like he owns the place. He offers us something to drink, which we politely decline. God knows what's in it.

We talk about the wedding. It isn't a topic of interest to me, but Hugh has asked and Peter is jabbering on about it, giving us the overall guest statistics (limited due to the virus hanging in the air), and details of the gourmet menu. He is careful not to gush out, to spare our feelings I suppose. His feedback is stilted. I take it all in: twenty-four invited, twenty-two attended. So it was just us who declined the invitation. The cheek of sending it to us!

Phillipa descends from upstairs to grace us with her presence. Her hair is still curled into those long spirals and it shines with glitter, or perhaps it is confetti. Her eye makeup is smudged. I can see her freckles breaking through the layers of rouge and foundation. Christopher fell in love with her freckles and her red hair. I did tell him redheads were false. Wasn't I right!

She is wearing a satin dressing gown. Metallic silver. It folds over her stomach which juts out of her hips, unusually enlarged. Her hand held protectively over it confirms my suspicion that she is pregnant. Six, maybe seven months, is my guess. She didn't waste any time... When she sits on the arm of the sofa and leans towards Peter to kiss him, the lapels open and I catch the sight of her left breast. It is already swollen with the new life she's carrying. You can see its ripe profile, complete with a nipple. Hugh catches it too. We exchange the look. He knows what I want to say about that slut. He knows I won't say it because I promised him I'd hold my tongue. Instead, I say, 'Congratulations are in order, I believe.'

'Thank you, Camilla.'

I am so glad Christopher never married her. When they first started dating I didn't think she would last any more than all the other floozies he brought home before her. But when she fell pregnant, I gave up the ghost. For the sake of the unborn, mind; not because she had somehow grown respectable in my estimation. We would have to have a quiet wedding, what with her already showing, I said to Christopher. He said they weren't thinking of getting married. It wasn't what Pip wanted – it wasn't *her scene*. Isn't it interesting then that it has taken her under a year following his arrest to marry his best friend? Suddenly, marriage is her scene, glitter in her hair, bridesmaids, tiered cakes and the all-inclusive package honeymoon.

The reception was at The Clifton Club. How they could afford it, I won't speculate. Joshua was a page boy. All that pomp and ceremony while his father was being sentenced to a jail term. On the very same day!

'The sentencing was yesterday,' she tells us as if we didn't know. *Unlike you, we were there!* I scream in my head since I am not supposed to say it out loud.

'What did he get?' Peter's eyes shine with excitement. I swear, they do – his pupils are enormous. It's either the excitement or he is as high as a kite. I always knew he was a bad apple.

'Five years,' Hugh answers. I couldn't possibly bring myself to say that, but Hugh is impervious to emotion when it comes to crime and punishment. 'He should be out towards the end of next year.'

'How's that?' Do I detect resentment in Peter's tone? The spark in his eye wanes somewhat.

'He only has to serve half of his sentence and if you take into account the eleven months he was remanded in custody, that gets us to Christmas next year.'

'He got away with it lightly, wouldn't you say, Hugh? I, for one, would have given him more than a paltry five years. Who was on the bench? A family friend?' Phillipa squinted, cynicism dripping from her forked tongue.

I wish I could rip that tongue out of her mouth. The wretched gold-digger! A lawyer herself, she was shadowing Hugh, serving her pupillage with his firm, when she met and ensnared Christopher. Now, she is one of those vigilante human-rights advocates.

I glare at her with a basilisk eye. Is she that stupid, or that spiteful? I can't make up my mind. I dare not test that theory but sometimes I indulge in covert jabs. So I inform them about the deprivation order. 'The house will be repossessed. You'll have to move out.'

'We were going to, anyway.' She shrugs and inadvertently flashes her left breast at us. Again. Hugh gazes at her chest barefacedly. Men!

'We've had an offer accepted on a place in Wick.' Peter sounds pleased with himself as if he has just announced winning the lottery. In a way, he has. Living rent-free in my son's house while saving up for their deposit on a place in Wick is a bit like winning the lottery.

I decide to put an end to this most awkward visit. I ask for

Joshua. Is he ready? He is the only reason we're here, and we must be going.

Phillipa is holding Joshua's hand as they descend the stairs. My heart skips a beat at the sight of my little man. He has had a haircut and all but lost his golden curls. His hair is darker – reddish brown. He has grown since we last saw him. He's wearing a pair of jeans and a navy-blue jumper. So grown-up! He looks just like Christopher did at the same age. I have photographs to prove it. A tear of joy and pride swirls in my eye.

'Look who's here!' Phillipa nudges him forward.

I run to meet him halfway. I bend down and pull him into my arms. I squeeze him. My little man! His fragile body is pressed against my chest. I can feel the sharp outline of his shoulder blades under my palms. He is thin and small for his age, but that can be sorted out. As soon as he is on his grandma's cooking, he will fill out. He will grow big and strong, like his daddy.

He wriggles out of my arms and mumbles, 'It's Grandma.'

'Grandad is in the lounge. Run over and say hello.'

Joshua pulls away from me, and I let him go because I know his grandfather is dying to take him into his arms too. He may be rubbish at showing affection but he loves this little boy as much as I do.

'Is that Josh I hear in the hallway?' Hugh tries to sound jovial, which doesn't come naturally to him. I give him top marks for effort.

Joshua doesn't exactly run. He lumbers to the lounge and I hear him say, 'Hi Grandad,' and, 'What's for breakfast?' in the same breath. As much as there is little enthusiasm in his greeting, at least the boy has a healthy appetite, I console myself.

Then again, I wonder where it all goes, what with him being all skin and bone.

'You'll have breakfast at your grandparents,' Peter informs him. 'Remember? We talked about it. Your mum and I are off on our honeymoon. We have a plane to catch.'

'Why can't I go with you?'

'Because you're going on a holiday to the countryside, to spend some time with Grandma and Grandad.'

'But I don't want to go with them. I want to come with you!'

Phillipa wheels in Joshua's suitcase and hands it over to me. She tells me that everything Joshua needs is in there. I peer at it doubtfully. It is a very small suitcase. I pass the suitcase to Hugh. It's too low for him to pull across the floor. He lifts it by the handle instead. Phillipa and Peter take turns to cuddle and kiss Joshua. He grimaces and hides his head between his shoulders, shaking it to avoid being kissed. He pleads with Phillipa not to leave him with us. He promises to be good. He floats the idea of stowing away in their luggage on the plane so that no one will ever know he is there. He doesn't mind the discomfort. There are lots of sharks in Australia. He likes sharks. He wants to see a live shark. He must go with them to Australia to see the sharks. His cheeks grow red and he purses his lips into a quivering downturned bow when Phillipa explains that cannot be done. She insists he is going with us. She nods to me and mouths, *go now*.

When I take his hand, he bursts into tears. I have to drag him out of the house kicking and screaming. Hugh follows with the suitcase in his hand and a mortified expression on his face. We pack the suitcase and Joshua onto the back seat of the car. I strap Joshua in and sit next to him. Hugh starts the engine. Nobody comes out of the house to wave goodbye, which is probably for the best. Joshua is sniffling. He has folded his arms on his stomach and refuses to look up at me.

'Let's just drive,' I tell Hugh. I feel exhausted – traumatised by this whole experience. This isn't how I envisaged it.

At breakfast, Joshua goes on hunger strike. Once he has established that we haven't got any Coco Pops, he loses his appetite and I lose my will to live. I take away the scrambled eggs on toast and come back with porridge generously smothered in honey and sprinkled with fresh blueberries. It's sweet, I reason with Joshua. He retches, and I fear he is serious about vomiting over the breakfast table. Hugh tells me to let him be. He will come back running when he is hungry. I heave myself from the table and remove the offending bowl of porridge. Alone in the kitchen, I pick out all the blueberries and eat them before throwing away the rest. I can't let fresh fruit go to waste. I can't remember Christopher being a fussy eater. It's down to how you're brought up and what you see at home. Joshua has been raised on junk food. I have one month to remedy that. I come back with coffee for us and a glass of fresh orange juice for Joshua. He takes a sip, screws up his face and squeals. So, he doesn't like *bits*. I could put the juice through a sieve, I say. Joshua gives a vote of non-confidence in sieves. Hugh tells Joshua that he can leave the table if he likes. He can go and watch the TV or play in his room. That's how Hugh's mind works: out of sight, out of mind. He let Christopher get away with murder as long as he stayed out of Hugh's hair. Look where that parenting approach has led us.

Over coffee, I raise the question of the appeal. I'm visiting Christopher today, you see. It would be nice to give him hope, something to look forward to. I can't imagine there is much to enjoy in prison to make time go faster.

'There're no grounds for appeal, Mills. Not as far as I can see.'

Hugh pours himself another cup of coffee. He drinks it in one go and twists his lips. He always drinks his coffee black and without sugar, and he always twists his lips violently as if he has just ingested poison. A drop of milk would make it less bitter, but he won't touch milk. He relishes the bitterness though you couldn't say that by looking at his contorted face. After the coffee, he will go to his study and punish his lungs with the sodding pipe. I tell him, I don't want Joshua to see him with the pipe hanging out of his mouth.

I pour more coffee into our cups so that we have more time to discuss the appeal before Hugh buggers off to his study to feed his addiction. It is a one-sided discussion – a monologue on my part, and more lip twisting on Hugh's. I may as well be talking to a brick wall.

'He got away with it lightly,' Hugh parrots Phillipa. Birds of a feather stick together, I ponder bitterly. Lawyers are not human in the way you and I are. This is Christopher we're talking about, and they behave as if he were some third-party delinquent from the wrong side of the tracks, or an abstract case study.

In what way is a prison sentence a lucky escape? I want to know.

'His sentence could easily be increased on appeal, Mills. It works both ways. Let sleeping dogs lie.' A last gulp of his bitter coffee, a satisfying lip curl, and Hugh departs to his den for his morning nicotine shot.

Someone has to mind Joshua at home, so Hugh stays behind while I visit Christopher on my own. I go through the indignity of surrendering my handbag and submitting to a body search with my head held high. They won't break my spirit by bullying me. I explain to the square prison warden with spiky hair and a tattoo that snakes out of her collar on the side of her neck that I'll keep beeping because I can't take off my ring. It's stuck. She retorts that I won't enter until I stop beeping as I go through the scanner. She adds that I can take off my rings, or my finger, she doesn't give a monkey's which. She growls at me in that thick West Country accent to step aside and let the next person through the machine. I head for the bathroom. I lather my fourth finger and begin to work on the ring. In the end I have to resort to licking my knuckle. It comes off. The ring, not the knuckle.

I return ring-free and pass through the X-ray machine without a squeak. I inform the square prison warden with the tattoo that I will be writing to the Prison Governor to complain.

'Be my guest, ma'am,' she says.

Christopher is sitting at a small table, waiting for me. He is without colour – sallow complexion and bags sagging under his eyes. I couldn't even say he looks grey. It's like all colour has been drained from him. I want to pull him into my arms and breathe all my colour into him – to inflate him with my life force. But I know I am not allowed to touch him. It pains me to sit in front of him at arm's length.

We hold a very civil conversation. We talk about everything and nothing in particular. I avoid mentioning the appeal, and he doesn't ask. Perhaps he already knows that the odds are against him. Conroy would have explained it to him. He asks after Joshua. I tell him he's staying with us. Why don't I bring him with me next time, I suggest. Phillipa has never once brought him to see his dad. Christopher won't have it. No, Mum, I don't want him to see me like this, in this God-forsaken place. His words make my ears bleed.

'What shall I tell him when he asks?'

'Does he ask?'

'No.'

'Don't say anything, then. I'll be out by Christmas next year. I'll make it up to him.'

So there is hope in this place after all, I discover, the hope of getting out when the time comes. It isn't forever that my child will stay incarcerated, it dawns on me. And just like that the great weight in my chest shifts and causes less friction when I breathe. I've been carrying it around for a year. To begin with, it was sharp around the edges like a brick lodged in my lungs. The sharp edges are being filed down and, blunted, they are now more tolerable. It makes sense. I couldn't possibly go around being ripped to pieces every day. One day, the serrations were bound to wear off.

Christopher wants me to collect his things from the house before they change the locks. I haven't thought of it, silly me. I am delighted to be of help. He explains where to find everything he needs salvaging before the bailiffs arrive. It's mainly his papers and items of sentimental value that need rescuing. Everything else is dispensable, he says. I can see how this conversation unsettles him. I can see the anguish in his eyes. Christopher doesn't belong in prison. He is too sensitive, too sentimental, too delicate to take it. I wish I could take his place. I wish I could give my boy a fresh start.

The odds and sods I retrieve from the desk in Christopher's study are few. I can't help wondering about the sentimental value of a broken biro, a calculator with a missing power button or a box of tissues. Do they hold memories meaningful and dear to Christopher? They obviously do. I wish I was privy to them. I empty the drawers into my Waitrose canvas bag and take it to my car. The tissue box falls out of the bag, and out of the tissue box falls a mobile phone. It's one of those old-fashioned ones with push buttons, from the days before they became smarter than us. I press the power button, but nothing happens. It needs charging. I will charge it at home and see what's on it. The eye of a camera looks promising. Maybe there are some old photos stored in the memory. I could have them printed and framed, and then I could surprise Christopher when he is out.

Clearing the desk is a piece of cake compared to the garage. Firstly, I have to reverse Christopher's Audi out of there. Everything is in the wrong place on the dashboard, and I am nervous, so I am not surprised when I shave off the wing mirror on the passenger side. Neither am I concerned. This car, like the house, is subject to the deprivation order. It isn't Christopher who will have to pay to have it fixed. I pick up the amputated wing mirror and throw it onto the back seat. On second thoughts, I wipe the thing clean. What if they found my fingerprints on it and accused me of vandalism? I wouldn't put it past them. I have always been a law-abiding citizen with an unconditional trust in the police, but since they hounded Christopher down the way they did and framed him for that woman's crime, I have lost my faith in them.

I have never been inside the inspection pit. Until now I didn't know it existed. But then, how would I know? Christopher's car would normally stand over it. There is no handle or anything to get hold of. I hook my forefinger over the trap door and try to shift it. It's heavy. I drop it and it falls with a loud metallic clank, raising a swell of dust. I consider calling Hugh to come and help, but decide against it. Christopher was adamant I do this on my own. I try again, this time hooking my four fingers under the edge of the flap. I manage to heave it open, but I break not one but two fingernails in the process. It was inevitable, I try to take it in my stride. They're only nails; they will grow back. Still, the sight of a broken nail is rather disturbing.

It isn't a real inspection pit with sophisticated levers and rails that you would find at the car mechanic's workshop. It is little more than a hole in the ground, but it has proper walls reinforced with solid grey blocks and a concrete floor. The trap door is lying on its back. It isn't going to flip over and fall on me when I am inside, I assure myself. I've always had a phobia of being trapped in a windowless dark cellar. Does this condition have a proper name? I wonder. I don't like closed doors. I fear I may run out of air. I know it's an irrational thing, like all phobias. But try telling that to my head. It won't listen.

I double-check that the trap door isn't going anywhere, especially not back where it was to entomb me, then I jump into the pit. The cardboard storage box is here, just where Christopher said it would be. It contains his personal documents – stuff one wouldn't keep in the house in case there was a burglary, correct? That's what I tell myself – that is the very reason why Christopher keeps important documents buried in his garage. This is a perfectly sensible hiding place, in case of a break-in. A burglar wouldn't look for personal papers in the garage, would he? One should keep one's most valuable possessions in the least likely places, like an inspection pit in the garage. Clever thinking, Christopher! Even the police didn't find his hiding place. They had searched the house from top to bottom, with a search warrant and all. They were not meant to find those papers, neither the burglars nor the police.

I heave the box over the ledge of the pit. It isn't easy, but my two nails are already broken so it doesn't matter if I break another one. I don't, as it happens. I have more trouble getting out of the pit than getting in. I leap several times, and slide back in. Finally, I jump high enough to heave my torso over the ledge, and I am able to scramble out. I slump on the floor and draw up my right knee to inspect it. I scraped it against the wall as I was climbing out. It's bleeding. My tights are torn. I start laughing. It is funny, believe me. It's really funny. I am like a little girl who got up to some seriously delicious mischief. I've had quite an adventure in that pit. I have two broken nails and a scraped knee to prove it. Still chuckling, I put everything back as it was: close the trap door, bring the Audi back into the garage and lock up. I drag the box with Christopher's belongings to my car and dump it in the boot. One last glance at my son's house, and I am off. Frankly, I never liked this house anyway. It has no character.

JOSEPH

This is the third Sunday in Lent. I don't have to preach about atonement for our sins and self-mortification. COVID-19 has been doing the job for me for some time now. It has made its way to the UK. I pictured it as Death, the Grim Reaper – in black robes, wielding a scythe, but it turns out that it looks more like a naval mine. This visual representation is quite apt in that the damned microbe has well and truly blown up in our faces. We're having an explosion of new cases. There is talk of a lockdown, like in Wuhan. We will be cooped up in our homes, watching repeats of Midsomer Murders for a few weeks until it blows over, I imagine. I'm sure they will find a vaccine soon. This isn't the Dark Ages. Medicine has made huge progress since then. Still, I am worried about my flock. Even if people's lives are spared, their jobs may not be. My parish is a poor one. It sits on the margin of mainstream society, covering the housing estates of Romley, Beechgrove and Windmore between Knowle West and Bedminster Down. People here can't afford to languish at home watching the telly. Those who do, have already lost their jobs or, never found them in the first place. Let's face it: the parish of The Sacred Heart is a hellhole. It is hardly by choice that people end up living here, but we have a community of sorts – born and bred Bristolians, Irish families who came here in the sixties, followed by Christian refugees from all corners of the Earth, and the recent contingent of ardent Catholics from Poland. Not everyone comes to church, but they do identify as Catholics and so they are my sheep and I am their shepherd.

Today, most pews are empty but my core parishioners are steadfast, and they are all here, COVID or not. They are led by the indefatigable Mrs Keating. Her body mass is sprawled across the pew, taking three-quarters of it. The remaining quarter is reserved for Mr Keating. He doesn't need more than that. He is a tickbird to his wife's elephant. And despite Mrs Keating's frequent grievances about her husband's character and earning capacity, they enjoy a symbiotic relationship. How otherwise could they have spent thirty years together in marital bliss? Then again, some people simply don't like change.

My sermon is about forgiveness and not throwing the first stone. I make several subtle references to that biblical harlot turned saint, Mary Magdalene. Every word I utter I direct at Mrs Keating. 'Don't judge lest you be judged yourself,' I say.

She sucks in her lips and scowls at me. She is having none of it. There will be no forgiveness for Jane Cuthbert, the whore, or for me. I have failed to listen to Mrs Keating's warnings. I have failed in my duty to cast away the rotten apple that is contaminating the barrel of our parish. I have failed to give the harlot the sack. She continues to lay her poxy paws on the holy relics. Shame on me! That's what Mrs Keating is communicating to me with her eyes alone, without saying a word. For a minute or two, I fear she will not come to receive the Holy Communion from my unworthy hand. Indeed, she seems to hesitate when the moment arrives, the internal battle between her indignation and piety raging for a few tortuous seconds. The piety wins. She heaves her bulk from the bench and approaches the altar, with me trembling before it. I offer her *the Blood of Christ*, and she takes it with a peevish screw of her face, as if it was a chalice of vinegar. I retreat.

When the last note of the last hymn of the Mass falters away, I step outside to shake hands with my parishioners and this is where Mrs Keating comes into her own. She withholds her hand but issues me with a word of caution.

'I'll be writing to the Bishop about it, Father. So that you know.'

I thank her sheepishly. I don't know why I should be thanking her for snitching on me and stirring shit in the parish. The gratitude just pours out of my mouth and floods the awkwardness of the moment.

In a heroic act of defiance against his wife, Mr Keating offers me a sympathetic glance and shakes my hand. He will pay a heavy price for this later, I'm sure of that. His wife is already sharpening her daggers. She shoots him one of those and pulls him by the sleeve. 'Get yourself here, Seamus. We going.'

God rested on the seventh day, but that doesn't apply to priests. It's late evening. The last Mass of this Sunday is behind me, but I am restless. It's Mrs Keating. She has a knack for sending me off-kilter every time she opens her mouth. Thanks to Mrs Keating I lose sight of my purpose, and my understanding of God's greater scheme for mankind becomes muddled up. I need to get out and get some air. I need to clear my head.

I untie my hair. It's long down to my shoulders. Behind my back but within my earshot, I once heard Mrs Keating refer to me as the Big Lebowski. In fairness, she was spot on. I do resemble the man and we share similar values. It's a generational thing. It's the hippie in me, you see. If I hadn't become a priest, I would definitely have become a faithful replica of the Big Lebowski. But I received the calling. I try to live up to it. I do my best to be less of a slob than Lebowski, and I dress fractionally better than him, but I draw the line on the hairstyle. I refuse to conform to the conventional image of a man of the cloth by having my hair cut short. For work, I wear it in a tight topknot. When I am on my own I let it down. In my case, letting my hair down means exactly what it says on the tin. It's cathartic. And when I take my motorbike out for a ride, I'm in seventh heaven. I rev it up and it takes off, possessed of a will of its own. It takes me out of the estate and out of the city. It knows its way to my mooring point on the canal. We fly past farmhouses, hedgerows and laybys. When we're on the final straight, I accelerate to full throttle. I leave everything behind and I'm catching up with God. This is the closest I get to Him.

I sit on my boat in the darkness. Anyway, the moon is big and bright. That's all the light I need to think. I am thinking of my conversation with Ruthie: about what's next for me when the refurbish is done. I know I have already decided, but I can't admit it to myself. The boat is finished, ready to sail. She is calling to me.

'I can't,' I say, 'I'm a priest,' but I know that all I need is a small nudge, and I will jump ship.

The nudge comes on Wednesday. It's more like a big push to send me free-falling from the cliff of my vocation.

Jane Cuthbert may have become a fallen woman, but she has never lost her work ethic. She is diligent and punctual, running on her internal Swiss clock like a busy little hamster in a wheel. She arrives at mine at 7am on Wednesdays, come hell or high water. She cleans the priory and the church, in that order. She returns on Saturdays to deal with the laundry and ironing first, then goes out to buy fresh flowers and replaces the flower arrangements at the altar. On Saturdays she also arrives at 7am sharp. Like I said, she has an inbuilt Swiss clock inside her. So, when she fails to turn up by 7:10am I know something bad has happened. I immediately think the worst. I was warned, and I did not heed the warning...

I am hearing an urgent whisper rustling in my head from the moment my alarm clock wakes me at six.

I open my eyes. I sit up and find myself drenched in a cold sweat. A sense of foreboding washes over me. I can't remember having a bad dream, and yet my body feels battered and exhausted. My mind is on high alert. I pant for a couple of minutes and peer around me for any clues as to my unsettled state. Everything seems calm and undisturbed, the way I left it last night. But the whisper permeates my brain cells. It transforms into a cry. At first, I think I am still dreaming but the dream doesn't take on any recognisable form. It's just a cry inside my head. I close my eyes to retrace my steps back into the night and catch up with my quickly receding dreams. This strategy often works, but not today. There is nothing there but a spine-chilling dread.

I climb out of bed and take a shower to wash off the sweat and the remnants of that dread. Gradually, I lower the temperature until the water runs cold. This should wake me up for good, I tell myself, but I'm wrong. The sense of foreboding swells my ribcage and the voice in my head grows in volume and urgency. I can't distinguish individual words, and perhaps there aren't any. It's a primordial cry that belongs to the time when man could not speak. But I can hear the fear and dread locked in that voice. What the hell was I dreaming about in the night? I ask myself. It must've been bloody traumatic for my mind to shut it out like that. Only the persistent voice has squeezed through my mind's defences and is haunting me, without an explanation. I go to the kitchen to make breakfast.

I switch on the radio to suppress the noises in my head. It only gets messier. I blunder about with the toaster and cafetiere. Everything is falling out of my hands. They are shaking. Perhaps, I've taken ill, a rational thought occurs to me. I take two paracetamol tablets just in case. Paracetamol is a miracle drug, perfect for all kinds of ailments. Apart from the aches of the body it can also dispel the aches of the soul. I realise that the moment the voice is reduced to a thin squeal. Good old paracetamol has done the trick. I have my breakfast, drink my tea, and listen to the 7 o'clock news on Radio 4. I'm told it is now ten past seven. That's when I realise that Jane is not here and that the dread-infused voice I've been hearing was real all along.

Jane's flat is on the fourth floor and, true to form, the lift is out of order. I leap the stairs two steps at a time. I knock on her door, call out to her to let her know it's me. A man with a clean-shaven head and bloated face emerges from the flat next door and tells me to shut the fuck up. I'll wake up his baby.

'I need to see Jane,' I tell him.

'You're keen,' he sneers.

'You don't understand. She didn't turn up for work. I'm her employer.'

'Is that what you lot call yerself nowadays?' He mocks me.

'I'm a priest. Jane works for me.'

'It takes all kinds, I reckon.'

I decide to ignore the filthy insinuations. 'Have you seen her this morning?'

'No. But we heard her. She been busy all night. We was minded to call the cops. Keep it quiet in there, or we will,' he warns me before retreating into his flat and gently closing the door behind him so as not to wake his baby.

I try the handle. I should have done it straightaway. I find the door isn't locked.

I find Jane on the floor in the bedroom. She appears dead. There is a bloody gash on her temple. A blow to the head with a sharp instrument is what killed her, will be the verdict. Or will it be death by misadventure: she fell and hit her head on a sharp edge. I slump next to her, not because I go weak in the knees but because I slip in blood. It hasn't come from her temple. The blood on her head has dried into a dark-red icing a while back. The blood on the floor is still warm. Now I can see its source – her wrists. The right one has been opened vertically along the line of her veins. It's still idly seeping blood. The left one is wrapped in a towel. On closer inspection I realise it's more than one towel. It looks like she was trying to stem the flow of blood with towels. They are saturated. The wardrobe is gaping open, a stack of towels leaning over the edge of the shelf like the Tower of Pisa. A clean towel she tried to pull from the top of the stack is hanging out limply. It's too high and out of Jane's reach. She must have passed out before she could grab it and cover her other wrist.

Sitting this close to her, I can tell she isn't dead. Although she is dead-cold, she has a faint pulse. I call 999 and shout her address at them. I tell them to hurry, the fucking lift is out of order.

The dressing of the two towels has helped, I'm told by a weary looking doctor at the hospital. It slowed the bleeding from the left wrist. Fortunately for her, she was clumsy with the other wrist and missed the artery. Veins don't bleed as fast, the doctor elaborates. It's usually the case with suicides – they cut clean across one wrist, but struggle with the other. Is Ms Cuthbert right-handed? The doctor guesses based on her *handiwork*.

'What makes you think she did it to herself? She wouldn't have. She's catholic.'

'Lost her faith, I imagine. That's all it takes.' The doctor's weary eyes slide off my face. He is young but looks and acts like someone twice his age: tired, cynical and indifferent. Nothing can shock him. He has seen it all already.

'Not Jane,' I assure him. 'If she'd done it to herself, she wouldn't have tried to stop the bleeding with those towels, would she now?'

'Changed her mind. That happens. At least she wasn't too late.' He is walking away, his stride heavy and slow. He tells me, without looking back, to come back tomorrow – I should be able to talk to her and find out for myself. And would I be able to inform her next of kin?

Matthew. I will have to call him and let him know his mother was assaulted by a madman but she will be fine. I won't be lying. I know who did it. I know it wasn't Jane.

'Say again?' Loki is gawping at me with those watery eyes of his, making me feel like an idiot. 'So you let the bugger get away with it because he confides in you?'

'It's more complicated than that,' I attempt to explain the arcana of the Catholic practice. 'The confession is a holy sacrament. He doesn't confide in me – he confides in God. God will judge him, not man.'

'This sounds pretty much bonkers to me. The bastard has near enough killed your woman'

'Jane is not my woman. She works for me.'

'He almost succeeded at killing her,' Loki stares me down, 'and you're covering up for him. Ain't that aiding and abetting?' Loki is good at criminal law. His intimate knowledge of the terminology must have roots in his past brushes with the law, but it's not my place to quiz him on that. He strikes me as a decent man, and I'll leave it at that.

But Loki seems to doubt my integrity, 'Doesn't that make you an accomplice? I say, it does.'

'I'm bound by the seal of confession. There's nothing I can do about that. It's God's law.'

'Some God you've got there. If I was you I'd find myself another one. Or just go without God. I do. It's done me no harm.'

'That's a conversation for another day.' And it's a conversation I am already having with myself, and have been having for a while. You could call it a crisis of faith, but that's between me and God, and no one else.

'Nothing there to talk about.' Loki shrugs. He may well have a point. Faith isn't a matter for debate. You either believe or you don't. Logic and reason don't enter the arena when it comes to religion. And then, there are rules and rites. You can't debate those either. They are there to be followed, not questioned.

'You're right.' I nod. 'Let's leave religion out of it.'

'First sensible thing you said today, Noah. Now, call the cops.'

'And tell them what? I don't know his name, where he lives... I don't even know what he looks like. And besides, I don't think the cops are looking for him.'

'How come? He kills women for sport. Whore or not, she's still a woman. And that makes her a human being. Right or wrong?' Loki can be quite philosophical that way. He is one of the most liberally-minded people I ever met. As a matter of fact, he is much more than a liberal – he's an organic anarchist.

I nod again, and in the same breath I reiterate that I can't report the man to the police.

'Back to the seal of confession, then?'

'No. It isn't just that. The Prophet is too clever to be caught.

He leaves nothing to chance. That's why the cops aren't even aware they have a serial killer on their hands,' I say and proceed to relay to Loki what I know about the Prophet's modus operandi. How he moves from city to city to get the cops off his scent. How he varies his methods – no two deaths are the same. Jane, for that matter, was supposed to have cut her own wrists. Suicides aren't investigated by the police. Nor are cases of accidental overdose. They don't even register on their radar. Hit-and-run cases go straight to the bottom of the in-tray. The police don't have the resources – or in some instances the inclination – to follow-up on drunk prostitutes fished out of the river or battered to death by their pimps, or unsatisfied clients. The Prophet counts on this inertia. He is a shadow in the night. You put the lights on and he's gone, as if he was never there in the first place. The cops will never catch onto him. He knows that. He knows he's above the law. He thinks he answers to God, and God is on his side. He will go on doing it, with God's blessing, he believes. Someone has to bring him down to earth and hold him to account.

'We have to do it, Loki,' I hear my voice go up an octave, 'to warn him off those women. We must tell him that we know and we're watching his every step. It's up to us to stop him – no one else will!' At last, I am beginning to formulate a plan of action. We will put the Prophet in the straitjacket of our constant vigil. He won't be able to take a breath without thinking of us.

'So,' Loki scratches his dreadlocks, 'let me get this right – you want us to track the bugger down and rough him up a bit. Is that it?'

'In a nutshell.'

'That will not stop him.' It's Jeremiah's voice: a deep, booming baritone. It flies right at us from beyond the radius of our dying campfire. Jeremiah follows his voice out of hiding (he must have been there all along, listening to us) and appears in front of us like a black angel of death. He gives me an almighty fright. Only when my heart almost stops do I realise that my nerves are wound into a tight spiral. Jeremiah's arrival makes the spiral snap. I can hear the ping in my ribcage. I curse, and Loki echoes my sentiment.

Jeremiah pokes the coals that simmer faint-orange in the drum. They don't come to life. The orange flecks shrink into ash. Jeremiah chucks a few dry splinters into the hearth and blows sideways to rekindle the fire. Orange flyspecks burst into yellow flames that crack the splinters open. Jeremiah adds a log to the concoction and spits some beer from his can on top. The flames drink it thirstily – the fire is resurrected. He rubs his hands over it and repeats, 'That will not stop him. Your pussyfooting won't stop him. He's a killer, not a petty thief.'

'What do you suggest we do, then?' I know I shouldn't ask this question because I can't possibly entertain the answer. Not as a priest. Not as a Christian.

'We kill the killer. An eye for an eye, like the Good Book says.' Jeremiah goes all Old-Testament on me.

'Yeah,' Loki sucks in his lips and nods, 'It's what I was gonna say. We kill the bastard or he'll go on killing them street girls under your nose. You want to have them on your conscience, Noah? Is your God alright with that?'

Despite the fire blazing sky-high in the drum, I shiver with cold. Thousands of tiny pins prick my skin. I've reached a point of no return. A decision has been made for me. I have to honour it. I came to these two good men for help and that's what they're offering. I have to take it even though this will change who I am for ever. This moment has been long overdue. I shift my gaze steadily from Loki to Jeremiah to make sure we understand each other. Loki lifts his chin and holds my gaze. Jeremiah is looking straight back at me. There is no hesitation. There is no misunderstanding.

'Yes,' I say. 'It has to be done.'

We put our heads together and plot the execution step by step. The Prophet will come to confess, sooner or later. He has the need to share his glory with me and the Almighty. He wants a pat on the back from God. I will be there waiting for him. Then I will follow him and find out where he lives. Maybe he has a family. We will have to take everything into account before our next move. But however and wherever we do it, we will kill him.

CAMILLA

So, we are going into lockdown. At very short notice, I'm afraid. I will have to drive into town and stock up. Apparently, toilet paper is in such short supply, that it is being rationed. This is like living through the war, only it may not be as quick as the Blitz. It may go on for a while, anyone who knows anything says so. I have made a list of life necessities to purchase: tin food, toilet paper, dry food, toilet paper, flour, sugar, powdered milk, toilet paper, Coco Pops, and some toilet paper. I realise I have mentioned toilet paper several times. That's because I am planning to visit several supermarkets. I'm determined we shan't be left feeling deprived during this lockdown due to loo paper shortages.

Hugh is in a state. He is making rushed arrangements to work from home. He has turned the whole house inside out, swamped the sitting room with archive boxes containing his law books. He is an old-fashioned barrister. He refuses to access reference books online so he has brought the whole lot of them home. He has been driving between his Chambers and the house since the early hours of the morning, like a shuttle bus. He can't possibly help me with the shopping or babysitting

Joshua, so I mustn't ask, he tells me imperiously before I open my mouth. Actually, I wasn't planning to waste my breath asking him for any help. When was the last time he helped with house chores?

I make sure Christopher's papers don't get mixed up with Hugh's. The boxes all look the same. It'd be only too easy for Hugh to make a mistake and open Christopher's box. Something tells me Christopher wouldn't like that. Something tells me I too should steer away from that box. It's best to leave it sealed. I am going to take it up to the loft and put it next to the boxes with Christopher's old school reports and art portfolios. Before becoming a banker, Christopher used to enjoy painting. Acrylics, watercolours. He was good at it, and it isn't just me saying that – it was his teachers.

For the time being, I leave the box in the sitting room, but in the opposite corner to where Hugh's junk is scattered. I will have to deal with it later. There will be plenty of time. Right now, I have greater priorities than shuffling boxes around the house.

I end up dragging Joshua with me on my shopping errand. Truth be told, I'd have to take him anyway. The clothes Phillipa packed in his microscopic suitcase are all too small for him. Little wonder the suitcase is tiny. Every pair of trousers stops an inch over his ankles, making him look like a clown. I couldn't find two socks that match. Soles are peeling off his shoes, his underwear with worn out elastic waistbands is sliding off his bum – it's a disgrace. This is what I call, plain and simple, *child neglect*. So, we will have to buy a whole new wardrobe and I need him to come with me to try things on. Once lockdown kicks in, I won't be able to exchange or return items that don't fit.

We do the grocery shopping first. His eyes lit up only once, and very briefly. It's when I pack a trolley-full of Coco Pops.

Half an hour later, in the aisle with household cleaning products, he throws a tantrum and runs away. The shop is buzzing with legions of half-mad panic-shoppers and there, hiding amongst them, is my seven-year-old grandson, God knows where exactly. I am beside myself with anxiety. My blood pressure must be shooting through the roof. I will have to have it checked at Boots later. Firstly, though, I have to locate Joshua.

I deploy the supermarket's entire security team to look for him. He doesn't respond to the loud-speaker announcement that his grandma is worried sick and she is waiting for him at the tills. Not that I expect him to respond, but his snub breaks my heart. Everyone is searching for him and every exit is manned so that no paedophile smuggles him out of the shop. I want to join the search party but the Manager – an Indian man with a Glaswegian accent and tinted glasses which don't inspire my confidence because I can't see his eyes – insists I stay put so that they know where I am when they find Joshua.

After a nail-biting wait, one of the shop assistants is leading my little man by the hand from the far end of the home appliances aisle. My knees buckle under me. My brain swims inside my skull. I feel faint. I find myself in the arms of the Manager.

'I've got you, ma'am,' he breathes reassuringly into my ear.

Joshua is unapologetic. I am told the shop assistant found him in the cafeteria, sharing a bowl of chips with a clergyman. My blood runs cold. I don't have to tell you what horrors pass through my mind. The things clergymen get up to! It's all in the public domain nowadays. It's so vile I couldn't make it up if I tried.

'I like chips!' Joshua shouts primarily at me, but everyone can hear him, and there is a sizeable crowd of well-wishers gathered around us. 'You never give me chips!'

Only when I cross-my-heart-and-hope-to-die in the solemn oath that I will buy him large fries and something called *Big Mac without lettuce* at McDonald's does he calm down. We head for the till to pay and get the hell out of this place.

I check my bag and my pockets. I spill the entire contents of my bag in front of the checkout assistant so that she can see for herself that I am not making it up. My wallet isn't there. I left it at home, I hope. That's the best I can hope for, because if it was stolen, it bears no contemplation. It could well have been stolen in all the commotion. I feel faint. I had my credit cards, my driving licence and all of my loyalty cards in that wallet. My PINs were there two, scribbled on a piece of paper crunched up and hidden in the compartment with the zip. I struggle to remember PINs. There are so many of them. I have to write them down.

The checkout assistant presses a button and a red light above her head lights up. We look at each other in stony silence, waiting for her supervisor. By we, I mean her and me, plus the line of some twenty people and their bursting trolleys behind me. They are shooting daggers at me. I can literally feel them piercing my back.

The Manager in tinted glasses arrives. I sigh with relief. He already knows me. I explain the situation to him and suggest I dash off home to drop the shopping and collect my wallet. I will be back in no time to settle the bill. He and the checkout assistant exchange a look that I am not entirely comfortable with.

'We can't let you walk away with the goods without paying, ma'am,' he says.

The shop shelves are almost empty. If I let go of my shopping, it will be lost for ever. The Coco Pops and the toilet paper! 'OK,' I say, 'in that case, please put my shopping to one side. Keep it safe for me until I come with the money.'

'It's not our policy, I am afraid.'

'This is ridiculous!' I look around me, seeking support from other shoppers. All I get is tut-tuts and rolling eyes.

A man shouts from the back, 'Are you serving on this till, or not?'

'If you come with me, please, ma'am.' The Manager touches my elbow. Despite his tinted glasses and shifty appearance, it is I who feel like a criminal caught in the act. Joshua is peering at me with fascination. He is temporarily appeased.

'Let me call my husband. He works at Albion Chambers, near the Crown Court. He won't be ten minutes and we can sort this out.'

The Manager eyes me with suspicion. He gazes at Joshua who is sitting in an office chair next to me, dangling his legs and gaping at the ceiling with his mouth open. The Manager ponders whether to call the police or to allow me to call my husband. I'm guessing he even doubts that Joshua is my grandson.

Joshua saves the day. 'I'm hungry, grandma. You promised I can have McDonalds. Can we go now?'

The Manager relents and agrees that I call Hugh.

Hugh arrives in a cloud of agitation. He is a busy man. He reminds me how he has told me over and over again to see a GP and to get a referral. My memory is going. He can't be bailing me out all the time. He bailed me out? That's news to me. When exactly was that? I don't ask him because it could just prove his point that I can't remember things. He hands his credit card alongside his profuse apology for the inconvenience his wife has caused to the Manager. The Manager smiles sagely and nods his understanding.

Before he flies back to work, I ask Hugh for his card. I

haven't finished shopping. Unless, of course, he wants to take over from here, I say. He looks as if I've lost my marbles (those few I had left in his learned opinion) and shakes his head in disbelief. He slips me a twenty-pound note. I glare at him and slap the banknote onto the palm of his hand.

'What's this? Is it a joke?' I ask him.

'OK.' He shrugs and puts the offending note into his pocket. 'Where is the cashpoint?'

The Manager directs us to the nearest one. He and Hugh exchange emphatic glances.

Joshua digs his heels in and refuses to try on a single item of clothing. He isn't a girl, he informs me and scowls. I can tell he is on the verge of another tantrum. I can't take another one without suffering a breakdown myself, so I fly through the shop, throwing various articles of clothing for boys aged 7-8 into the basket. I am desperate for a new bra. My old ones are a bit tired and tatty. They may not last through lockdown if it endures for longer than a month. Planning ahead, I thought I'd buy one today. But right now, I just want to get out of the department store before all hell breaks loose. Even if it means I will have to go through lockdown with my tits hanging out. Please excuse the vulgarity, but I'm at the end of my tether and I need to sit down somewhere, and unwind.

We go to McDonald's. I suspend my strongly-held beliefs about child obesity, obscene salt content levels in junk food and the type 2 diabetes epidemic while I blissfully watch Joshua devour his large fries and a Big Mac, and noisily suck his Coca Cola through a plastic straw. His eyes roll with pleasure. He resembles a junkie who has just pumped his veins full of crack cocaine. I am having the lettuce leaf he discarded from his Big Mac. We have called a truce. If I am to be honest with myself I must admit that it is an unconditional surrender on my part rather than a truce. Joshua has made no concessions. But he is content at long last. I am thoroughly enjoying this moment of tranquillity and togetherness with my grandson. I remember how I used to take Christopher for fish and chips served in newspaper on the beach. It became our ritual. The day after he came home from his boarding school for the summer holidays, we would drive to Weston-super-Mare for a donkey ride followed by fish and chips. I worry what they feed him in prison. He may develop scurvy if it's as bad as I think it is. I tell Joshua that Coca Cola will rot his teeth if he has any more of it.

I'm doing some hard thinking. How will I explain this to Hugh? I don't know why I did it. We have a policy of no pets in the house, and here I am driving home with two goldfish, a 4-foot long fish tank on the back seat, an assortment of aquarium accessories, and two bags of fish feed, all purchased with Hugh's cash.

We had left McDonald's and were walking to the car, past a pet shop. Joshua spotted the shark-like fish in the window. He stuck his nose to the glass, mesmerised. 'Look Grandma, sharks!' He waved to me to join him. I stuck my nose to the window too and we watched them together. I found it cathartic to watch fish swim in green water illuminated with lights that made their scales twinkle. It occurred to me that this was my chance to win over my grandson. Perhaps my only chance. I remembered how hard he fought to try to go to Australia with Phillipa and Peter just to see sharks. Sharks were key to conquering his little heart.

'Shall we take one home?' I heard myself say.

We bought two because, quite rightly, Joshua felt one would be very lonely and could die on us. Once we acquired the sharks, we also had to purchase the tank and everything that went with it.

There is no going back. Joshua is sitting next to me with a bag containing two Bala sharks in his lap. They are only small at the moment, about 3 inches each, but we were told they could reach up to 20 inches in adulthood. 'Sharks grow big, Grandma,' Joshua confirms that, his eyes as huge as saucers, 'bigger than you and me put together.' He is staring at them, watching them grow.

'They're definitely mine, yeah? We don't have to give them back when they grow up, or ever?' He quizzes me for the second time just as we approach our driveway.

For the second time I say, 'Definitely. I paid for them so they're yours.'

I flick on the indicator.

'Good,' he smiles at me most graciously. 'It's good you're not a cheating – thieving bastard, like Daddy. Daddy is a cheating – thieving bastard. And he got caught and he had to give everything back.'

'Who told you that?' I say it calmly, displaying only passing interest in the identity of the *cheating – lying* bastard. I don't want to alarm the boy. He is only a child. He doesn't know what he is saying.

'Peter.'

'Did he, now?'

'Yep.' Joshua nods and pokes the bag, forcing the sharks to retreat in panic to the other side.

I grab his arm and demand that he looks at me. 'Listen here!' I think I am shouting when I tell him that his Dad is a good, honest man, unlike that scumbag, Peter.

My blood reaches boiling point. I see red, and that could be the reason why I don't see the motorbike until it's too late.

JOSEPH

I give the taxi driver my address. Jane shoots me a quizzical look. She is as pale as a starched sheet. In her ghostly face her eyes seem like black puddles. I had to push her in a wheelchair to get her down to the taxi, and yet something makes her think that she is ready to go back to her fourth-floor flat. Considering that the sodding lift is out of action, she is sorely mistaken. And I won't even mention that the Prophet is out there, lurking in the shadows. He is probably watching her flat in the expectation of her funeral so that he can bask in the glory of his handiwork. What will he do when he realises she is still alive?

'Not today, you're not.' I inform her with the highest level of authority I can muster. 'You're in no state to go back to your flat. We'll talk about this at mine later, not now.' I gesture towards the cab driver who is eavesdropping on our conversation. His eyeballs turn away from the road. They are huge and they jut out of his skull and move as if they are on stalks. I look into his eyes which are peering at me through the rear-view mirror. They narrow with curiosity: what is an old priest doing taking a vulnerable young woman home? Is she related to him, or is he one of those predators hiding behind a dog collar? The world is full of them. I smile benignly at him. He scowls and his eyes – thank God – return to the traffic on the road.

'What did you tell Matthew? I don't want him to worry.' Jane can't wait until we are out of the nosy taxi driver's earshot.

'I told him you'd be fine.'

'Good,' Jane says, but she doesn't look reassured. Her face is crumpled with anxiety. 'How did he sound to you?'

'Well, you know young people these days...' I earn a few seconds to order my thoughts. I can't repeat to her what Matthew said. She is too fragile to hear it. I promised him I'd talk to her gently and prepare her for what's coming, but this isn't the right time for revelations. I am not ready and the taxi isn't the place to discuss such matters, so I say, 'He sounded busy, overall.'

'Is he not coping?'

'No, it's not that. He's busy, but happy. He loves it there. You can be sure of that.'

'He told you, did he? He doesn't tell me much. Kids, eh?' A smile lifts her cheeks. Her eyes brim with motherly pride. It looks like I have put her mind at ease. She relaxes, drops her head on the headrest and sighs her relief. I can't relax. I still have a mountain to climb.

We are sitting over a welcome-back-home cup of tea and an accompanying packet of biscuits (I only have Hobnobs). We are facing each other so I have nowhere to hide when I finally blurt it out, 'I'm leaving the priesthood.'

This conversation should really be taking place in the confessional because leaving the priesthood is only the tip of an iceberg: an inevitable consequence of the mortal sin I am about to commit. I yearn to be able to unburden myself, to tell someone – to tell Jane in particular. She stands in the centre of this. What happened to her is the trigger for my actions. But we are in my living room, not in the confessional, and I have no right to saddle her with my guilt. If I were to tell her and she kept my secret, I would be taking away her innocence and turning her into an accomplice. I can't have that on my conscience as well as murder.

She puts down her cup and gapes at me while she slowly processes what I have just told her. A sharp vertical line cuts into her forehead as she finally understands. 'You can't do that!'

'I believe I can.'

'You have lost your faith.' It's funny how her face speaks for her, and sometimes, contradicts her. Her tone is disapproving and harsh, but her face tells a story of anguish and fear.

'It's a long story, Jane. My faith is still here,' I place my hand on my chest to demonstrate my point, 'but my plans have changed. I've a narrowboat, did you know?'

Her face tells me that she didn't and that she cannot fathom why she should.

'I'll be moving there. I always fancied sailing, living close to nature. It's my retirement treat.'

'You're retiring from being a priest?'

'I am, yes – retiring. Precisely that.' I lie through my teeth as I smile at her.

'Is that even allowed?'

'I'm sure it's been done before.'

'I don't believe you.'

It isn't disbelief that registers on her face – it's panic.

'I am leaving, Jane, but I've made arrangements for you. I'm setting you up on the payroll as a live-in housekeeper. You can have the room in the roof. It's got its own ensuite. You'll have your privacy. And with me gone nobody will say that you're a kept woman. A new priest will probably be a hundred years old. We aren't getting any younger. So, how's that for a plan?'

She is shaking her head.

I will not let her foil my plans. I say, 'You've no choice. You can't go back to what you were doing before... After what happened... You know that damn well. This is your best bet: a roof over your head, a secure income, a stable job. You'll have to sign here,' I shove the backdated employment contract in front of her and hand her a pen. I watch her sign it. I am pleased with myself. I took her by surprise. Given time to think, she would have said no. I know Jane Cuthbert only too well.

Later, after the News that I watch and she ignores, I ask her about the man who attacked her. I want to be sure I have the right man.

'It wasn't any of my regulars,' she says. She can't tell me much more than that. The man had a beard, a thick and untidy facial growth. He was wearing a hat – a beanie. It was too big for him. It drooped over his ears and sat on the bridge of his nose. He had to lift his chin to look at her. His eyes peered from under that weird hat like two thieves in the night. She should have known better, she tells me. She took a stupid risk because she was worried. What with lockdown coming, social distancing, people trapped in their houses, she would have no income for God knows how long. She took a risk on a stranger. She led the way to her flat; he followed behind her. The lift is out of order.

'Yes, I know,' I comment, and add, 'Did he say anything?'

No, he didn't. Not to Jane. He had nothing to say to her, unworthy of his words as she was. He will have a lot to say to me when he comes to confess. He will sing his heart out. But he didn't utter a single word to Jane apart from the initial inquiry of *how much*. She led him to her fourth-floor flat in silence. She unlocked the door. They stepped in and then it all went blank. The cut on her head – he must've bludgeoned her... Her fingers hover over the shaved patch on the side of her head from where the stitches sprout. She didn't feel a thing when he opened her wrists.

'I'm sorry.' The weight of guilt compresses my chest and obstructs my airways like a fallen boulder that comes to rest across a shallow stream. I let this happen. I let him do it. I did not stop him.

'It's not your fault, Father. I made my bed...' Her voice trails off.

I beg to differ. The boulder sits firmly on my chest.

'In my defence,' Jane frowns, remembering, 'I had the feeling I knew him from somewhere. Like, you know, something in his voice, in how he moved – something about him... I can't put my finger on it, but I'm sure I've seen him before.'

I have an audience with Bishop Hillary.

His Personal Secretary has managed to squeeze me in before lockdown begins and we have to wait for God knows how long. Given the nature of my *inquiry,* the Personal Secretary pronounced the word with a pointed slowness, it would be best if it was discussed in person. I didn't argue that this wasn't an inquiry, but my resignation, and that the Bishop and I had nothing to discuss because I wasn't changing my mind. I would have preferred to simply give in my notice. I had completed it in the early hours of the morning after numerous failed attempts to compose it throughout my sleepless night. It had taken a lot of out me to put down on paper the three short paragraphs that felt like a suicide note. I certainly didn't wish to prolong the agony by debating my decision with the Bishop. But the Personal Secretary was adamant His Excellency would wish to see me in person. Despite his very busy schedule, he added.

The audience is at 2pm. That should give His Excellency sufficient time to conclude his lunch in peace and perhaps indulge in a short nap afterwards. He is an old man, in his mid-eighties. He deserves a nap. Come to think of it, he deserves to hang up his skull cap and put his feet up permanently. He will put me to shame, no doubt: me resigning my holy post at the tender age of fifty-seven while he plods on, like the Queen, till death does him part from his duty. Oh well, I have other fish to fry, I ponder glibly. I am trying my best to calm my nerves before the audience. I fear it will take the shape and form of giving me the third degree. I half expect the Holy Inquisition to turn up. My palms are sweaty. I have not sweated like this since puberty.

I don't want to be disrespectful by arriving late so I am there with more than an hour to spare. I loiter about for a while until it starts to rain, then I seek shelter at Sainsbury's. There is a café at the back of the store. The food smells good and I didn't have lunch, so it's a no-brainer. I join the queue. I buy fish and chips (it is a Friday after all) and a pot of tea. The place is buzzing with customers and the only table I can find is plonked by the stairs that lead through to the shop. There is a constant flow of foot traffic accompanied by the squeaking of overloaded shopping trolleys. People must be panic buying today in preparation for lockdown which is to start on Monday. I feel a bit awkward in my best cassock, sitting at Sainsbury's over a plate of fish and chips. I've tied my hair so tightly that my face feels like I've been injected with Botox (not that I would know how it feels, but I can imagine).

'Can I have some of your chips?' A boy of about eight is standing in front of me, reaching to my plate before I say yes. He has reddish-blond hair that would be angelic if it was a touch more curly. As it is, it flops over his eyes. His determination to have my chips is evident in his hungry scowl. He grabs the chunkiest chip he can find and asks me for ketchup. He can see I have unopened sachets on the table. I can't deny him. Chips go with ketchup so if he is having my chips he may as well have the ketchup. I squirt it onto my plate and he dips his chip in it. He takes big bites and chews with his back teeth (his front ones being temporarily unavailable). When he goes for the second chip we smile at each other.

'Are you lost?' I ask him.

'No,' he responds. 'I like chips. My grandma doesn't give me chips and my mummy's gone to Australia without me.'

I can feel his pain, so I push the plate towards him and nod my encouragement at him. 'Well, help yourself then.'

He does. We squirt out more ketchup, all over the chips, the way he instructs me to do.

I ask his name (it's not right to share a meal with someone without making your acquaintance first).

'Joshua Bramley-Jones.' So now, we aren't strangers anymore.

'That's a fancy name.'

'I know. It's like I am an apple.' He laughs so I laugh too. I'm having a good time chatting to Joshua Bramley-Jones, so good in fact that I almost forget about my audience with His Excellency.

'Do you like apples?'

'I love apples. They're good for you.'

'I don't like apples. I love chips.' He is chomping away, and pauses to ask me what my name is.

'Joe. It's Joe.'

'OK. Are you a ninja, Joe?'

I think my cassock may be misleading. 'Not quite, Joshua. I'm a priest,' I dispel the confusion.

'My dad is a cheating – thieving bastard.'

'Is he now?'

'Aha. He's in prison.'

'I see. Well...'

'I like sharks.'

'To eat?' I jest.

'No, silly. You can't eat a shark. A shark can eat you!'

We chuckle.

I become acutely aware of the fact that this doesn't look good: a priest sharing a plate of chips and a laugh with a young boy. I can feel people's eyes burning into my back. The horror stories they will share with their families over their dinner tonight! *So, he bribed the poor child with chips... In broad daylight, it was. No shame, them paedophiles! It's an urge for them, an illness. I was minded to call the police but-*

'Joshua?' A shop assistant with a name tag that says *Maggie* peers at my new friend, and then at me. A big question mark is plastered on her face. I raise my eyebrows and try to look like I'm no more than an unsuspecting bystander.

'Who wants to know?' Joshua retorts.

'Your grandmother's looking for you. She's very worried. Didn't you hear the calls through the loud speakers?'

I didn't, I want to say, but I shouldn't really dig myself deeper so I remain neutral.

'She never gives me chips. I like chips.'

'Let's go.' Maggie, the shop assistant, extends her hand to Joshua and he clasps his greasy one into it. He goes with her obediently, but I am guessing his compliance is more to do with the fact that there are no more chips on my plate than with him being a good boy.

He definitely has good manners though for he turns his head and chimes, 'Thanks for the chips, Joe.'

I mock-salute him and grin despite a few accusatory glares

trying to burn through my skull and appeal to my conscience. I finish the fish, no chips, and leave the tea untouched. I'm late for my audience with the Bishop.

The heavy swollen bags under the Bishop's eyes look like upended eyelids. His whole face seems to be the wrong way up. His lips are shrivelled and drained of colour. They are no more than a thin slit. Two pronounced folds created by wrinkles on his forehead could pass for his real lips. And then there is the bald head, narrowing into an oval shape towards the top. It could easily be his clean-shaven chin. When he frowns, the illusion of a flipped-over head is irresistible. Indeed, this could be the case as I have just turned his world on its head.

'Dear me, dear me...' he mutters. He has a lot to be unhappy about. A priest abandoning his calling on Bishop Hillary's watch is a PR disaster, and a personal affront. It's a failure of leadership. I feel for him. 'Is there anything I can do to change your mind, Father Joseph?'

I shake my head with a contrite expression on my face. 'I wish there was,' I say, 'but no. I'm sorry.'

'I'd be happy to give you some time off, a sabbatical. It can be done. You could go to Wroughton Retreat. Take as much time as you need. A year, even longer. Think about it, Joseph. Think deeply about it. Leaving the priesthood is not a decision to be taken frivolously.'

I listen. I don't attempt to interrupt him in order to put him straight. In fact, I am glad he does all the talking. When he asked to know why, I couldn't even begin to explain my reasons, not without making things up, and I didn't want to lie. So, I said I couldn't talk about it. He was baffled, but didn't push me. Now, he is making a valiant effort to convince me to stay.

'Take a break, Joseph. We could organise counselling for

you. It's not unusual to experience a crisis of faith. Even St Paul denied our Lord – thrice...' His Excellency fixes me with eyes that nestle in the sacs of his heavy eyebags. 'If you leave there'll be no return.'

'I won't be returning.'

'And you will leave your parishioners without a second thought?'

'I will stay in post until you have a replacement – throughout lockdown at the very least. Six weeks? Months?' I am amiable. I have to be. With lockdown upon us I will have to sit it out and wait until the church doors are open again and the Prophet is back in my confessional. No one knows when that will be. I won't be leaving The Sacred Heart until I've *dealt* with him.

'That's very thoughtful of you. I will let you know when we have a replacement.' The Bishop lets me kiss his ruby-red signet. As I bend down to do so, I can feel his hand on my head and hear him whisper a blessing.

I only stop at the priory to shed my cassock and release my hair from the shackles of the elastic band, and to change into something motorbike friendly. I don't even pause for long enough to have a cup of tea. Jane scowls at me and climbs up the step ladder to take down the curtains. The dust trapped in the thick velvet rises in a grey cloud as they hit the floor. In reply to my offer of help, she informs me she is perfectly capable of handling ladders and curtains on her own. Indeed, she is back on form: agile and strong. Her bandaged wrists look like they belong to a tennis player and give little indication of the attempt on her life. She doesn't ask what the Bishop said to my resignation. She has already told me what she thinks of my decision. Not much, let's leave it there. The Bishop's comments won't change that. She does want to know however if I will be back for tea. That's an affirmative from me. It's a fish pie, she says. And that will be a welcome deviation from my earlier fish and no chips.

I am heading for the canal. I have a few things to discuss with Loki and Jeremiah before the Monday lockdown begins in earnest. They – we – will have to arm ourselves with bags of patience. The church will be closed for the foreseeable future. The Prophet will be prevented from confessing. On a positive note, he will also be prevented from preying on women. Even he won't take chances on scouring the streets at night and getting caught by the curfew police (I'm guessing that there will be police patrols making sure that people stay at home and that no carnal liaisons take place between strangers in dark alleys). In a way, I welcome the lockdown with open arms. It will give us all time to think – a stay of execution. Maybe, I ponder uncharitably, God will change his mind and strike the Prophet dead with the virus. That would save me, Loki and Jeremiah from having to commit mortal sin.

The country lanes feel glorious. It isn't quite that I have the wind in my hair (the helmet prevents any such romantic notion), but the sense of freedom gives me wings. I don't mind the rain, either. I am the only one on the road, charging ahead with a clear mind and purpose, and it feels like an allegory for my new beginning. I was reluctant to embark on this journey but now that I've taken the first step and shaken off my inhibitions, I'm sailing with favourable winds. I have no doubts and no regrets.

The road follows a sharp bend that is edged with untrimmed hedgerow. There is a concealed driveway there. A car cuts in front of me but doesn't make it to the safety of that driveway. I slam on my brakes but the road is wet and slippery and I know that I won't be able to stop. The brakes lock the wheel and my bike topples over itself. I am catapulted at the car.

I just about register the face of the woman driver. The look in her eyes.

It is true what they say about that fraction of a second before a collision. Your soul leaves your body. Mine does exactly that. It evacuates the scene of the accident just before the final impact and it shoots across towards the car, and towards the woman driver and her wide opened eyes. It drowns in the black of her irises.

PART 2

PICKING UP THE PIECES

HUGH, IN CAMILLA'S ABSENCE

Hugh Bramley-Jones, QC, was in the middle of a strategic meeting about business continuity in lockdown when his mobile phone rang. It was his wife, Camilla. Again. Only a couple of hours ago he'd had to rescue her at Sainsbury's. She had left her purse at home and embarked on a shopping expedition without it. Whatever was going through her head it had nothing to do with life on this planet. He would have to insist on her seeing a GP. She would need a referral for one of those MRI scans to have her head examined. Hugh didn't mean this in a nasty way. He was genuinely worried about Mills. However, right now he had no time to run and rescue her from yet another self-made crisis, so he pressed the Ignore button. His attention returned to the tricky matter of how to install Microsoft Teams on his home computer. He was a pen and paper man, but needs must.

His phone rang again. Everybody in the room gave him the look. Being of a certain age, none of the senior partners were technically minded and all that IT stuff was doing their heads in. Hugh's ringing phone wasn't helping. He excused himself and answered the bloody thing in the foyer.

'Mills, this isn't a good time.'

'Mr Bramley?' a male voice addressed him, truncating his double-barrel surname in the way that always made Hugh cringe.

'Bramley-Jones, yes,' he pronounced the full version of his name pointedly. His quick mind drew an instant conclusion that Mills had lost her phone and that this interlocutor had found it and pressed the first number on the speed dial. Hugh wasn't concerned to hear a stranger's voice on Mills's mobile, but he was marginally annoyed. He would never know how to install the sodding Microsoft Teams now.

'This is PC Jenkins. I'm afraid your wife's been involved in a motor vehicle collision.'

Hugh puffed out his cheeks. His first reaction to the news was that of a lawyer rather than a husband. Thoughts of insurance claims, premiums going up and possibly a court hearing crossed his mind in telegraphic succession. Mill's recent absent-mindedness had to be a contributory factor to the crash. Since Christopher's arrest, her mind was all over the place. She shouldn't be driving in her state, and he partially blamed himself for letting her. But what was he to do? He was a busy man. He would have to settle any third-party claims out of his own pocket to protect Mill's clean insurance record. He asked matter-of-factly, 'What happened? Was she at fault?'

'We don't know yet, sir. But your wife is in hospital. She's in a critical condition.'

'Where? Which hospital?'

'University Hospital Bristol.'

The A&E department was absolute bedlam. Hugh pushed through a crowd of the sick, the injured and the dying to queue at the reception. When he leant over the counter he was told to maintain a two-metre distance by a masked nurse who refused to answer his questions until he did as he was told. He stared at her wide-eyed and swept his arm over the waiting room packed like a box of sardines. That was his tacit protest, but she didn't relent, so he did move a step back under the nurse's implacable glare. She then asked if he was experiencing any symptoms of coronavirus.

'No, I'm fine, as you can damn-well see. It's my wife.'

'Please don't swear, sir.' The receptionist was icily composed as she recited the rules for him, 'If your wife has symptoms, please take her home. Your household must self-isolate for fourteen days. Should her condition deteriorate, call 111 in the first instance. Do not visit your GP or bring her to the hospital.'

Hugh let her finish her pointless sentence. He was trained not to butt in when others were speaking (no matter what nonsense they were spewing) and wait his turn. When it came, he said, 'My wife was in a car accident. I received a call from the police telling me that she was admitted here. Camilla Bramley-Jones. Can I see her please?'

The nurse fixed him with a scolding gaze that implied that people who were reckless enough to have accidents in the middle of a pandemic should be shot, alongside their meddlesome spouses. She didn't say it though, and maybe Hugh only imagined that look in the first place. The nurse just happened to have those dead-cold eyes and deep frowning wrinkles. She asked if it was Bramley Jones *with a dash*, and he nodded, glad that this dialogue was moving in the right direction. She tapped away on her computer, read the screen and advised him to sit down and wait. 'You can't see her right now – she's in the operating theatre. Someone will come and talk to you as soon as she's out and we have some news.'

Hugh was not used to taking orders, but he sat down and waited. Time dragged on and no amount of checking the clock on his mobile phone made it go any faster. Hugh couldn't even stretch his limbs. He was squashed between two people: a man of Hugh's age, who patently couldn't stop coughing, and a youngster, probably still a teenager, judging by his angry acne, whose sleeve was saturated with blood. There was so much of it that it trickled down his hand and dripped from his forefinger onto the floor. If he was not seen by a doctor soon, Hugh pondered, he would bleed to death.

His coughing neighbour made him anxious. If Hugh didn't have the virus when he arrived here, he would certainly have it by the time he left. He scanned the waiting room for an alternative seat, but there wasn't one unless you counted the chair used by a mother to change her baby's nappy. Hugh decided to take his chances with the virus. He didn't like children overall, but babies in particular gave him a severe allergic reaction.

The unpleasant sight (and smell) made him think of Christopher and the day he had been brought home from hospital. After her c-section Mills had been unable to tend to Christopher, or so she claimed, so Hugh had ended up bathing and changing nappies, and cursing heavily under his breath. He had never wanted children. The world was overcrowded without him adding to the headcount. Still, despite his misgivings about parenthood, Christopher had grown on him. He was an agreeable child, knew his place and as soon as he reached school age, he had been dispatched to a boarding school. For the best part of Christopher's childhood and puberty, Hugh hardly knew that the boy was there. In fact, that blissful oblivion extended into Christopher's university days, and beyond. Christopher studied away from home, in London. Straight after uni, he had found a good job with a decent income and was able to afford to buy his own house. Thinking about it now, Hugh mused, it was as if Christopher had never really entered the equation of what one would call their family life. Hugh's memories of Christopher growing up were rather sketchy. He vividly remembered Christopher cry, kick and scream when they were about to drive him to his boarding school in Hampshire. Not unlike young Joshua the other day when Hugh and Mills had gone to pick him up from Phillipa's...

...Joshua.

'Joshua!' Hugh heard himself exclaim in horror. Somehow he had lost his grandson in all the mayhem and confusion of this surreal day. The man to his left stopped coughing and gazed at him quizzically, and the young man to his right nearly jumped out of his skin and raised his arm over his head in a gesture of self-defence.

Hugh rose to his feet and pressed his weight to the front of the queue to the reception, ignoring many heated protests and recriminations.

'What about Joshua Bramley-Jones?' He demanded from the stern nurse. 'He was with my wife in the car. Is he here? Is he alright?'

She scowled and reminded him of the two-metre rule before checking her computer. The man she had been dealing with before Hugh's intrusion groaned and announced that this was a fucking circus, not a hospital. The nurse remained uncompassionate. She peered at Hugh from above her screen and told him that there was no Joshua Bramley-Jones on record. He hadn't been admitted to this hospital. She suggested Hugh try Bristol Royal Hospital for Children and apologised to the *circus man* for the interruption.

Hugh had exhausted all the hospitals within the area as well as his phone battery. The little battery symbol was flashing red when he called the police in a last-ditch attempt to locate

Joshua. He should have thought of it earlier. By the time he had made it to the correct person, he was hyperventilating and praying to the non-existent god not to cut him off now. He gave the female officer at the other end of the tenuous line the hazy details he had in his possession about the accident. Luckily, Mills's full name was sufficient for the officer to find the traffic police accident report. She started skim-reading it under her breath. Hugh informed her that he had no battery left and all he wanted was to know where his grandson was.

'There's no mention of your grandson,' she said at last.

'Whatever do you mean! He was there with my wife!'

'I'm sorry, but no child was found at the scene.'

'He can't have evaporated!'

Another alarmist beep of his phone told him this inquiry was nearing its unscheduled conclusion.

'Would you like to report a missing child, sir?'

Hugh shouted that yes, he damn-well would, but the policewoman can't have heard him. His phone was dead.

Hugh had been making those frantic calls from his car in the car park outside the hospital. It was dark and dreary by the time he started the engine and headed home. It was still drizzling – it had been all day. His car headlights fanned out onto the wet tarmac and made it glisten like quicksilver. Though he was tempted to put his foot down, Hugh drove carefully. The last thing he wanted was to roll off the road and not be able to call for help. He was at his wits' end and not quite clear on the way forward. His immediate emergency was to charge his mobile phone and report Joshua missing. Then, he would call the hospital to inquire about Mills. This whole situation felt utterly improbable, like a bad joke. An irrational idea took root in his head that the moment he arrived home Mills and Joshua would jump out from behind the sofa and scream *Surprise!* Though why would they? His birthday wasn't until September.

As he approached the driveway, he saw Mills's Volvo. It was hanging over the ditch with its nose leaning into it. The rear wheels held it back from rolling down. Police tape was draped over the car in several layers. The access to the driveway was obstructed by the Volvo whose rear squatted across it. It must have been quite a spin for the car to enter the driveway sideways. There was no way Hugh could drive past it. He parked his car by the roadside and hurried towards the wreck.

It was dark and difficult to see what the hell had happened. The other car involved in the collision was nowhere to be seen. Perhaps there had been no other car – perhaps it was just Mills losing control of her vehicle and crashing into the ditch, Hugh speculated. But one glance at the driver's door and he was sure something had been rammed into it. The door was badly damaged, sporting a deep dent as if something hard had ploughed right through it. The door was hanging by its bottom hinge. Hugh peered inside through the window with great care. The teeth of broken glass stuck out around the base of the frame. More glass shards were scattered on the dashboard and the driver's seat. The passenger side with Joshua's bumper seat was sprayed with glass. Hugh pulled the back door open, hoping against reason that he would strike it lucky and find Joshua there. Instead of Joshua he discovered a huge glass tank taking up the whole width of the back seats. Miraculously it was unscathed. It contained bags with fish feed and a box containing an air-pump. *What the fuck,* Hugh asked himself, baffled. For a second, he contemplated the possibility of one huge mistake being made by the cops and of this being somebody else's car altogether while Mills and Joshua were safe and sound at home, having supper. He even glanced towards the house to see if the lights were on. Of course they weren't, and this definitely was

Mills's Volvo. He double-checked the number plate. His wishful thinking received one final blow when he opened the boot to find it full of shopping in Sainsbury's Bags for Life.

Feeling faint, Hugh slumped to the ground, next to the car. The cold wet grass under his hand brought him back to reality. Where was Joshua? Rather hopelessly, Hugh stared into the night. There were no streetlamps on this road, not even road markings. To the left, some fifty yards away, the road bent sharply. That was where the other vehicle would have come from. Mills had been turning into the driveway. She had swerved into the path of the oncoming traffic on the other lane in order to execute her trademark wide turn. He could picture it because she always did that. He would always tell her it was unsafe; you could not see the oncoming cars beyond that bend. She never listened. Her door would have taken the main impact of the collision, Hugh concluded. In his seat on the other side, Joshua would have been less exposed. So where was he?

The passenger side of the car was tipping over the ditch. After days and days of rain the ditch was knee-deep. Excess water had been draining into it from the fields beyond the house. Hugh felt fear squeeze his stomach in a vice-like grip. He heaved himself to his feet and stood by the overgrown bank, trying to see into the water. It was murmuring beneath him, revealing none of its secrets. A child could have easily drowned in there.

His feet sank into the mud. Doubled up, Hugh was raking the water with his hands, searching for a body. He tripped and fell onto his all fours. The water level was up to his mouth. He kept feeling among weeds and slimy rocks. He came across a solid object that didn't feel like it belonged in the stream. He pulled it out. It was a shoe. Hugh's heart halted halfway through a beat. He stared at the shoe. It was a large-size leather boot; definitely not Joshua's. Hugh's heart resumed its beat and he resumed his search. Oily muck was pouring through his fingers. He had covered a few yards of the ditch up to the point where its bed rose and it became a shallow puddle. Nothing. He didn't know whether to celebrate or to weep. Where was Joshua?

There was no use blundering about in the night looking for him. He could be anywhere. He could be far, far away from here. There was a possibility that he had been abducted. Hugh had to go back to plan A: charge his phone, call the police and report Joshua missing. He pulled himself out of the ditch and stumbled into his house, dripping with water and leaving behind a trail of slime and seaweed.

The landline phone rang just as Hugh entered the house. It gave him a jolt of surprise. Hugh had forgotten they had a landline. He flicked on the lights in the lounge and grabbed the receiver. News! Someone was calling with good news! They had found Joshua safe and sound!

'Yes?' he croaked into the phone.

'Hugh? It's Phillipa. I've been trying to get hold of you all evening. We were supposed to be having our Facetime with Josh.'

'What?'

'Facetime. An hour ago. More than an hour – more like two hours! Camilla's offline. What's going on there?' This sounded like an admonishment rather than a genuine inquiry. Phillipa was clearly not amused by Camilla's failure to facilitate regular contact between Joshua and his mother, as she had promised. 'We agreed seven-thirty every other day. This is not on!'

'There's been an accident. Mills is in hospital. She's in a critical condition. You need to get off the phone, Phillipa. I've got a few urgent calls to make.' Hugh had to get rid of Phillipa before she asked to speak to Joshua.

'Oh my God! What happened? What sort of an accident?'

'I'll have to call you back. I'll explain everything later.'

'Can I at least have a quick word with Josh?'

'No! Not right now.' Hugh rang off. He felt rotten, but he had no choice. And he had no guts to tell Phillipa that they had lost Joshua. He wouldn't know where to begin. He had to think, and he had to follow his plan – report Joshua missing. The police had to act urgently: call a search party, blockade the roads, do whatever they are supposed to do. This was a priority. And then Mills. He had to ring the hospital and find out how she was. There had to be a method to this madness.

The phone rang again. He knew it was Phillipa. She wouldn't be shaken off that easily. He picked up the receiver and slammed it down again. He held it down to make sure it stayed silent, then ripped it off the cradle and dialled 999. 'The police,' he spoke into the phone, his voice trembling, 'I want to report a missing child.'

Triggered by motion, the security lights flooded the garden. Someone – or something – had crossed the lawn. Hugh couldn't remember the last time this had happened. The garden bordered an ancient wood which stretched all the way to the Kennet and Avon Canal. The garden was fortified with a five-foot dry-stone wall. It was home to many birds who could be assured of their safety. No cat, nor a fox, no matter how resourceful, had ever made it over the wall. Hugh had altogether forgotten he had security lights installed over the patio. They never came on. Until now.

He crept towards the French doors and pressed his face to the glass pane. It was being battered by rain. The visibility was poor despite the security lights blazing through the sheets of water. Droplets crashed against the stone pavers of the patio and splattered in mini-grenade explosions. A small figure was huddled just within the perimeter of light. In front of it, inconceivably, hung a large balloon. Hugh strained his eyes. No, it wasn't a balloon – it was a plastic bag full of water. Two small hands were holding it in a tight grip. The figure lifted its head allowing the light to penetrate under the hood it was wearing. Joshua's tear – or rain – streaked face emerged into plain sight. The security lights went off and everything turned black.

Pushed out by a surge of adrenaline, blood drained from Hugh's arteries. He raced outside, calling out from the door, 'Joshua! Is that you?' He squinted into the darkness. Silence, peppered with the incessant rain, answered him.

'Josh! It's grandad! Where are you?'

Hugh stepped out into the rain. After a few steps, he was detected by the sensors and triggered the security lights. And there was Josh.

He was cowering next to the burning bush plant, jittery and ready to dive into the darkness behind him. He was quivering. The still inexplicable water balloon he was clutching in his hands appeared to contain fish. Two fish. Hugh gaped. 'Joshua, my boy...'

'Grandad, I swear it wasn't me! I didn't kill Grandma!'

'Nobody killed Grandma. Come here. It's OK,' Hugh cajoled and slowly stretched his arm towards him. The poor child was in shock. His shivers were so violent that they looked like fits.

'It was an alien. I swear it was!' Joshua stammered. 'He flew at Grandma. He broke her window and he killed her. It wasn't me!'

'I know. I believe you. Let's go inside. You must be cold. Your teeth are chattering.'

'I won't go on the naughty step?'

'Why would you?'

'I didn't do it. It was the alien.'

'Aliens are like that, yes.'

Hugh clasped his hand on Joshua's shoulder. Until now, until he could feel the boy's skinny body under his hand, he doubted this conversation was really taking place. He had thought he was talking to a ghost.

'Come inside. It's raining.'

'I know. I'm not blind. And I swear to god – I didn't kill Grandma.'

Hugh smiled at his grandson. 'No, you aren't and no, you didn't,' he conceded the two points.

They crossed the patio and entered the house. Hugh shut the door behind them. He peered at Joshua, looking for signs of injury: blood, torn clothes, bruising. There was nothing. Joshua stood rigid, his neck shrunken into his raised shoulders, water dripping from his clothes, his chin and the tip of his nose. He looked like a melting snowman who for some unfathomable reason was dressed as a child. And then there was the balloon housing two fish. Joshua clung on to it.

'What have you got there? May I have a look?'

'It's sharks.' Joshua's eyes lit up. 'We bought sharks. Grandma paid for them so they're mine.'

'I see... Shall we release them into the sink – watch them swim?'

'They'll grow big. Bigger than you. They won't fit in a sink.'

'Bathtub then.'

The phone rang again. It was Phillipa. Hugh passed the receiver to Joshua. The boy went on for a while about the alien flying his saucer through the car window and killing Grandma, and followed that seamlessly and without stopping for breath with a story about the two sharks and their exponential growth expectations. Hugh couldn't begin to imagine what Phillipa made of it all, and he didn't care to find out. He took the fish to the upstairs bathroom.

'I really need your help, Yvonne! I wouldn't be asking if I didn't!' Hugh gazed hopelessly at Joshua's muddied clothes piled in a soggy heap on the floor. He had no idea how to deal with them, or with anything else for that matter. He had made Joshua undress where he stood in the lounge because of his shivering and his lips going blue. He had towelled him as well as he could and told him to go to his bedroom and put on his pyjamas. He had crossed his fingers in the hope that Joshua knew where to find them. In response to the boy's demands for food, he had shoved a bar of chocolate at him. The groceries were still in the boot of Camilla's car, he knew that, but what he didn't know was how to turn them into a meal. It seemed like squaring a round hole. It was totally outside his field of expertise. He truly needed his sister to come and sustain him and Joshua until Mills was back. He had been told it could be a few days or a few months. She had suffered a head injury which resulted in significant swelling of the brain. The doctors had to induce a coma. All of a sudden, Hugh was on his own, looking after a seven-year-old child (he estimated Joshua to be around seven for he hadn't kept up with his birthdays) and facing God knows how many weeks of lockdown. 'Yvonne, I beg you,' he whimpered.

'I have a school to run, Hugh. You need a housekeeper.'

'Where will I find one on such short notice?'

'It's not my problem.'

Hugh decided to resort to emotional blackmail. 'I have nearly lost my wife. For all I know, she may yet die. I'm all over the place! I have a small child in the house on the brink of starvation, concussed and possibly suffering from some form of mental breakdown. He's hallucinating about aliens, for crying out loud! If I can't rely on my own sister, who can I turn to?'

An hour later, Yvonne dropped her suitcases in the hallway and hung her coat on the hook. Extracted from her puffy red overcoat like a pit out of a cherry, her tiny figure seemed no more than that of a child. It inspired little confidence in her ability to hold things together in Mills's absence. She had lost weight since Hugh last saw her. That must have been last Christmas. She had stayed with them for two days, spewing her nonsense about climate change. Stray dogs, unjust wars and the imminent Armageddon were her life's passions. Yvonne had never married and had no children – out of choice. Hugh approved of that but he didn't approve of her Extinction Rebellion activism. Apart from chaining herself to tree-trunks in her spare time, she was also Assistant Headteacher in one of the Bristol comprehensives. How she could reconcile those two irreconcilable pursuits was anyone's guess. Hugh never asked her. Her life was hers to run the way she liked, no matter how eccentric and downright bonkers it was.

'Thank God you're here!' He embraced her with genuine fondness and instantly forgave her for not reciprocating it.

She shook off his arms and frowned. 'Is that Camilla's car outside?'

He nodded.

'That's grim.'

'Tell me about it!'

'There are groceries in the boot.'

'Yes, I know.'

'Well?' She eyed him in a challenging fashion.

'Well what?'

'Go and bring them in! There's stuff there that must go in the fridge.'

Hugh braved the rain without an umbrella. He needed his hands free to grab as many bags as he could in one go. He didn't fancy making too many trips in the bloody downpour. After all the groceries, plus a few intriguing items of underwear, were deposited in the hallway, he decided he had enough energy left in him to drag the fish tank in from the car. He was dying for a hot bath so the damned fish had to go somewhere else. It had taken him ages to install the fish tank and equip it with an oxygen pump. Hugh didn't believe in reading instructions. They were in any case usually written in Chinese and translated into English using Google online dictionary. That rendered them utter, incomprehensible tosh. But putting together an oxygen pump without instructions carried its own challenges. After forty-five minutes, Hugh succeeded, having followed his trial-and-error method to hell and back. The two fish could at last be evicted from the bathtub.

As he was finally soaking in the bath and watching the bubbles circle the island of his protruding stomach, he contemplated the unpredictability of even the best organised life, such as his own. Yesterday, he had been a professional man with sacrosanct daily routines, a loving wife waiting for him at home with a hot meal and a glass of decent French wine, and not a worry in the world. Tomorrow he would wake up to his worst nightmare: an enforced domesticity with his sister and grandson, both of whom would rather be somewhere else. Just like Hugh.

And he was worried – worried like he hadn't been in a very long time, if ever. He was worried about Mills. He had never thought much about her mortality. She would remind him often enough about his own, nagging him about his smoking, drinking and his unhealthy body mass index. Hugh was on his way to an early grave, fair enough. But Mills was supposed to be immortal.

Looking at Mills, Hugh did not hold out much hope for her. He wanted to stay positive and the doctor had told him that she was stable, but she wasn't yet out of danger – not by far. *Critical but stable*, those were the good doctor's exact words. They didn't inspire confidence in her swift recovery. What's worse, Hugh pondered, was that she looked like she had given up the ghost. Hugh would have given up if it was him lying there like a zombie. Her face was swollen, bruised, cut and stitched up as if a mad plastic surgeon had taken to it with a scalpel and left the job unfinished. Tubing protruded from her gaping mouth, attached in a criss-cross of plasters. Her head was bandaged. She was perfectly still and silent – dead-still and dead-silent. The only sounds were those made by the machines: the ventilator that was doing Mills's breathing for her and the device that was monitoring her heartbeat and other, so-called, *vital signs*. The screen wasn't particularly busy. If that lazy white line was meant to trace Mills's brain activity then Mills was doing very little thinking.

'Oh Mills,' Hugh sighed, 'what did you do to yourself, you silly girl?'

He sat on the edge of her bed and stroked the side of her hand. At least, it felt warm. He feared it may be cold. It had a drip attached to it with a needle. Mills had lost lots of blood. Her brain had been deprived of oxygen for longer than was considered safe. When – if – she woke up, her brain functions could turn out to be severely inhibited. It could be her speech, her memory, her balance, her mental faculties, moods – anything – that might have suffered damage beyond repair. All of it, some of it or none of it, the doctor wasn't very specific.

Time would tell. For now, Mills had to wait for the swelling to go down in her brain before she could be brought back to life. Hugh couldn't believe it. It couldn't really be happening. Not to Mills. Yes, he had been banging on about her having her head examined, but this... This was way over the top.

'I'm meant to talk to you, Mills,' he began awkwardly. 'Can you hear me in there?'

Unlike her, she didn't respond.

'It's only today. I mean, I won't be able to see you anymore – for a while, at least. I won't be allowed in. It's the damned lockdown, you see.'

She couldn't possibly see that. She couldn't see anything, full stop. Her eyes were shut. From time to time, something fluttered beneath her eyelids, Hugh observed, or maybe it was just a trick of light. The fluorescent lights in the room were crackling and flickering. Someone should come and fix them. They were a source of irritation to Hugh. God knows what they were doing to Mills. She couldn't tell him.

Hugh was supposed to be talking to her, so he did, 'Just to put your mind at ease, Joshua is fine. As are the fish – flitting about in their fish tank. All set up, oxygen pumps and all... Whatever possessed you to go and buy the damn goldfish!' He checked himself. 'No, don't answer that.'

She had no intention of answering anyway.

He prolonged his vigil by Mills's side as long as he could even though he had nothing else to say to her and she didn't seem to care whether or not he stayed. In the end, a nurse kicked him out. In a perverse way, he was grateful to the nurse for making that decision for him. He wouldn't have the guts to just up and go. He needed an excuse. The nurse provided that.

'Thank you, nurse,' he heard himself say. The nurse scowled

at him quizzically and pulled the curtain around Mills's bed while he watched. There was something final in that gesture – the proverbial final curtain. Hugh shuddered.

He wanted to be alone and wasn't in a hurry to get home to Yvonne and Joshua, so he snubbed the lift and headed for the stairs signposted to the fire exit at the back of the building. He pushed the swing door into the landing and found himself face to face with Aiden Turner.

Hugh's first thought was that it had been Turner – that Turner had made an attempt on Camilla's life. He had driven into Mills's car and was now lying in wait to finish the job. He had threatened Mills before – repeatedly. But on a closer look at the man's face Hugh knew he was wrong to suspect him. Turner was crying.

He appeared to have his back rivetted to the wall as his legs, bent at the knees, didn't seem able to carry his weight. His hands hung by his sides, long and lifeless. He recognised Hugh and his face twisted as he gave a harrowing sob.

'Aiden? What are you doing here? Are you OK? Do you need help?' It certainly looked like the man needed something, at least somewhere to sit before his legs gave way altogether.

They did. He slumped onto the floor and pressed his palms to his forehead. 'No, leave me alone,' he croaked.

'You sure? I could call a nurse.'

'And what good would that do? Sally's dead.' Turner fixed Hugh with a bloodshot eye. 'She's dead. I had her taken off life support. This morning.'

It was now past six pm. Had he been standing here on the landing of a fire escape all those hours, crying? It was possible. It was conceivable that a bereaved man would do that. Hugh didn't feel like going home either, and Mills wasn't even dead. He lowered himself with a heavy groan, and sat next to Turner. 'I'm sorry,' he said, and meant it.

'There was no hope. No detectable brain activity.'

'I see. I'm sorry.'

'And they need beds. Bed shortages. The pandemic, and all that.'

'I see.' Hugh had an idea: 'Do you want a lift home? I'm on my way out.'

Turner shook his head. 'I'll stay here a while, I think.'

'OK.' Hugh nodded but didn't get up. His knees felt too weak to take his weight.

'What you doing here, anyway?'

'It's Mills. I'm visiting Mills. There was a car crash. She's in a coma.'

Turner jerked his face at Hugh. His large nose almost stabbed Hugh in his forehead. 'Camilla Bramley-Jones is in a coma?' He repeated slowly.

'Afraid so. It's fifty-fifty, the doctor tells me.'

All considered, Turner's reaction was predictable. He burst out in laughter. He rose to his feet and gazed down at Hugh, shaking with laughter.

'It's karma, my good man. Karma!' He was rapt with joy. He skipped down the stairs, light on his feet and carefree like a little boy. But his parting shot was hardly one of childlike innocence. 'I hope the bitch dies. She's had it coming!'

Turner's malignant laughter lingered over Hugh long after the man was gone.

Hugh reflected. Turner had really hit the nail on the head. It was karma, wasn't it? If it hadn't been for Camilla and her meddling, Christopher wouldn't be in prison and Sally Turner would be alive and well, managing a successful Investment Department of a large banking corporation instead of taking an overdose. If Mills hadn't spotted Sally and Christopher leaving a seedy hotel late one evening two years ago and hadn't jumped to conclusions about the nature of their liaison, nobody would have been hurt. If Mills hadn't engaged that private detective who went on to uncover the scam Sally and Christopher had cooked up, no one would have ever been any the wiser. Life would have gone on as it always had: not perfect, but comfortable. Christopher would be enjoying family bliss with Phillipa and young Joshua. Aiden and Sally Turner would continue to take long cruises to tropical destinations way into their eighties. Hugh's professional reputation would have remained untarnished and he would be looking at joining the High Court Bench in a few years' time. Even if he didn't do that in the end, he would still have had that option. But Camilla had to do what she thought was right: to meddle and jump to conclusions, to run to Turner to tell him about his wife's supposed affair with a younger man, to confront Sally with threats, and finally to try to move heaven and earth to *put things right*. She wouldn't rest until everything fell to pieces.

It was karma, wasn't it?

JANE, IN JOSEPH'S ABSENCE

The fish pie was stone cold. As soon as the heat escaped, the peas had shrivelled and their skins wrinkled. They were spoilt now, leathery and not fit for consumption. Jane chucked them into the bin. What a waste! She was seriously displeased with Father Joseph. Although she would have never admitted it, she had been trying to impress him with her culinary skills in case he had second thoughts about employing her as his fulltime housekeeper. She had deep-cleaned the entire priory, waxed the floors, washed and pressed the curtains that were so stiff with dust that it could be safely assumed they hadn't been cleaned since the turn of the last century. She had shopped and cooked the fish pie from the raw ingredients. And all along, she had been harbouring a twinkle of hope that with some home cooking and an upgrade in creature comforts, Father Joseph might yet change his mind about leaving the priesthood.

Sadly, he hadn't given her a chance to prove herself. He had not even come home. Jane couldn't tell whether this meant that he had already left for good, or if this was just his normal behaviour and that he would turn up in the morning as if nothing had happened and go to bed to sleep off his hangover.

She assumed that he was out on the town, celebrating his early retirement and getting drunk with friends. She didn't begrudge him that. Everyone is entitled to a bit of harmless fun, even a priest. Only why hadn't he mentioned that to her before he left? If he had done so, she wouldn't have gone to all that trouble of making the blinking fish pie.

She had called his mobile phone endless times, and on her last attempt left an ill-tempered message, letting him know that this was not on and that the blinking fish pie was going into the bin, hot on the heels of the peas. She slammed the phone down.

By ten o'clock she decided that she couldn't let a decent pie go to waste altogether. Her anger had subsided. Her hunger had risen to the surface. Her stomached rumbled. She shoved the pie back into the oven to warm it up. Fifteen minutes later she was devouring her late supper and muttering furiously between mouthfuls, 'Whatever he gets up to in the night, I don't want to know. Calls himself a priest! A holy man, my arse! He won't find his way home till the morning, I bet. Smashed out of his skull, lying somewhere face down in a ditch. Lost to the world!' Little did she know, she wasn't far from the truth.

She polished off the whole pie. She couldn't bring herself to throw away a single crumb – it was too good for the bin. She washed up, rang the Father's phone again and when it went straight to the answerphone, voiced a couple of blasphemies and told the Father to *sod off, then, and goodnight.* She was well and truly cheesed off.

The chime of the doorbell woke her up at two minutes to midnight. Startled, she sat up in bed and scanned the dark interior of her room, expecting to uncover some paranormal activity: demons and such-like haunting in the night. The doorbell boomed again and she finally realised what it was. This was the first time she had heard it. Father Joseph had chosen a blood-curdling tune for his doorbell. It sounded like the trumpets of the Apocalypse. Nobody could sleep through that, not even the dead.

Jane fumbled around her bed in search of the bedside lamp. She knocked over a glass of water and swore as she heard it crash into shards on the floor. The doorbell bawled again.

'Piss off, and bloody well wait!' Jane instructed the visitor, contradicting herself without realising it. She dangled her feet from her bed, trying to locate her shoes with the tips of her toes. The last thing she wanted was to step onto the broken glass scattered on the floor and bleed to death. Her blood reservoir was already seriously depleted after her wrists had been cut open by that psychopath. She slipped her feet into her trainers with caution. Pieces of glass could be hiding inside them. She felt her way towards the door. The light switch was next to it.

She turned on the lights and felt reassured. At least, there weren't any demons in sight. The doorbell trumpeted impatiently.

'Coming! Hold your horses!' She muttered under her breath. There was no point raising her voice. Her room was in the attic. Father Joseph could wait. He'd made her wait longer than was acceptable in civilised society. Coming down the stairs, she was preparing her chastisement for him. Who did he think he was, rolling home at this ungraceful hour? And couldn't he use his blinking key instead of dragging her out of bed in the middle of the night?

She pressed her eye to the spyhole. After her encounter with the psycho, she had become a bit jumpy. As things stood, she wouldn't take a chance on a stranger ever again. She expected – hoped – to see Father Joseph looking contrite and slightly tipsy. In his place stood a man disguised as a policeman.

Jane pulled away from the spyhole and leant against the

door, her breathing shallow and rapid. What would a policeman be doing, standing on the doorstep of the church priory at midnight, demanding to come in? What if this was the psycho? She wouldn't recognise him without his beanie and his beard, and certainly not if he was masquerading as a policeman. It could well be him. What if he had found her and come here to finish the job?

Her first instinct was to pick up the telephone and call the police, but she had only just moved into the priory and didn't know where the phone was.

The rampant doorbell rang again and made her heart jump to her throat. Jane swore like a trooper to stir some courage into her gut. She clenched her small fists.

'Anyone home? It's the police!' The intruder shouted on the other side of the door.

She peeped through the spyhole again. The policeman's face moved in and out of focus as he was trying to peer inside. He took a couple of steps back and a female copper pushed to the fore. That convinced Jane. She could trust a woman. Maybe they had some news about the psychopath. Maybe they were here to tell her that they had apprehended the bastard. She opened the door.

'Sorry, you had to wait. I was asleep.'

The police constables introduced themselves. The woman asked if Mr Steedman lived here.

So, this was a false alarm – they had the wrong address. Jane shook her head, 'Nobody here by that name. This is a priory – a priest house. I'm the housekeeper.' It pleased her to be able to introduce herself as such.

'You're sure, ma'am? This is the address we have on record for Joseph Steedman.'

'Joseph? Father Joseph?' Jane was catching up. 'Well, yes.

Father Joseph lives here. I didn't know he was Steedman... I suppose even priests are bound to have surnames.'

The policewoman nodded to Jane with encouragement. 'So, this is his address?'

'Yes, but you're not in luck. He's not in.'

And that was when they told her about the accident, and the name of the hospital where he had been taken.

Jane's anger transferred promptly from Father Joseph to herself. She sat at the table in the dark kitchen, propped her chin on the base of her palm and tapped her index finger furiously against her tightly pursed lips. It was the closest she could come to self-flagellation. She should be kicking herself big time! She had been nothing but an ungrateful cow. After all that man had done for her. He had saved her – literally saved her life, and her rotten soul on top of that — given her a roof over her head and a chance to make an honest living for herself. And how did she repay him? By cursing and bad-mouthing him, accusing him of all sorts!

She should have asked the coppers to give her a lift to the hospital, but the charitable thought of visiting the sick hadn't occurred to her at the time. She had been too busy swaying on her feet in shock and worrying about what it meant for her. The question of whether Father Joseph would pull through seemed to carry more relevance to her future prospects than to his.

She shouldn't be sitting idly and waiting until the morning bus, assuming there was one at all. On Sundays there weren't many scheduled and even the few that were ran erratically. Some didn't turn up, others didn't stop. Bus drivers were known to give Romley Estate a wide berth if they could get away with it. Most of the time they could, especially on Sundays. Jane decided not to wait until the morning. She called the hospital to inquire. The phone rang and rang, but nobody was there to answer it. In the end, it would cut out. Each time she became disconnected, she re-dialled the number and started counting the rings all over again.

'...thirty-one, thirty-two, thirty-three–'

'University Hospital!' A breathless female voice jerked Jane out of her counting reverie. Shakily, she gave Father Joseph's name and inquired about his condition. When asked about her relationship to the patient, she lied. For some unfathomable reason, she said she was his wife, Mrs Steedman. A fraction of a second later, she considered the repercussions of this falsehood for Father Joseph. If it somehow came to the Bishop's attention that one of his priests was married, all hell would break loose. Then again, she remembered that Father Joseph was beyond reach of the long arm of the Church – he wouldn't be a priest for much longer; after all, he had handed in his notice.

'Yes, we have your husband. He's stable though in a bad way. Let me see...' Jane could hear the nurse tapping the keys of the computer keyboard. 'His left lung was punctured. Um, a broken arm, in two places, plus the collar bone. Yes, a few serious injuries, but he'll live.'

'When can I see him?'

'You can't. He's sedated and waiting for surgery. That'll be some time this afternoon. You can telephone to inquire, but you can't visit. From six pm tomorrow the hospital is in lockdown.'

'Before six?'

'It'd be a wasted trip, Mrs Steedman. We're already on full COVID alert. They won't let you near the critical care ward.'

'So, you mean... How am I supposed to... see him?'

'He'll be coming home as soon as we can release him. Even sooner. We need every bed.'

She must have fallen asleep at the kitchen table and, despite the discomfort, managed to oversleep. Her usual waking hour of six am had come and gone, and Jane was still slumped over the table, her face cradled in the crook of her elbow, her eyelids flickering full of dreams.

The trumpets of the Apocalypse brought her back to the land of the living. The doorbell was being pushed furiously and repeatedly. Jane jumped to her feet, disoriented. It took her a while to narrow down her coordinates and realise she was in the kitchen of the priory which was now her home. Her left arm had gone to sleep. For a moment, especially because of the trumpeting doorbell, she feared she was having a heart attack. The numb arm regained feeling and the bell went transiently silent. That gave Jane a chance to recover her wits and answer the door.

'Holy Mary, mother of God! What are *you* doing here?!' Mrs Keating's double chin shook with horror. Dressed in her Sunday best, wearing bright cherry-red lipstick and carrying her faux Gucci handbag, she was evidently on her way to Sunday mass, Jane quickly deduced.

'I work here,' Jane said simply.

'As a what, exactly?'

'A housekeeper, as it happens. What's that to you?'

'What, in God's name, is going through the Father's head? To have you brought here, of all places! It's a disgrace! A blasphemy! Do you hear me?' Mrs Keating wagged her finger in Jane's face.

Jane raised her eyebrows and twisted her lips contemptuously.

'He's gone mad as a hatter! God have mercy on his soul.' The old trollop was clearly referring to Father Joseph's soul; it was her learned opinion that Jane Cuthbert, the whore, didn't have one.

It wasn't only that Mrs Keating didn't like the sight of Jane at this holy establishment, but she also didn't like the look of her. She scanned her critically from head to toe. It was at that point that Jane realised she was wearing her rather skimpy pyjama shorts, a vest displaying the obvious absence of a bra underneath and a pair of squashed trainers on her bare feet. Not quite the Sunday look of a priest's housekeeper, she had to concede the point.

'This is an outrage! The Bishop will hear about this. I'll be writing to His Excellency tonight.' Mrs Keating said.

'Do what you like, see if I care.' Jane wasn't one to be easily intimidated by the old windbag. She made to shut the door in Mrs Keating's face.

'Oh, I will and you'll be out on your face faster than you can say–' Mrs Keating checked herself, swallowed the profanity that was quivering on the tip of her tongue (it just wouldn't be right to blaspheme on a Sunday) and asked in a more formal tone, 'So, is Father Joseph planning to grace us with his presence? He is late for Mass. We've been waiting fifteen minutes. It's unheard of!' She peered over Jane's shoulder and shouted, 'Father, you coming?'

Jane clasped her mouth. She should have stuck a note on the door about Father Joseph's indisposition, and perhaps called the Diocese to ask for another priest to deliver the service today. She had failed on all accounts. There was a whole congregation, the choir, elderly ladies, mums with toddlers in tow, all fidgeting in the pews, waiting for their priest to intone the first hymn. Jane meanwhile was fast asleep on the kitchen table.

'Oh my,' she muttered. 'Father Joseph is in hospital. He was in an accident... There'll be no Mass today.'

'An accident...' Mrs Keating's lips moved soundlessly, but Jane could read the words on them. Mrs Keating was digesting the news and her mouth continued to move without emitting any sound. Finally, she uttered a question, 'So why did nobody tell us?'

'I'm telling you now, ain't I?'

Mrs Keating snorted.

'He's due to have surgery today. But you can't visit him–'

'And you can?!' The indignation in Mrs Keating's voice was palpable.

'No one can, you stupid woman!' Jane snapped. She wanted to add that it was due to the lockdown but Mrs Keating didn't take kindly to being called stupid.

She pushed her fists into her wide hips, her Gucci bag bouncing off her thigh like a pendulum, and shouted: 'Don't you go getting ideas above your station, Jane Cuthbert! We all know what you are! A whore! Once a whore, always a rotten whore! You're no more a housekeeper than I'm the Pope. And you trust me on this – don't get too comfortable 'cos you won't be a housekeeper here for much longer. Fancy that – Sodom and Gomorrah ... Over my dead body! Over my dead body,' she huffed as she turned on her heel and waddled away with the vigour of an enraged rhino.

'Then go die, cow,' Jane hissed under her breath and slammed the door.

'Yes, it all went to plan,' the doctor assured her for the second time after she had questioned whether he was sure. It had sounded too good to be true. Maybe she had misheard him. 'Your husband is recovering, but he is not yet able to receive calls – too groggy. It's too soon after the surgery. Try again tomorrow. The anaesthetic will have worn off by then. He should be fully alert, unlike today. And I'm positive you should have him home by Easter, Mrs Steedman.'

Jane thanked the doctor gushingly as if she were indeed his

patient's eternally grateful wife. Father Joseph would be back soon. She would have to get the house ready for his arrival – cleaning, baking and all. She would have to get herself ready – make herself presentable. She had been wearing her pyjamas all day. It was fine today when she was home alone, but when he returned she would have to start taking more pride in her appearance.

She ran to her room in the attic and rummaged through her wardrobe, pulling out revealing tops and tight jeans, trying them on and parading in front of the mirror. She pushed up her breasts inside her bra and pinched her cheeks to instil some colour into them. She applied lipstick and experimented with the Cleopatra look by drawing thick black lines over her eyelids and extending them towards her temples. She tousled her hair, loose locks falling across her face as she shook her mane with the flair of a catwalk queen. She pouted, all along thinking of Father Joseph's return – all along imagining that he was already back, here with her, watching her. She put on a show for him. She strolled across her room, one leg crossing seductively in front of the other, her hips wiggling, and on a couple of enthusiastic occasions, twerking. She pondered if Father Joseph was into this sort of thing.

She sobered up and frowned at her reflection. 'You're such a rotten tart, Jane Cuthbert,' she heard herself echo Mrs Keating's sentiment. She deserved it. This was Father Joseph she was fantasising about. She was a thirty-six-year-old woman – no longer an affectionate, daft teenager. She had no excuse to act like that. He was her priest! He had known her since she was a girl. He would be appalled and disgusted by her behaviour.

She wiped the lipstick from her face with toilet paper and flushed it down the loo. She gave her face a vigorous wash with hot water and soap. If only she could do the same to her sick mind! But even though her mind was full of filth she could not cleanse it.

She had strayed into wickedness quite early in life. She couldn't remember when she had started fancying the priest. She had been a teenager – thirteen or fourteen years old. It had been a safe crush – nothing would come out of it. Jane could fantasise to her heart's content about kissing the priest in the privacy of the bottom bunk, while her young sister in the bunk above slept, oblivious. A small tinge of guilt stained her conscience for it was one sin she could not confess and had to keep back from Father Joseph, thus rendering her confessions null and void in God's eyes. That had been a year or two before she had fallen head over heels for Dr Curry. Thinking of it now, and Jane didn't like to think of it at all but sometimes she couldn't help herself, it wasn't she who had seduced Dr Curry. She simply loved his subject – physics. Physics made perfect sense to her and she dreamt of one day coming up with a theory that would explain how God fitted into the Universe, and once and for all put an end to the conflict between science and religion. Jane used to dwell a lot on the matter. She wanted to study physics at university and in preparation for that began to spend quite a bit of time debating the mysteries of the Universe with Dr Curry – Elliot. He had soon become just Elliot. He'd insisted on the first name basis. It had got out of hand from there, and before Jane knew it, she was pregnant and Dr Curry (he'd stopped being Elliot by then) had accepted a new post in a school three hundred miles north of Bristol, and taken himself and his family (wife and three kids) there without leaving a forwarding address. Matthew was born six months later and Jane's dreams of reconciling God and science were replaced by nappies.

Father Joseph had been there – always there, unwaveringly

supportive throughout all of that – like her guardian angel. He was the one and only constant in her life, especially after Mum died. Even though his intentions were bound to be pure and honourable, Jane's fantasies of kissing the priest had soon returned to haunt her. It was clearly because she wasn't pure, and possibly because of her postpartum hormonal imbalance. She had read a lot on the subject, but she never talked to anyone about it. How could she?

Even now, twenty years later, she fancied the pants off the middle-aged priest with his hippy leanings and the fumes of petrol from his motorbike hanging over him. He was her unattainable macho idol, her young girl's fantasy that had survived her loss of innocence, child-rearing, adulthood, failure and disappointments, and lived on to see a brighter day. Whenever – if ever – that day may come. For the time being, she was celebrating his miraculously successful surgery and his imminent homecoming. She just had to stop making a fool of herself and start acting with the propriety that was becoming of a priest's housekeeper.

A week into lockdown, Jane was feeling acutely alone. It was strange because, on the whole, she wasn't particularly sociable. One, she didn't like people that much, not enough to talk to if there was no need, and two, because she was a busy woman. With her many jobs on the go, she didn't have time to sit down and finish a cup of tea, never mind nattering about yesterday's snow. Jane was a busy bee – always on the go, with her finger in many pies.

But that had been before lockdown. Nowadays she was a housekeeper for an absent priest. That meant there was little to do in a day. She had dropped all her other jobs and focussed her energies on this one alone. As a result, the priory was pristine.

You could see your reflection in all the surfaces and smell wood polish in every room. Every rug had been cleaned, aired and brushed. Every window pane gleamed. Jane had run out of chores and simply didn't know what to do with herself.

On Monday morning, which would be late Sunday evening in Boston, she decided to call Matthew and tell him about Father Joseph's misadventure. And to find out about Matthew's latest. They hadn't spoken in three weeks – since before her *accident.*

Jane concluded that it'd be cheaper to call her son using the priory landline. In fact, it wouldn't cost her anything. She couldn't remember when she had last topped up her mobile phone. That must have been before her *accident* too. It was funny, she mused, how her *accident* divided her life's chronology into before and after. That insane psychopath had changed her life for the better. That can't have been his intention, but there it was. Jane's life had changed direction and acquired new meaning.

She was gratified to hear Matthew's voice when he answered the phone and immediately inquired how she was – was she now fully recovered *after her accident?*

'Oh, I'm fine, Matthew! As good as new,' she chirped, 'but I can't say the same for Father Joseph,' and she went on with his story. Her knowledge about the circumstances of Father Joseph's accident was sketchy, but she compensated for that by elaborating on his injuries and treatment. Matthew was naturally shocked, and said as much. Jane told him not to worry and assured him that the Father was on the mend and would be home by Easter. It would be nice, come to think of it, to have everyone home for Easter, Jane said hopefully. It was just wishful thinking that Matthew would visit. His post in America, at the Center for Astrophysics at Harvard no less, was for one year, ending in July. In the meantime, he couldn't afford to jet between the USA and the UK on a whim, and Jane knew that. She just found it hard to face Easter without her son. This would be their first Easter apart since the day he was born. Still, it would be the first and only time.

'So, Father Joseph didn't tell you? He wouldn't have got a chance, I guess.' Matthew's voice sounded weak and distant as if he had turned away from his phone.

'Tell me what?'

'About my job offer with the Center.'

All Jane could utter was a faint *Oh?*

'So, he didn't tell you?'

'No, he didn't tell me nothing.' Irritation stole into Jane's voice. She knew it wouldn't be good news by the way Matthew was meandering around it. 'Out with it, then! Tell me what exactly?'

'It's good news. Great news, actually! I'm stoked. You'll be too, Mum, when it sinks in.' Jane's worst fears were confirmed by that vehement assurance and by Matthew's unconvincing enthusiasm.

'Let me hear it.'

'I've been offered a permanent post with the gravitational research team. It's one in a million!'

'So it is... Well, what can I say? Congratulations, Matthew.' The words departed Jane's lips without her willing participation.

'Thanks. I knew you'd be happy for me.'

'I am. I'm proud of you.'

'But that also means that I'll have to stay put here in the US for a while. It's their daft immigration rules. What I mean to say is—'

'I know – you won't be coming for Easter. Anyway, about you coming – I just said it without thinking. I don't expect you to come. Due to the lockdown, for starters, and then there's the cost.'

'Nor for Christmas. I won't be travelling home for a while.'

'I've gathered as much. Yes, such is life,' she sighed and instantly kicked herself for sounding so glum. This was her son's greatest chance at a better life. She should be happy for him. A bright idea occurred to Jane: 'I'll save to come and visit you there, how about that?' She would be saving bags of money in her new job.

'Sounds like a plan.' Jane could hear a smile in Matthew's voice. He was definitely happy about the prospect. 'And you'll meet Bridget.'

'Who?'

'My girlfriend, Bridget. Hang on, I'll put you on loud speaker so she can say hi.' There was some frantic whispering and a chuckle at the other end, which gave Jane time to recover her wits.

'Hi, Mrs Cuthbert. You alright?' Bridget sounded confident. Her voice was husky and low. She stretched her vowels in the typical South American drawl.

'Jane – it's just Jane.'

Bridget and Jane exchanged a few superficial pleasantries and the conversation promptly fizzled out.

'I'd better be going,' Jane said at last even though she knew damn well, as did they, that she had nowhere to go.

She stayed where she was – sitting on the bottom step in the hallway, with the phone in her lap. Firstly, she heard the continuous flat sound of a disconnected telephone line and then the frantic drip-drip-drip sound of an engaged one. She replaced the receiver in the cradle. As she stared into the claustrophobically narrow hallway which seemed to shrink further towards the distant door, she felt her head spin and with it the hallway, the distant door and the cross on the wall. She could not get up and walk towards the exit. She was like a mouse who, seduced by a piece of cheese, had wandered into a trap. She was the victim of her own success – she had the cheese but she was trapped.

Of course, Jane was happy. All her dreams had been realised. Her son had found a way out of Romley. A promising future lay ahead of him in the land of endless opportunities. She had escaped, too. She was a respectable woman – a priest's housekeeper with a steady income and a roof over her head. And yet Jane Cuthbert had this disturbing feeling that something had come to an end and that she was to lose everything and everyone worth living for.

In Jane's experience troubles always arrived in busloads. Days before Father Joseph was due to be released from hospital, he had contracted coronavirus and within forty-eight hours had to be put on a ventilator. His lungs were badly affected and he was unable to breathe unaided. It was probably due to the fact that one of his lungs had been punctured in the accident, the doctor told Mrs Steedman. Her husband's prognosis was poor but the doctors were doing everything in their power to save him.

Jane was devastated. She had been following the news of COVID deaths rising day by day, but until now it had been just a whole lot of anonymous statistics. It was horrifying but it applied to other people. Now, it applied to her. She fell to her knees, and prayed. Her prayers, she believed, weren't worth that much in God's eyes for she was a woman of little value, and she didn't expect a miracle. But there was nothing else she could do. She prayed humbly and fervently, and waited for a phone call from the hospital. They would call if there was any change in Mr Steedman's condition.

Easter came and went, and there was no change. When the phone rang a week later, Jane's heart jumped to her throat.

'Mum, are you there?' It was Matthew. She couldn't understand why he would be calling. She had only been on the phone to him a few days ago with wishes of happy Easter and to thank him and Bridget for the card. She hadn't sent them one. She didn't do cards.

It wasn't convenient to talk right now. He was blocking the line. The hospital could be trying to get hold of her. 'Matthew! It's not a good time. I'm on my way out.'

'I thought you were in lockdown.'

'Still, I'm allowed to go out – to do my weekly shop, and such. I was just... Anyway, what is it? Be quick.'

'It's the money. The money hasn't come.' He sounded worried and aggrieved. 'Did you cancel the direct debit? It looks like you misunderstood, Mum. That job offer... I mean, I've got the offer but I don't start until after graduation. I'm counting on that money from you, Mum. I've had to borrow from Bridget, and I feel shit about that.'

'Hang on,' Jane interrupted his diatribe. 'I didn't cancel anything. Are you saying the money didn't come through?'

'Yes, that's what I'm trying to tell you. I need that money, Mum.'

'I know you do. I wouldn't stop those payments without telling you. Let me call the bank and find out what the hell is going on. I'll get back to you.'

Jane's account was in the red. She had already exceeded her credit limit and was being charged extortionate interest rates on her overdraft. But what about her pay, she asked the customer service adviser. Jane was a salaried housekeeper in the employ of the Catholic Church! The bank had no record of any receipts from that quarter in the last two months. In fact, payments of her cleaner's wages had been stopped too. The bank could not shed any light on this. Jane would have to take it up with her employer.

Had she missed some trick with the furlough scheme everyone was talking about? Should she have made an application to claim it? She rang the Diocese and asked for Accounts. They confirmed payments had indeed been stopped on her account but couldn't say why. She was then transferred from one department to another, pushed from pillar to post and back again, until eventually a man from Human Resources explained to her in a patient and non-judgmental, if slightly bemused, tone that her contract was *under query*. Her salary payments had been frozen until her references could be verified. A letter had been sent to Father Joseph about this.

Jane's mind raced back to the pile of unopened correspondence on Father Joseph's desk. It wasn't her place to read his letters, personal or business. Jane was a housekeeper, not a private secretary.

'But Father Joseph is in hospital,' she protested. 'You know he can't answer your letter. And anyway, I know my rights. We signed a binding contract, Father Joseph and me, before his accident. He told me all the paperwork was in order. I've no money! Do you understand? My son... Please–' Jane's voice snapped into sobs. She wasn't the crying type and she hated all forms of soppy weakness. She would never ask for charity. Begging was below her. But it wasn't for her – it was for Matthew. And she was lost. Father Joseph wasn't here to fight her corner. She could not go out there and find some odd jobs to tie her over until this *query* business was resolved. She couldn't go back on the game even if she wanted to, which she didn't because she was too scared. She didn't – she couldn't – she was desperate. She was locked down in the empty priory unable to fend for herself and confronted by the bureaucratic machine of the Catholic Church which she could not even begin to understand.

'Can your *query* not wait until after Father Joseph is out of hospital?' she whimpered. 'I'm sure he'll clear everything with you. Meantime, if you could just pay me my–'

'I'm sorry Miss Cuthbert, we can't do that. A serious allegation has been made against you, and it has to be fully investigated before–'

Jane slammed down the phone. She didn't need to hear the rest of that sentence. She had got to the bottom of the problem. She had found the cause of her misfortune. It was that trollop Keating! Jane's blood boiled. She was going to kill that nasty interfering bitch!

Jane Cuthbert stormed out of the priory and stomped towards the back of the Romley Estate, cutting through the graveyard and taking the shortcut under the railway bridge where some homeless man shouted an obscenity at her and was rewarded with her middle finger in reply. She charged along the empty streets, trampling over uncollected rubbish bags abandoned next to overflowing wheelie bins. She was fuming. She didn't care how and she didn't care at what cost to her, but she would make that wicked cow pay.

Jane kicked a half-full beer bottle standing by the lamppost. It somersaulted towards the wall, spraying yellow liquid like a runaway garden hose, and crashed against a low red-brick window sill. It shattered into pieces. Jane picked up the top half of the broken bottle by the neck. Judging solely by her expression and that bottle in her hand she could easily be mistaken for one of the Peaky Blinders.

A couple of random passers-by sensed a woman possessed and crossed the street to avoid colliding with her. A man saw her from the top of the road and halted there, watching her with his head tilted to one side, probably keen to witness a street fight. A few cars slowed down as she bulldozed on.

She reached the end of the terrace in Riding Close – Keating's nest. She curled her hand into a tight fist and banged on the door. A man with the face of a rat and a scrawny body to go with that face opened the door and glared at her. She recognised the bastard as Rory, Keating's son. She shoved him out of the way with a swipe of her forearm.

'Where is she? Where is your fucking mother!'

PART 3

FURTHER UNFORESEEN DEVELOPMENTS

JOSHUA

Joshua smelt a rat. That's what people said when things were not quite as they should be. Right now, in Joshua's opinion, the rat was very, very smelly. Firstly, Mummy told him she and Peter weren't coming back home *just yet*. She blamed the lockdown. Joshua didn't mind so much about Peter not coming back, but Mummy was a different story. He was missing her beyond words. He was missing her cuddles and kisses. Although, if someone asked, he wouldn't own up to being such a baby. It was his shameful secret. It hurt badly not being hugged by anyone, especially Mummy. He was missing her bringing him hot chocolate in bed and reading him his favourite *Famous Five* stories, and leaving the lights on until he well and truly fell asleep. There were no *Famous Five* books in Grandad's house, not a single one. Grandad offered Joshua *Winnie the Pooh*, which frankly was an insult. Aunt Yvonne tried to read some weird story about a boy called Tom Sawyer and his friend Huckleberry Finn, but Joshua couldn't follow any of it, apart perhaps from one intriguing bit about Huckleberry Finn living in a barrel. It was something Joshua would be willing to try out himself. The sharks, whom he named Flip and Flop, provided some distraction but nobody in their right mind could spend the whole day watching fish swim (although theoretically sharks weren't fish at all. It was a discovery Joshua had made while paging through Grandad's Encyclopaedia Britannica. There were some illustrations in there worth checking out. Joshua had annotated some of them with labels using his felt-tip pens. He also coloured in some diagrams and tables which were otherwise a bit bland and boring). But however hard he tried to entertain himself he missed his mum awfully and counted the days to her return. And now, to his unspeakable grief, she wasn't coming – *not just yet.*

After dropping that bombshell on Joshua during their usual Facetime chat, she asked to talk to Grandad alone. 'Why don't you go play with Auntie Yvonne?' Grandad suggested so that he could get rid of Joshua and speak with Mummy in secret.

There was no way Joshua would voluntarily go and play with Auntie Yvonne. Auntie Yvonne didn't know how to play without wanting to sneak some school work into it. She always tried to *touch on* jolly phonics or some silly number lines, and called that playing educational games. That wasn't playing – that was school. Joshua wasn't fond of school. So, although he left the room, he didn't go far. He lingered outside the door and listened to Mum and Grandad talking behind his back.

Mum: And on top of everything else, it's my blood pressure. I'm advised against long-haul air travel. Until the baby's born. And then... It's complicated, Hugh, and I want to play it fair.

Grandad: What's the game we're playing, then?

Joshua's ears pricked up. He also wanted to know what the game was. Were they going to play without him?

Mum: There was always a chance of us settling in Aussie. With Peter's parents and sister here, we'd have a good support network. I just wanted to see it for myself, and I love it. It's a great place to bring up a family.

Grandad: So, you're staying there for good?

Mum: Yes, we've decided.

Grandad: And what about Christopher? How will he fit into this? He's still Joshua's father.

And how about me? Joshua asked, but only inside his head. He didn't want to be discovered listening by the door. Not just yet.

Mum: That's what I mean. We want to play fair. When he's out we'll sit together and agree custody arrangements. Amicably, I hope. Until then, we felt the least disruption in Joshua's life the better.

Grandad: So he stays here, with us.

Mum: At least until after the baby is born and the pandemic is over.

Grandad: It makes sense. When are you due?

Mum: The eighteenth of September.

Grandad: Add a couple of months to settle down with the newborn, that takes us to Christmas.

Mum: Christopher is likely to be released by then.

Grandad: Good.

Mum: Good.

Joshua didn't think it was remotely good. He didn't understand everything they were saying, but it sounded wrong. Definitely not good.

Grandad: What about school? We won't be able to drive him every day to his old school in Bristol. It's all good now with the remote learning, but from September...

Mum: Yes, I realise that. Your village school?

Grandad: That won't work, Phillipa. I can't cope with Joshua on my own, I hope you can appreciate that. As for Mills, we still don't know...

Mum: I should've asked, I'm sorry. How is she?

Grandad: No change means no improvement. That's where

we are with her. Going back to Joshua's school, the only way forward I can see is a boarding school. I can make inquiries with Tiverton Park. That's where we sent Christopher. But I'll need your consent. I've no parental rights.

Mum: Yes, absolutely. That might be for the best.

NO! Joshua screamed, again in his head, though the scream nearly jumped out of his mouth on its own. He was not going to be locked up in a boarding school! It was like a prison. Dad had once told him all about boarding schools. He would never send Joshua to any such place, he had said. It was a bad place. It had made Dad cry a lot. There were days that it was worse than a prison, Dad had added. And Dad knew what he was talking about because he was in prison right now.

Joshua walked away on tiptoe so that they wouldn't hear and try to stop him. He went straight to his room to pack his rucksack. He knew to pack his toothbrush and a change of underwear as well as a pair of warm socks even though it was almost summer. He knew about survival. He had learned about it at Beavers. He took his teddy, Ted. He wasn't going to leave him behind all by himself. Joshua knew how that felt. It wasn't a feeling he would wish to inflict on Ted.

He felt sorry for Flip and Flop. He had to let them stay where they were. He'd briefly considered scooping them into a plastic bag, but he wouldn't be able to keep them there for ever. Releasing them into the wild had crossed his mind. The ditch outside the house was the only fresh water reservoir he was aware of, but somehow it didn't seem big enough for two sharks with their huge growth potential. And what if the ditch dried up? It did that sometimes, when it didn't rain. No, Joshua had to leave Flip and Flop behind. He said his goodbyes to them. They seemed to listen. Flip (or Flop. In truth, nobody could tell the difference between them) swam to the glass wall and waved his flipper. Joshua waved back.

'I'll be back for you, alright?'

When he made a promise, he kept it. Unlike Mum and Peter. They had said they would be back after one month, and that one day they would take him to the Great Barrier Reef to meet real sharks living out there in the wild. They had lied. Joshua was done with the lot of them.

He crept downstairs. In the dining room, Aunt Yvonne was talking to her laptop. She was in a conference call with other teachers from her school, or maybe it was her Climate Change buddies. She spent hours conferencing with people about saving the planet and free school meals.

Joshua made a stop in the kitchen to raid the fridge for food. He also armed himself with a nice kitchen knife with a wide serrated blade. There were lots of dangerous predators in the wild, he imagined, and he would have to be able to defend himself against them.

He slipped his feet into his muddy trainers in the hallway and slunk through to the lounge, leaving behind a trail of gradually fading footprints. He exited via the patio door. The dry-stone wall had crumbled in the corner behind the raspberry bushes, just enough for a small boy to squeeze through. Joshua had discovered it a couple of weeks ago and explored a little way into the deep and slopy woodland beyond it. He would now go much, much further, and never come back. Well, except to get Flip and Flop because he had promised them.

On the other side of the wall, Joshua was free as a bird. He inhaled that freedom together with the fresh air that he drew in through his nose like the sweet smell of hot chocolate. Though, of course, he wasn't stupid and knew that air didn't really smell of chocolate. It smelt of dry wood and something musky Joshua couldn't quite place. He was surrounded by trees, some of them with thick trunks narrowing towards the sky like well-sharpened pencils and ending with green canopies that teemed with birds. There were other types of trees, too. Their branches hung low. They couldn't be asked to compete for the sky so they made themselves comfortable close to the ground. They were the sort of trees that Joshua could climb if he wanted to. He did, but this wasn't the time. He was on the run.

As the ground was sloping, he had to take care not to step awkwardly and twist his ankle, and land back at Grandad's with Auntie Yvonne fussing over him. Not to mention that it would be painful. He had sprained his ankle once on the football pitch. It hurt, and Joshua had squealed in pain. The coach pulled a sorry face and declared that a sprain like that would hurt like hell, and that clenching his teeth could make it feel better. He said Joshua had to be brave. From then on, Joshua knew what hell felt like. Finding out that Mummy was having another child and didn't want Josh with her in Australia and that Grandad was planning to lock him up in a boarding school hurt like hell too. Joshua clenched his teeth and began a slow, zig-zag descent down the slope, minding the jutting roots and rabbit holes.

He soon reached the end of the woodland and emerged onto a pasture to find himself face to face with a cow. The cow didn't look very surprised to see Joshua. It hardly noticed him. It gave him a passing glance and didn't stop moving its jaw for one second. Joshua on the other hand was slightly rattled by the beast. From the safety of the dense brambles, he inspected the creature head to hoof. He discovered that it had udders. Joshua had learned that from Grandad's Encyclopaedia Britannica that this meant it was a cow. Cows were placid animals who usually minded their own business. It would be an entirely different story if this was a bull. Bulls had a bad reputation, especially in Spain where they liked to trample over people in narrow, cobbled streets with dead ends. Anyway, it was all academic, because this was a cow. Reassured, Joshua pushed through the brambles, ignoring the cow but making sure he didn't scratch his bare arms and legs on the thorns. The brambles were the thorny variety, not that Joshua knew for sure whether there was an un-thorny one. Being a city boy born and bred, Joshua hadn't had much experience of the country, or of brambles in particular.

He was relieved to emerge unscratched on the other side where he waded into the innocent-looking, waist-high undergrowth. He soon realised the error of his ways for he had entered a patch of nettles. They stung his legs and forearms without mercy, sending electric shocks through his body. He knew jellyfish could do that but he had never dreamt of plants being capable of such malice. Joshua yelped and cried, running deeper into the patch and breaking out in nettle rash all over his exposed limbs.

In the end, he lost his footing and fell. As the slope was steep and Joshua was no longer in control of his footing, he began to roll down the hill, bouncing on a large stone which changed the direction of his fall. The cow was watching him with moderate interest until he disappeared from sight.

His tumble was also being witnessed by a black man who was fishing on the other side of a canal. For it was a canal towards which Joshua was heading. There was not a tree, nor a bush or boulder to halt or even slow his fall, so it was inevitable that sooner or later Joshua would end up in the water. Which he did, with a large splash.

The water closed over him and Joshua found himself drifting to the bottom. He watched wide-eyed as sinuous weeds twisted and swayed around him, pushed by air bubbles inadvertently expelled from his lungs. Joshua and his lungs had been taken totally by surprise and all they could do was to continue dropping, especially because his rucksack was full and very heavy, and it was pulling him down rather persistently.

The fisherman on the opposite bank jumped to his feet, also very much taken aback. It had taken him a couple of seconds to decide what to do next, but once he'd made up his mind he was like a spitfire. He dived into the canal and swam across it in search of the little boy who fell from the sky.

He was very lucky to find him for Joshua was now at the very rock bottom of the canal and helplessly watched the huge bubbles that carried the last remnants of air from his lungs to the surface. Water pushed into his lungs to replace the bubbles.

The fisherman's large hand gripped Joshua's hoodie and yanked him up, together with his rucksack and all that water in his lungs. Joshua was dragged onto the opposite bank and received a big bang to his chest, followed by some rib-crashing compressions, until at last, he spat the naughty water out of his lungs.

Overwhelmed by panic, Joshua sat up and wheezed like an old man. To his relief, air returned to his lungs.

The black fisherman gazed at him like a wolf, with his head lowered and his eyes flashing from under his brows.

'You alright?' he asked.

'I'm not supposed to talk to strangers,' Joshua retorted.

'I just saved your life,' the fisherman said in a low booming voice. 'You can talk to me.'

Joshua reflected on that. It made sense. If this stranger was dangerous, he wouldn't have bothered fishing Josh out of the river. 'OK,' Joshua said, 'tell me your name.'

'Jeremiah.'

'OK. I'm Josh. But you mustn't tell anyone. I'm on the run.'

Wrapped in a dirty blanket, Joshua was shivering. He was still wearing his wet clothes (someone should have taken them off and towelled him, but it didn't occur to anyone here to do that).

Joshua wished, but only in passing, that Grandad was here to dry him and maybe run his bath. Auntie Yvonne would do too if Grandad was busy. Grandad was often busy smoking his pipe and looking out of the window of his study.

It was already dark and Loki started a fire. He said his name was something else, but everyone called him Loki so there was no point in memorising that something-else name. Loki had fish-like pale eyes and impressive yellow dreadlocks tangled on his head like Medusa. Joshua knew about Medusa from when they had been reading Greek myths in class. The log bench Joshua was seated on was carved with many battle scenes from Ancient Greece. Joshua was fascinated. The fantastical scenes held his attention for a good while, firing up his imagination as the flames from the camp fire flashed at them and animated them with light. Loki explained some of those scenes to Josh. There was one from a place called Thermo Pile (or so Joshua misheard it) that was especially interesting. There were lots of dead bodies piled up in a mountain pass. That's why, Josh deducted, the place was named Thermo *Pile*.

Ruthie – she was a funny woman dressed in colourful skirts and wore so many silver bangles with so many charms that her arms rang like small bells when she waved them – she was preparing yet another fish Jeremiah had caught for dinner. This one would be for Josh. They were going to cook it over the camp fire like the others. Joshua was looking forward to it. Not because he liked fish (he didn't unless it was made into fishfingers) but because he liked the idea of turning the fish on the spit. It was going to be fun. He was also very hungry, so hungry that he could eat a cow. And there was one on top of the hill, standing there in the full glare of the moon.

Waiting for his fish to cook, he explained to his new friends, who were no longer strangers at all, about his escape from Grandad's and his reasons for doing so. They all nodded their understanding. Joshua was pleased to have them on his side. They all had narrowboats and he could catch a ride with them to the mouth of the river and maybe into the open sea where, of course, sharks were likely to be found.

'You came all the way from that house on top of the hill?' Loki looked very impressed.

'Ahem,' Joshua nodded, proud as Punch. It had been quite a journey for a boy of seven and a half. It was only a beginning.

Loki finished his fish, licked his fingers and said he had to be off. And off he went. Joshua's fish was almost ready. It was beginning to smell like proper food.

Seeing Loki walking back into the camp with Auntie Yvonne by his side should have felt like the ultimate betrayal. A sob shook inside Joshua like the shudder of an awakening volcano. Joshua gasped and tears rolled down his cheeks, but he couldn't tell exactly why. He was torn: worried about what Auntie Yvonne was going to do to him for running away, but also strangely comforted by her arrival.

Auntie Yvonne shrieked his name and ran towards him with her arms wide open. She scooped him into them. Even though Joshua didn't like to admit it, being in Auntie Yvonne's arms felt better than just good. He wept some more, his nose dripping onto Auntie Yvonne's shoulder. Small as she was, she was able to lift Josh off the ground and swirl with him firmly in her embrace, his arms and legs dangling. Then he couldn't help it – he wrapped his arms around Auntie Yvonne's neck, so desperate to hold on to her, not to let her go, that he nearly strangled her. She coughed.

She sounded croaky when she finally put him down, grabbed his shoulders and, looking deep into his eyes, said, 'Let's go home.'

'But...' Joshua tried to have his say.

'No, don't you worry. I know everything. Loki told me all about it. You've made your point – loud and clear — and you won't be sent to a boarding school. If I have anything to do with it, and I do, your grandfather had better sit up and listen. I'll have words with him. That's a promise.'

That promise was credible and reassuring even though it came from such a small person as Auntie Yvonne. Grandad was scared of Auntie Yvonne and he always did what she said. Joshua breathed a sigh of relief. Although there were still a couple of unresolved issues that needed addressing, at least he wouldn't be going to prison. It'd be nice to sleep in his own bed tonight and to see Flip and Flop. Maybe he could still raise the possibility of a narrowboat trip with his new friends during the half-term break. That would be as soon as the next month, and the next month was only six sleeps away.

'Let's go home.' Auntie Yvonne reached for his hand.

He withdrew it. He wouldn't be pushed around now that he had *made his point*. He had another point to make: 'But I want to have my fish first. I cooked it myself, and my tummy is growling with hunger. I need to eat something or I may die.'

Showing him all due respect, Auntie Yvonne took a seat on the carved log bench, and waited for Josh to finish his supper.

THE PROPHET

He was stunned – winded, speechless and literally disembowelled. It was a shock to his system to see the woman he thought he had dispatched to hell two months ago alive and well. It shook him to the core. His stomach turned and he threw up violently, painful cramps pumping bile to his throat, muscle spasms squeezing his windpipe and cutting off his air supply.

The whore was flaunting herself without shame, walking the streets as if she owned them. Her putrid stench was offensive to him and to God. She was bloated with sin and disease, arrogant and dangerous. She was contagious. She had to be contained, like a deadly virus, before she infected the weak and the vulnerable that he had taken upon himself to protect.

She had proved herself harder to eradicate than he had expected. He had bled her like a slaughtered pig and left her for dead. She had looked dead. Drained from her face, blood had been oozing steadily out of her forearms. He had watched her for a few gratifying minutes, then sheathed his bloodied knife in a plastic sandwich bag and taken it home to wash. He had been pleased with his day's work. He had clearly made a huge mistake.

He was mortified to discover where she had been hiding, licking her wounds and consorting with the Devil right under his nose – in God's house. She had holed up in plain sight, where he would least expect to find her. The whore was cunning. He had underestimated her and that sorry excuse for a man of God who was harbouring her. It was a travesty – a further, unforgivable insult to the Lord. He would have to deal with the priest too. He would have to deal with both of them and put things right.

He fell to his knees and prayed for the Lord's forgiveness. He had failed Him. His sorrow cut deep into his soul, but he wouldn't seek absolution. It would be his actions that would earn him absolution. What he did ask for was a second chance. He begged for it. And he punished himself severely for wasting the first one. The hooks from the whip clawed the skin on his back and tore through it, each lash deeper and more satisfying. He was rewarded with a partial arousal, spiritual rather than physical. That spurred him into action. He had to take it further, all the way.

He had arrived at Junction 15 and left the motorway, taking the A-road towards Oxford. The night seemed young, but then this was the longest day of the year. Daylight stubbornly lingered in the shadows. He decided to cruise through the industrial outskirts of Swindon, looking for laybys and graffitied bridges, disused warehouses and lone women. No self-respecting lady would be prowling the streets in the night, and those who did were fair game. He drove past a group of four prostitutes, each occupying her own spot along the kerb, giving each other space and custom. It looked as if they were social-distancing, though, in truth, whores and social distancing was a contradiction in terms. He gave them a wide berth, and drove on. They looked after each other. One of them, or maybe their pimp sitting in the car in the adjacent layby, was bound to take down his registration number. Even without his number plates, they would recognise his van. It was distinct in colour and design, and it had his name and telephone number splashed across the back. He carried on without slowing down.

He was beginning to lose hope when he spotted a figure emerge from a bus shelter. It was a young woman. She tottered on high heels, clearly unaccustomed to them. Her long hair was bouncing provocatively against her shoulders with every unsteady step. Her skirt fell five-inches short of her knees. She paused to light a cigarette and to exhale a cloud of foul smoke over her head. Everything about her was a disgrace. She had obviously missed the night bus, or it had never arrived. Her bad luck had only just begun.

He changed into second gear and let his van roll silently behind her. His eyes darted from wall to wall of each building along the way, searching for CCTV cameras. The damned things were everywhere these days. As far as he could make out, there wasn't one in this God-forsaken place. It was his good fortune and the young whore's final hour. He accelerated and pulled up beside her. He then leant across the passenger seat and wound down the window. She would find it less intimidating if he spoke to her without leaving his van.

'Excuse me, miss, can you point me to the town centre?'

She started and peered at him with frightened large eyes. They were red and glassy in the light of the street lamp. He noted with interest that she was crying. He also noted, with disgust this time, that her top was low cut, revealing her heaving chest. She was panting heavily which wasn't surprising considering she was a smoker.

'I don't know, sorry.' She was foreign – Eastern European, or such like.

'Are you OK, miss?' He twisted his face into a spasm of concern.

'No,' she sniffled, 'I got off at the wrong bus stop... My stop is next.'

'Bad luck, but nothing we can't fix.' He pushed the passenger door open. 'Hop in, I'll take you to your stop.'

She didn't move. Her expression was wary. 'No. No, thank you.'

'Look here, miss, it's up to you. No skin off my nose, but I'd hate to leave you here alone. It looks like a dodgy area. Pretty girl like you... Oh well, suit yourself. Be safe, yeah?' He reached out for the door and began winding up the window. He watched hesitation creep into her eyes.

She stepped forward and grabbed the door. 'OK. You are very kind.'

She sat next to him. The smell of her cheap perfume mixed with cigarette smoke was overwhelming. It would take hours to air his van afterwards, he mused.

'Buckle in, miss.'

As soon as she did, he locked the doors. He performed a three-point turn and sped off, heading towards a flyover pedestrian bridge a couple of blocks away. He knew it to be a quiet and desolate place – perfect for a desperate woman to end it all and jump to her untimely death.

'It's the other way... Stop the car!' She screamed in panic. She started fumbling with her seatbelt. 'I change my mind. I want to go.'

'Shut up,' he growled at her, but the stupid tart wouldn't listen. She rammed her shoulder into the door and fought with the handle. To no avail – he had locked the doors as soon as she had got in. Only when she tried to reach for his steering wheel and cause him to come off the road did he take the pre-emptive action of striking her across her head with his hot flask. She went limp. Blood trickled out of her ear. He wasn't worried about the injury he had inflicted. It would blend nicely with the injuries from the fall.

He pulled up under the bridge and switched off the engine. He sat still for a while, steadying his breath. He scanned the shabby surroundings: a pavement ending abruptly in a rubble of broken bricks, slabs overgrown with weeds, and some unsavoury old litter he'd rather not identify. This wasn't a regularly frequented beauty spot. It was a dump. He checked that there were no witnesses about and switched on the internal light. He examined the girl. She was young – younger than her high heels and makeup would imply. Her cheeks were full and her skin soft and fluffy like a peach. She was slumped in her seat, her knees indecently apart with her hand wedged between her thighs. He clenched his teeth, his jaw muscles twitching. He couldn't help hating the whore even though hate was so unchristian. She left him with no choice, parading her body in the night, inviting sin. She was still alive. Her breath brushed his face as he bent down to undo her seatbelt which despite all her scrabbling she hadn't managed to unclip herself. There was time, he thought, to take a photo.

His camera was an old-fashioned Kodak with film roll. He didn't trust smart phones and wouldn't go near digital cameras – not with the kind of photos he took. He wasn't stupid. A smart phone would keep track of his movements. Printing digital images at the superstore would leave some form of indelible trace that would lead directly to him. He'd heard, and had no reason to doubt it, that no digital content could be permanently erased. If uncovered it would be easily linked back to the author.

He took two photographs: one a close-up of the girl's face with her jaw slack and her mouth slightly ajar, and the other one of her body splayed in the seat without a care in the world. She was a little whore after all.

Dragging her several steps up to the crossing was strenuous. He wasn't a big man, and not particularly athletic. Years behind the wheel with little exercise to tone his muscles, were beginning to take their toll on him. He had to stop once to catch his breath and re-arrange his grip on her body. He hooked his hands under her armpits and pulled. She groaned and opened her eyes, shouted something in some foreign tongue and tried to scramble to her feet. No way would he let her. After a short scuffle, he kicked her, his heavy boot making contact with her temple, and she passed out. He did his best not to leave any other marks on her. A few bruises would make no difference. They would be compatible with the fall.

He stopped in the middle of the bridge and looked down to find the street beneath tranquil and empty under the night stars. Satisfied with the situation, he flung the little whore over the barrier. There was a muffled thud as her body hit the tarmac surface below. She sort of curled in and out, and froze in that position. Her knees were awkwardly bent and pointing in the same direction while her head turned the other away, as if she couldn't bare the sight of her disjointed limbs. He spotted her stiletto wedged in a crack in the concrete slab near his foot. He picked it up and tossed it over the barrier. It landed neatly next to her foot.

He set his camera on flash and zoomed in on her body. He held his hand steady. He really wanted a clear image. The flash lit momentarily as the camera clicked immortalising the moment of another harlot's death.

He had set up the dark room in the roof. It was the perfect place for it with a direct access from his bedroom. Nobody ever ventured here, not since he had announced that the hatch mechanism in the ladder was jamming and could be dangerous. There was no need to fix it as there was no need to climb up to the loft. It stored spare blue bathroom tiles which had since been replaced with new white ones. There were a couple of end rolls of lino and a few pots of dried paint. And there was the table with the film processing equipment on it, trays with liquid paper developer and stop film baths, a dry-plate area and a lockable cabinet, all illuminated by the warm red safelight fixed to the rafters.

With the new photographs he had taken last night, the film was now full and could be developed. It contained the pictures of the last one and the previous two women he had mercifully rid the world of. It also contained the images of Jane Cuthbert, but to his immense disappointment she was still very much alive. Thank God the other three were dead or his head would explode with white fury.

He processed all the pictures and hung them to dry. As they were drying, he contemplated what to do with those of Jane Cuthbert. They did not reflect the facts. He examined them. They looked deceptively real. He wished he could keep them, but they weren't true trophies. God would not accept fake offerings no matter how well-meant. They had to be destroyed. He would take new – authentic — ones soon. He pulled them off the line and, one by one, fed them through a shredder.

His attention moved to the remaining images. Three other harlots had been successfully dispatched to hell through his unwavering vigilance, hard work and unflinching dedication to God's calling. He had something to celebrate after all. He scrutinised each of them with relish, enjoying every detail. The way the latest whore's shoe sat upright next to her twisted foot – not exactly a Cinderella moment, he pondered with a smile. The pinkish foam blistering on the Stroud woman's mouth reminded him of candyfloss. The third woman's hair splayed out in the bathwater like the leaves of a black spider plant. It seemed almost like a work of art. In a way, once they were dead, they had become beautiful again, in God's true image.

Having enjoyed the artistic aspect of his photographic efforts, he allowed his eyes to drift towards other, less godly aspects: their exposed thighs and breasts, the mysteries of their pubic areas, the curvature of their waists. He fed his eyes and his imagination and grew hard. These were the only times when he could achieve an erection. He didn't want God to know about it. He was playing with himself under the table.

'Dinner's on the table!' His mother's voice carried faintly from the kitchen downstairs. It jolted him upright and he lost his momentum.

'Coming!' he shouted back, though he wasn't anymore, was he?

He locked his new photographs in the cabinet alongside the others. All in all, he had thirteen dead whores to his name, and one pending.

PART 4

THE NEW NORMAL

CAMILLA

A man, a woman and a child have collected me from the hospital. The man is in his mid-to late sixties, rotund and flabby. His idea of casual is a white shirt with cufflinks but without a tie. His head is a shiny dome dotted with liver spots, reminiscent of a duck egg. The egg sits in the nest of his messy, faded-blonde hair that stretches in a horseshoe shape around the lower back of his head. He sounds posh. He could easily be on a first-name basis with the Queen. His name is Hugh and, apparently, he is my husband. The woman is called Yvonne. She is his sister, which makes her my sister-in-law. I take diligent mental notes of who is who. I need to be able to put a face to the name. Her face is nothing like his. It is long and narrow, and very economic with fat tissue. In fact, she is skin and bone all over. Her gauntness makes her appear stern, but based on what I have already learned about things, I like her. I daresay, I like her more than him. And vice versa, by which I mean to say that I have a feeling that she likes me more than he does.

The boy, going by the name of Joshua, is my grandson. I am relieved to experience a glimmer of recognition when I see him. I recognise his eyes, his chubby cheeks and his part-cheeky, part-guilty scowl. I recognise his voice. I might have previously seen the navy-blue hoodie he is wearing. The sleeves are too short. He must have grown since I last saw him. I think I am beginning to put it all together. But there are huge gaps that need filling. Questions that need answering. Pieces of my life's puzzle that need to be found to complete the picture.

I mustn't panic, I tell myself, reassured that some things are slowly coming back to me. I have been out of circulation for three months. I need time and head space to find my bearings.

We leave the city. We travel along a road that cuts across rolling fields and dips in and out of small hamlets. We live in the country, which I find pleasantly surprising. I envisaged myself as a city dweller.

We approach a narrow bridge and stop to give way to two cars travelling from the opposite direction. The arch of the bridge and the curve of the road beyond it, flanked by a terrace of stone cottages on one side and a windowless barn wall on the other, spark another flicker of recognition in my head. Yes, I have been here before and probably driven over this bridge many times. It seems promisingly familiar.

'Just take a look at that – it's bone dry, and it's only June.' Yvonne points to the riverbed below the bridge. The water level appears to be low, but I wouldn't call it *bone dry*. Even if it doesn't tumble in gushing rapids, there is some water there. It sits in shallow pockets and it is teeming with green frogspawn. That isn't good enough for Yvonne though. She will accept nothing less than flowing rivers and lush woodlands. From the little I already know about her I am in no doubt that Yvonne Bramley-Jones is an eco-warrior.

By the way, we are all Bramley-Joneses. I am looking forward to meeting the rest of the family in the hope that I may recognise a few more faces. I am thinking of my children. I am bound to have at least one considering that there is the grandchild. I tell myself that as a mother I will definitely know my children's faces.

Our house is an impressive country mansion shielding behind a six-foot high, dry stone wall. We are rich, I gather, and that thought fills me with distaste. I have to assume that like Yvonne I may be a bit of a leftie. How did I end up with someone like Hugh? I marvel. I don't even like the man. I hope this aversion to my own husband passes quickly. I will surely discover his redeeming qualities and my love for him will reignite. For now, I have to keep an open mind, and my gob shut. I can't possibly have any defensible opinions without having all the facts in front of me. I know that, and they do too. The good doctor explained it all to us. I suffered multiple head injuries. My body shut down. I have been in a coma for three months. My brain has been concentrating on nothing else but healing my body. Now that my body requires no further attention, my brain will start retraining itself in remembering my life. It is normal. I have nothing to worry about.

But I do. Nothing seems right. I don't feel comfortable in my own skin, in my own home. I am surrounded by strangers – all but one.

Hugh takes me to the lounge. He has to show me the way because I can't remember. He points me to the sofa and invites me stiffly to take a seat while Yvonne organises some tea. Joshua demands to go out into the garden – he wants to play outside. I mustn't take it personally. He is not running away from me. He has been cooped up in the car, being a good boy, for nearly an hour. He has earned some fresh air and the freedom to do what he likes. I wish I could follow him. I feel bereaved when he leaves. He is the only familiar face I have.

Hugh stands on the patio and lights a pipe. A whiff of

smoke swirls inside the lounge and teases my nostrils. I crave a cigarette. Am I a smoker? This may be a good time to give up. On the other hand, I may as well give in. I get up and join Hugh on the patio.

'Can I take a puff?' I ask him.

He gapes at me. His jaw hits his chest. I can tell he is gobsmacked. Maybe he doesn't know I smoke. Maybe I've been hiding this fact from him. Maybe I used to be a smoker in my distant – blank – past. Maybe I gave up years ago. Maybe my accident bumped my old vices up to the front of my mind.

'Yes, of course.' He passes me his pipe.

I take it from him, put it in my mouth. The mouthpiece is a little wet – Hugh's saliva lingers on it. I ignore it. He is my husband after all. I take a couple of puffs and release a rather successful series of rings in the air. I am good at it, and it feels great.

It has been a hell of a day. I am exhausted. It is Yvonne who puts Joshua to bed. I hear their voices upstairs, a bit of mischief, banter and laughter, then the flapping of wet feet on the floorboards of the landing as Joshua runs out of the bathroom, evidently without a towel. I hear him tease Yvonne, 'You can't catch me! You too slow!', and Yvonne patently proving him wrong as, after some commotion, he screams, 'That wasn't fair! You always cheat!'. Yvonne accepts none of the blame. In a firm tone of unwavering authority (she is a teacher, I understand), she tells him to jump into bed, it's time for a story. 'I don't like your stories!' Joshua protests. 'I want my mum!'

Downstairs, Hugh and I are listening to the boy sobbing.

'It's the same story every night,' Hugh shrugs, 'In the end he just cries himself to sleep.' I wonder where Joshua's mother is. Why is she not here to put Joshua to bed? Is she dead? I don't ask. I'm sure that with time everything will become clear – I will remember myself.

Yvonne comes to join us. She has the expression of a martyr splashed across her face together with bath water and patches of foam in her hair. She collapses on the cushions next to me, with her wet bare feet propped on the arm of the sofa. 'Get me a bloody drink, Hugh.' She gives a sigh loaded with frustration.

'The usual?' Hugh asks, casually, and gets up.

Upstairs, Joshua is screaming his head off. They don't seem to be able to hear him, but I can't take it. 'Why don't I go and see what I can do?' I offer.

'You'll only make matters worse. Stay, have a drink with us. He'll stop sooner or later – fifteen — twenty minutes of this din and then he is out, fast asleep,' Hugh informs me as he is pouring drinks for Yvonne and himself. He glances at me. 'What would you like?'

'I'll go, have a word with him.' I decide.

The door to Joshua's bedroom is open, but I knock and ask if I can come in. He doesn't answer. Instead, he pulls the duvet over his head and hides from sight. I take this as an invitation to enter. I sit on the edge of his bed.

'Go away...' he mumbles tearfully from under the duvet.

'I've only just sat down,' I counter. 'Let me catch my breath.'

'You can catch it somewhere else!'

Feisty little rascal, I smile.

'I'd like to catch it here, with you, if it's all the same... Come to think of it, if you don't come out from under that duvet, you may run out of breath, too.'

'I won't!'

'You won't come out, or you won't run out of air?'

Silence. At least, he is not crying.

'Running out of air is not a good idea. It's really scary,' I inform him.

'How would you know?' a muffled grumble sounds from the depths of his bed.

'It happened to me once. I nearly died.' I suddenly remember. I rejoice to have this memory, disagreeable though it may be. It is vivid in my head – it's real.

'How?' Joshua's head pops out. His face is flushed red, his eyes the same colour from all the sobbing he has been doing.

'I was about your age, I'd say. It was winter. A very cold winter, I remember – the lake was shackled with ice–'

'What's shackled?'

'Well, the lake was frozen.'

'You had a lake?'

'There was a lake where I lived. There were hills and lakes. It was very pretty.' I distinctly remember the topography but I can't remember the name of the place.

'So how did you run out of air?' Joshua prompts me. He isn't after the descriptions of landscapes and names of villages. He wants action.

'Me and my friends went on the lake to play, as you do when you're seven. There was a collapsed jetty that led towards the middle of the lake – that's where the ice is thicker. It's usually thin around the edges.'

'Why?'

'I guess, it's warmer where it's shallower, towards the bank.'

'OK. So what happened?'

'So, we jumped off the jetty and ran across, pushing and shoving each other, as you do... I tripped and fell. Ice is slippery – you trip and fall all the time. But I tripped on the handle of a plastic bucket. Someone must have chucked it in the lake and it drifted to the surface and floated there until it froze over. The handle was sticking out – just so,' I show Joshua the space of two inches between my thumb and forefinger, 'and it was enough to trip me up. I fell. The ice over the bucket was thin and weak. I heard it crack. I thought it was my bone, or something... It happened very quickly. The ice gave under me and I went down. My jacket took in water and started dragging me under. I tried to push myself to the surface. It was hard, what with the heavy soaked clothes, but I managed. But you see, there was a problem.'

'What problem?' Joshua's eyes are burning with interest.

'I became disoriented and entangled in the damned bucket,' I bite my tongue for saying *damned* – not quite the bedtime story language – but it is too late to take it back now. I have said it. I go on, 'Suddenly I was trapped between the bucket and the layer of ice above me. I punched it with my fist, but it wouldn't give. I tried to scream for help, and that was when all that water gushed into my lungs. No air – it's a very scary thing...' I can still feel the sensation of my ribcage being crushed. I don't want to stop on this particularly grim note, no matter how educational it may be. I quickly move on to the mandatory happy ending, 'Luckily for me, there were some older boys – teenagers – playing a game of ice hockey on the lake. They saw what had happened and ran to my rescue, with my friends scattering in panic. The big boys grabbed the handle of the bucket and pulled it out, with me in it, breaking the ice, and all...'

'Wow!' says Joshua. 'It happened to me too, Grandma. I nearly drowned in the canal – when I ran away – because...' There is a little sniffle, but he deals with it like a man by wiping his nose with his pyjama sleeve. 'I couldn't catch my breath, and my chest started squeezing. Honest, Grandma, if Jeremiah hadn't pulled me out, I'd be... you know... drowned. He pulled me out and pumped my chest until I was alive again.'

'Jeremiah?' I recognise that name. I don't know who it is, but I know that name. Of course, I realise, I may recognise it as a name from the Old Testament. Maybe Joshua is telling *me* a bedtime story, a little myth he'd heard at school, slightly adapted for his needs. Because, in all honestly, this can't have happened: Joshua being fished out of water by a holy man.

I tuck him in. 'Let that be a lesson to both of us,' I say.

'What about?'

'Well, about catching breath, I suppose.'

'OK,' Joshua agrees.

'Goodnight, Josh.'

'Goodnight, Grandma.'

I switch off the lights and all I can hear when I close the door is his soft, steady breathing. He is asleep.

When I arrive in the lounge, both Yvonne and Hugh stare at me in awe.

'That was... something,' Hugh says. 'How did you do that?'

'A bedtime story,' I tell him. 'I'm ready for that drink now.'

'Sherry, then,' Hugh heads for the drinks cabinet.

'Make it double Scotch,' I say, and again, both he and Yvonne stare at me in shock. Am I really a sherry drinker?

After two double whiskies, my head is spinning and my feet are out of step with each other. I fear I have overestimated my body's ability to handle drink. Somewhere in my gut sits the firm conviction that I could tackle half a bottle on my own, no questions asked. And I mean half a bottle of strong spirit, not some pissy sherry. Yet, I'm pissed as a newt. I blame my three months in hospital, being drip-fed mushy peas.

'I'm knackered,' I slur. 'I tink I gotta lie down.'

Hugh gives a cockeyed look, 'Are you pickled, Mills?'

'I am not!' I lift my hand to my forehead, which I intend as a goodnight salute, but my hand drops and for a second I wonder where it has gone. I look for it on the floor, but to my relief I quickly discover it is right here, hanging by my side, rather aimless and numb, but it is still attached to my body.

'And where did you acquire that Irish drawl?' Hugh continues with his interrogation.

'What you mean?' I am genuinely puzzled by his stupid question, 'I am Irish – tazz where. I should go to bed, I tink.'

Yvonne and Hugh exchange bemused looks. I am standing there, swaying, wondering which way to the bedroom. I could stay here, in the lounge. I'd be perfectly content with the sofa if only Yvonne would shift a fraction. In fact, she gets up and squeezes my elbow, 'Let's go, Camilla. First thing, first – you need to shower.'

There is a moment when I am trying to work out who Camilla is, but as soon as Yvonne shoves me towards the stairs, I realise it is me.

The shower does me a power of good. I finish it on a cold jet stream. It has a sobering effect on me. I step out of the glass cubicle and shuffle gingerly towards the towel rack. I grab a towel – I assume it belongs to me – and wrap it around my hips. It occurs to me that I may need a shave. I have been three months in hospital without a razor. There is a body length mirror next to the towel rack. It is steamed up. I wipe away the mist and check my reflection, rubbing my chin to feel the stubble. There is none, I realise, and that surprises me. It shouldn't, but it does. I am a woman and I am looking at an image of a woman's face: soft skin, regulated eyebrows that don't appear entirely natural, and full lips. There should be a crooked tooth – bottom left. I seem to expect to find it, but it isn't there. My teeth – I bare them at the mirror – are all straight and pearly white. By all accounts, I am a good-looking woman. I really like the picture before my eyes, but I don't identify with it. Bloody hell, a voice screams inside my head, I'd better have my memory back soon or I will go bonkers!

I lower my gaze to find an ample bosom gazing back at me with the two beady eyes of pink nipples. I avert my gaze, and shamefully, pull the towel from my hips and wrap it around my chest, high under my armpits. For some unfathomable reason, I feel guilty, like a rotten Peeping Tom caught red-handed. What in God's name is wrong with me!

Enveloped in the bath towel, head to toe, I tiptoe to the bedroom and fumble on the shelves, looking for some nightwear to cover my decency. I find a pair of sensible striped pyjamas. I am relieved to be able to put them on. They are way too big for me. I have probably lost lots of weight in hospital, so that would explain it.

I sit on a king-size bed, and scan the bedroom. It is large and cosily furnished. Two piles of books sit on two bedside tables. I examine them. One set consists of mainly military non-fiction and Hilary Mantel's *Wolf Hall*; the other lot is a neat stack of *Agatha Raisins* plus something that looks like chick-lit judging by the idyllic cover. I shift to the side of the bed featuring cosy mystery and chick-lit. I gaze at the wall opposite the bed. That area is occupied by a chest of drawers on top of which numerous family photos vie for attention. My curiosity aroused, I leave the bed. I examine the photos one by one to re-acquaint myself with my nearest and dearest. I am pleased to recognise Hugh and myself in our wedding photograph, the two of us in a loving embrace against the background of an arched chapel door, my veil trailing on the stone steps. I find pictures of Joshua. I soon realise that only some of them are of Joshua – the other little boy, a spitting image of my grandson, is wearing a posh private school uniform and a cap with an emblem. There are more pictures of him. The snapshots follow his progress as he grows through the gangly awkwardness of puberty and becomes a man. Here he is on a boat, wearing black sunglasses, with Joshua, just a toddler, clutching his arm. They are the spitting image of each other, and there is that copper tinge to their blonde hair that I have just seen in the bathroom mirror. That man must be my son.

I pick up the boat photograph, mounted in a quaint frame with nautical accents of anchors, ropes and seashells. I peer at the man and will myself to know him. He is my flesh and blood. Our connection should be buried somewhere in my gut. I fail to retrieve it.

Hugh enters the room without knocking. It's his bedroom after all – our marital bedroom – and his arrival shouldn't bother me, but it does. I regard him as an unwelcome stranger who has invaded my personal space. My first instinct is to hide, but I don't know any hiding places in this house. He scowls at me and asks why I'm wearing his pyjamas.

'I couldn't find any of mine,' I reply, quick on my feet, I fancy.

'Yours are on the same shelf as mine.' He cocks his head and gazes at me with concern. A deep vertical line cuts his forehead. His gaze travels down to the framed photograph I am holding in my hand.

I have no choice but to level with him. I turn the picture his way and ask, 'So, that's our son – Josh's dad? I seem to... remember. The names are a bit fuzzy.'

'Yes, it's Christopher.'

I've got a name. I cling to it even though it still means nothing to me. But I've got it! It feels like I have just won a badge in the Scouts – a badge for one of the hardest challenges out there. I experience a gratifying sense of accomplishment. It swells in my chest. Although, it surely isn't the Scouts I remember – it is the Girl Guides, of course. I swiftly correct that discrepancy in my mind.

'Christopher,' I repeat my son's name with budding confidence.

'Yes, our only child, in case you wondered.'

'So, tell me, Hugh, why is Joshua living with us? Why is he not with Christopher? What happened to Christopher? Is he–' The only option that comes to my mind on this short notice is *dead.*

'Christopher is in prison.'

I didn't expect that, and I am shocked. Being in prison isn't one of those badges of honour I had contemplated earlier, but I suppose having a son in prison is infinitely better than having a dead son. That would ultimately boil down to not having a son at all.

Alive, though he thankfully is, he is also a criminal. I need further clarification. 'What has he done?' I ask.

'Nothing serious, Mills – um, a white-collar misdemeanour,' Hugh shrugs his shoulders, making our son's crime appear trifle, 'but yes, he made a mistake and is currently enjoying Her Majesty's hospitality.'

'What sort of a mistake was it?' Do I really have to drag it out of him? I have the impression that Hugh is still working on his sanitised version of our son's crime. Flippancy seems to be his preferred way of putting it into words.

'He got caught,' Hugh says, and then I hear him mutter something else under his breath, 'largely thanks to you, dear.'

'Oh? Can you explain that?'

'Look, Mills, you're tired. Your memory is shot. I don't want to go scratching at old scabs – at least not this very minute. But we have copies of all the disclosure papers from the trial. If you really want to relive every fine detail all over again, do it tomorrow. I'll give you the files. But for now, can we just go to bed?' He begins to undress. He unbuttons his shirt, revealing a flabby bare chest. I shudder internally. Blind panic makes me break out in cold sweat. What if this man decides to claim his conjugal rights tonight? I couldn't stomach it. I really need to get to know him first – to get used to him and his physique (which right now I find nothing short of repulsive).

'Is there a spare room where I can go tonight?' I ask. 'I'm so sorry, Hugh, but I still... I still don't know you. I mean, I do but... but I need some time.' I plead. I hope to God I haven't offended him.

His alcohol-reddened face begins to lose colour, the blood draining from his bloated cheeks. He opens and closes his mouth without emitting a sound. For a couple of seconds, we gawp at each other. I don't know what to say, but I'm not prepared to change my mind – I don't want to share the bed with him. I let him deal with it in his own good time. I watch his face regain colour and composure. He smiles, an indulgent expression softening his eyes. 'Yes, sure... What was I thinking! It's like landing on a different planet for you, isn't it? Inconsiderate old goat, me!' he manages to make light of the impasse, and briskly — though untidily – does up his shirt buttons. 'I'll sleep in the spare room. You stay here, Mills. I insist.'

'Thanks, Hugh,' I breathe with relief.

'Don't mention it,' he mumbles. He binds his hands on his stomach, looking about the room. He points to the wardrobe. 'I'll just grab a pair of shorts and a change of clothes for tomorrow. I get up at six – wouldn't want to wake you.'

I give a permissive nod. 'That's very kind of you.'

He fumbles in the wardrobe, behind the door. He emerges, holding striped pj's, identical to the pair I am wearing, and a coat hanger with a fresh light-blue shirt and a pair of trousers on it. 'And some underwear,' he narrates as he heads for the chest of drawers. I step aside. He takes what he needs. I don't want to be intrusive, but I am watching his every move, longing for him to be gone. At last, he is by the door.

'Good night, Mills.'

'Good night, Hugh. Sweet dreams.'

He cocks his eyebrow, but doesn't comment.

In the night, my mind is bombarded with dreams – snippets of memories, or imaginings, depending on what I am supposed to believe to be real. I recognise people's faces: my parents, my sisters and my Nana.

Nana lived with us until she died of old age. She would make herself useful by staying out of Mum's way in the kitchen and trying to mind her own business. She would often impress on Dad that she wasn't used to the *treatment* she was getting from Mum. Dad would bite his lip and do absolutely nothing about it. Nana would go on whingeing. I liked her a lot. She was my ally against my sisters. There were five of them – the scourge of my childhood. They were older than me and loved to alternate between babysitting and bullying me. I hated it when they kept ordering me around, outdoing each other at making me sit straight, blow my nose into a hankie or take my shoes off on the front step before entering the house. It was a small red-brick terrace house – one of five. I seem to recognise the front door in my dream – the fan of yellow-glass panels letting light into our otherwise dingy hallway. On sunny days, at a certain time in the afternoon, the light would hit the picture of Jesus with his red heart on full display, sticking out of his ribcage. The light would bounce off the glass and shine into my eyes, like a torch. When that happened, Nana would take the opportunity to remind me that Jesus was a miracle maker, and here was the proof. I remember it like it has only just happened, only none of it can be real, surely.

In my dream I am sitting by the door, in a patch of gold-tinged sunlight, playing with my lead soldiers. They are fighting in a battle against the multicoloured cotton reels I recruited from Mum's sewing kit. The cotton reels are the baddies, and they are on the losing side. They are dying one by one. Helped by an expertly executed flick of my forefinger, they fall down and roll off towards the bottom stair. Four of them are already dead.

My big sister (well, all of them are big – bigger than me – but this one is the eldest) is tumbling down the stairs. She is wearing her nurse's uniform, and as always, she is in a hurry. She pays no attention to the corpses of the cotton reels scattered on the battlefield under the bottom step. The inevitable happens: she slips and she falls, face down into my victorious army of lead soldiers. She wreaks havoc. It is too late for my troops to regroup. Many fall to their untimely death. It was an ambush by my evil sister. And she isn't finished. She screams at me to get out of her way, *the little shit* that I supposedly am. Mum runs out of the kitchen, wooden spoon in hand, looking perturbed and wanting to know what the matter is.

'Take him out of my face, or so help me God!' My sister seethes and rubs a droplet of blood from her cheek. I am delighted to discover that at least one of my soldiers managed to inflict harm on the enemy. We didn't surrender without a fight!

Nana's face materialises from her room (she is occupying the small front room on the ground floor as she can't deal with the stairs any more). Her quick, milky-hazel eyes assess the situation and she delivers her verdict, which as always is in my favour. She scowls at my sister and says, 'Next time watch where you step, young lady.'

I grin at Nana. She grins back at me, which isn't the prettiest of pictures as she has forgotten to put in her dentures.

I smile, lying in my bed, the dream fresh before my eyes. It is so vivid that I can't believe it isn't real. But it can't be. Apparently, I am an only child.

I'm fully awake. I check the radio-clock on Hugh's side. It's ten past six. I fear I may have overslept. I jump out of bed, feeling as fresh as a daisy and full of beans. I embark on push-ups with the window wide open. I am slightly disappointed that my body can only perform three of them before collapsing in a heap. Something tells me that I should be able to do at least twenty, even with one hand behind my back. My hospital stint has taken a lot out of me, I commiserate with myself. It will have to be a slow process but I will rebuild my stamina.

After cleaning my teeth, I head for the wardrobe. After last night's faux pas, I am careful to locate a set of clothes that fit me. I can't find anything particularly sensible, so I end up wearing a pair of white (!) linen trousers and a t-shirt. It's six-thirty and I am more than ready for a hearty breakfast. I'm dreaming of full-English: a couple of Cumbrian sausages, two fried eggs, rashers of bacon (I like them well-done, but not burnt) and a hash brown, if we have any.

I head for the kitchen. I know where that is – I was taken on a house tour when we arrived yesterday; the location of the kitchen is one thing that stuck in my mind. Hugh and Yvonne are already there, sitting at the breakfast table over their respective dishes: hers – fresh fruit and what smells like strawberry yoghurt, his – scrambled eggs with bacon. Tea is steaming out of their mugs, teasing my nostrils.

'Good morning,' I say brightly.

They stare at me in the same way they stared at me last night. Hugh stops chewing, pushing his scrambled-egg mouthful into his cheek. With his cheek bloated with food he looks like a spooked hamster. Yvonne drops a piece of pineapple into her bowl.

'What you doing here at this hour, Mills?'

'What hour is that?'

'A very early hour...'

'It can't be that early – you two are already up. Anyway, I am an early riser.'

'No, you're not. You don't leave bed before nine!'

'Well,' I reflect, and modify my earlier statement, 'I'm hungry. I could eat a horse, but I think I'll settle for a full English.'

Hugh's eyes turn into two bulging discs. He nearly chokes on his bacon. 'But you're a vegetarian!'

I consider this, but only briefly. I arrive at a decision. I can take a lot and I'm pretty adjustable (I think), but I will not compromise on meat. Deep in my gut, I am a carnivore and I intend to remain a carnivore for life. My vegetarian phase isn't even a distant memory. I can't imagine ever surrendering myself to a diet of nuts and cucumber. I simply do not identify with the greens. I reply resolutely: 'News flash! I'm a vegetarian no longer. I've had a change of heart. Three months in a hospital bed taught me to live life to the fullest, and that puts meat firmly back on the table.'

JOSEPH

We are having a welcome-home dinner, in my honour. After eleven weeks of lying unconscious in a hospital bed, attached to a ventilator and unable to deal with any of my basic bodily functions, my recovery seems a real miracle, almost like the Second Coming. I don't say that out loud in front of my guests so as not to sound disrespectful or insensitive. After all, I am having this dinner with the Right Reverend Hillary Irwin, his Private Secretary Brother Augustine (of the Franciscan Order) and Father Jacob, who stood in for me during my long hospital confinement (notwithstanding the fact that he had his own parish to run in Kingswood).

Since I am too weak to walk, I have been wheeled into the dining room by my housekeeper apparent, Miss Jane Cuthbert. I say *apparent* as I had no idea who she was when I first met her, which was only this morning.

When she appeared by my bedside, she told me she was taking me home. *Home* sounded good, like a salvation, and Jane Cuthbert had instantly become anointed as my guardian angel. I readily put my fate into her hands. I had no reason not to trust her. She was the person the hospital had called to collect me. She would have to be my next of kin or, since I am a priest, one of my flock. She could potentially be a nun, though I eliminated that option based on what she was wearing. It was a pair of skinny jeans with a rip just below her left buttock, and a tank top. When doctor Khatri arrived and greeted her, I could have sworn he addressed her as Mrs Steedman. He probably – incorrectly– assumed that she was my other half. I am guessing that doctor Khatri, being a Sikh, doesn't know that catholic priests don't take marriage vows. They take chastity ones instead and live celibate lives (those few, that is, who don't stray into carnal pleasures and indulge in a spot of sinfulness as a sideline). Jane Cuthbert didn't trouble herself to enlighten Dr Khatri on this moot point and let him call her what he wanted. *Mrs Steedman* seemed to go down well with her. She thanked the good doctor for taking care of me in reply to which he wished us good luck and good health.

She pushed my wheelchair along a wide hospital foyer to the accompaniment of hearty applause by a group of tearful nurses and hospital porters lined against the walls at two-metre intervals. I confess tears welled up in my eyes, too. Those were the people who had brought me back from the dead and nursed me to health. Those were the first human faces I saw when I woke up. Theirs were the first names – indeed, first words – I learned to say.

Jane Cuthbert bundled me into a taxi (with the help of the taxi driver as I was rather wobbly on my feet) and gave the driver the address of the Sacred Heart church in Silver Lane, Romley. Having no recollection of the place whatsoever, I had the niggling feeling that I was being abducted. Some strange, deeply buried instinct told me we were heading in the wrong direction altogether. I was disoriented and lost. Jane Cuthbert wasn't making things easier for me. We spent the journey in wooden silence. I sat there, strapped into the back seat like a toddler in a booster seat, marvelling at who I was – who I *really* was.

I kept revising my credentials in my head: I was a catholic priest. My name was Joseph Steedman. My parish was The Sacred Heart in a Bristol suburb called Romley. I had managed to gather this intelligence from my hospital bed shortly before my release. But now I was entering the wider – and deeper – waters of the outside world, and I had very little to go on.

As soon as Jane and I reached the priory (an impressive Victorian edifice behind the actual church building), I finally mustered the courage to ask her who she was.

'Jane!' She scowled at me the way a school mistress would scowl at a mischievous little boy who was playing silly buggers with her. 'Jane Cuthbert! Who else?'

And that was where I confessed to her that my memory of her and everything else for that matter had deserted me.

Her face softened with an expression bordering on empathetic. 'I see,' she said, and upon more reflection, added, 'What do you want to know?'

'Everything,' I said. 'Let's start with who you are? I know your name, but are we related? Who are you to me?'

'Your blinking housekeeper, Father! That's who I am. How could you forget? You begged me on your knees to work for you! And you'd better remember this quick 'cos you'll have to vouch for me to the Bishop. I haven't seen a penny of my wages since you gone down with COVID. It'd be the third month running that I been living on baked beans from the food bank.'

I dug deeper into the matter while I sat in the kitchen watching her prepare the feast for my welcome home dinner with the Bishop later. Apparently, I had recruited Jane

Cuthbert on the same day I'd had the accident. I had clearly failed to finalise the necessary paperwork. The *diocese* had been resolutely refusing to pay her wages, demanding references and for Jane *to bend bloody backwards* (or so she told me with an indignant expression on her face). I made her a solemn promise that I would sort this mess out with the Bishop this very evening.

'Or else I leave too, and then there be no one here to keep this sorry place going,' she threatened. 'So, do it before you go, Father. Once you're gone, I won't know where to look for you, and frankly I won't bother,' she elaborated, but still left me none the wiser. I wondered what she meant by any of that but I didn't get a chance to ask as she despatched me from the kitchen *to go have a rest, and stay out of the way.* Apparently, I was getting under her feet.

Six hours later, my housekeeper apparent, Jane Cuthbert, wheels me into the dining room and places me at the table where I am about to dine with said bishop, the Right Reverend Hillary, as well as Brother Augustine and Father Jacob. We are celebrating my miraculous recovery and triumphant return to duty. I imagine catholic priests don't get holidays or sick leave because what they do isn't a job – it's a vocation. I may be totally wrong about that. I will soon find out. I also cannot fathom why I keep thinking of priests in the third person. After all, I am supposed to be one of them.

One of us, I mean.

'So glad to have you back to health, Joseph. You beat the damned virus! Well done, my son,' His Excellency pats my hand affably, just as you would a dog's head. His hand feels soft on mine, and it is pleasingly manicured. Pure perfection! My hand, I note with dismay, looks awful by comparison. My hands are the hands of someone who has spent years doing hard labour in some wretched quarry. My nails are unkempt, chipped in places and haven't been trimmed in a lifetime. The cuticles are ragged and dry. It will take hours of soaking in lemon water plus tons of quality hand cream to bring my hands back to an acceptable condition. Embarrassed, I withdraw my hand from the table and hide it in my lap.

'Well, thank you, *sir*,' I respond gracefully. I can't understand why all three men exchange looks of mild alarm. 'Although I must say, I didn't do much to save myself. It was all down to the NHS.'

'We all prayed for your recovery, Joseph.'

'...and that too,' I am swift to add. I should have probably placed the divine intervention at the top of the list in the first place. 'The power of prayer is immense. Thank God you were all there for me to do your bit. Praise be!'

'Yeeesss,' Bishop Hillary enunciates slowly and appears to be taking the measure of me. His eyes are narrow slits under his heavily hooded eyelids.

The door is kicked open (I say *kicked* because it flies open following a muffled bang, the sort of bang one would expect to hear when a boot makes contact with solid wood). My housekeeper enters carrying a tureen and a ladle. We all smile brightly at the prospect of the soup starter being served. Brother Augustine, tucks his cloth napkin into the collar of his shirt (no, he isn't wearing hooded robes despite being a monk. Perhaps he is off duty, as this is, after all, a private function among friends – or so I am led to believe). Father Jacob places his napkin on his lap while Bishop Hillary just sits there and waits to be served.

Jane Cuthbert plonks the tureen in the middle of the table and says, 'Fish soup. Enjoy.' She turns on her heel and heads for the door without offering any condiments or even the faintest of smiles. She is still wearing her skinny jeans (with the slit under her buttock) and that dreadful tank top. When she leans over the table to deposit the tureen I notice she hasn't shaved her armpits in at least three days. The stubble is disconcerting.

Bishop Hillary also appears disconcerted. He watches Jane with palpable discomfort as she swings her wide hips on her way out. When she kicks the door shut and is safely out of earshot, the old man addresses me with a pained grimace on his face, 'We've had a complaint about your housekeeper.'

'Oh?' I beg clarification.

'About her dubious moral standards, I'm afraid.'

'Oh...'

'Are you absolutely positive that she is the sort of woman the Church can trust to...to look after a clergyman? I don't mean you, Joseph, of course, but say, a young novice priest fresh out of a seminary...'

Ah! Here it comes – the unfinished paperwork, Jane's references, and something unspecified about her character. I have no idea what *sort of woman* Jane Cuthbert is, but that isn't the point. I promised her that I would champion her cause and get her employment status with the Holy Church positively verified. But that's not all. I have my own, selfish reasons to fight in Jane's corner: I need her. Without her, I will be lost, even more so than I am now. She holds the key to who I am, to my memories and, I daresay, to my future. She is my guardian angel in torn jeans and a tank top. Yes, I will have to work on her dress code and manners, but I am certainly not losing her. I say, 'Yes, sir! Absolutely positive! Jane Cuthbert is a... a paragon of virtue. And let me be perfectly honest with you – it's all rumour and false accusation. People are jealous and some are gossip mongers, that's all there is to it.'

Bishop Hillary heaves a sigh of relief. 'I'm glad to hear that, Joseph. We'll keep her on the payroll in that case. Brother

Augustine,' he shoots a passing glance towards his private secretary, 'let HR know everything is in order as far as the housekeeper is concerned.'

Brother Augustine nods, eager to please. 'Of course, Your Excellency.'

The Bishop's attention returns to me. 'But, Joseph dear, please do something about her attire. A uniform, perhaps? I don't mean she has to wear a habit, but for goodness' sake, can she at least cover her buttocks?'

'I was thinking just that,' I agree, and I am not lying.

Father Jacob's jaw is twitching nervously. I hope he hasn't got a fishbone lodged somewhere in his throat. I offer him a glass of water.

After a satisfying dinner, courtesy of Jane Cuthbert's fine culinary skills, we say farewell to Father Jacob who is due to hold evening mass in twenty minutes at his own church in Kingswood. The Bishop instructs Brother Augustine to wait for him in the car (that being the black limousine parked in the church car park outside the priory). The Bishop has private business to discuss with yours truly.

'Let's go to your drawing room, Joseph,' he suggests, and I cross my fingers that he knows where it is. He does. I follow him in my wheelchair, violently bumping over two thresholds. Something will have to be done about ramps, I make a mental note of that. I have a few of those notes stored at the back of my head already. Changes have to be made around this place. Even though I don't recognise this as my home (I can't possibly imagine voluntarily choosing such heavy, dark curtains that would block out all the daylight and make this house feel like an underground vault, for example), I take it as it is for the time being. As soon as I have my feet firmly on the ground, in more ways than one considering that I am both wheelchair-bound and emotionally unhinged, I will start on some major alterations. The curtains will have to go.

In the drawing room, Bishop Hillary whips out a box of cigars from his pocket and offers me one. I cringe inwardly. My windpipe tightens. Not only will I not submit to this vile and unhealthy habit, but I would also prefer if His Highness took his filthy fags outside. Naturally, I don't vent my objections. I can only bring myself to politely decline, 'Not for me, sir. Thank you.'

He raises his bushy eyebrows in surprise. His milky-blue eyes round on me and hold me in a steady grip while he re-examines my mental faculties. 'Since when did you refuse a prime Cuban cigar? Have you given up smoking or lost your mind?'

OK, so I am supposed to be a smoker. That is quite a conundrum as I find tobacco repugnant in its every form. Even the faintest whiff turns my stomach. I am already feeling sick. From the moment the Bishop lights his cigar and expels a cloud of smoke, I begin to feel nauseous. I swallow the bile coming up to my throat and stammer, 'I... I must've given up... I think. A few weeks on pure oxygen pumped into my lungs must've done the trick. Got off cigarettes altogether, I imagine...'

'You did? Commendable.' He doesn't look as impressed as he does sceptical.

'I weened myself off them, I don't know how, but I did.' I tread deeper, 'Couldn't touch the nasty things now. Not anymore.'

'You don't mind if I do?' he asks in a challenging way. I don't believe he is giving me any option other than to say: *No, not at all. Go on and gas yourself to your heart's content.* Which I do, but not in so many words.

'Good,' The Bishop grins. His teeth are stained. No wonder!

It's all those nasty tobacco fumes he ingests. 'But you will join me for a small brandy. I seem to remember you have a decent Armagnac in that cabinet over there.' He gestures towards a dark-wood piece of furniture with carved doors.

'I suppose I should have one. Only a very small one for me,' I say demurely. Again, somehow I don't think alcohol is my thing, but if it is, brandy doesn't seem to strike the right chord with my palate. Sherry perhaps, but not brandy. Be it as it may, I wheel myself over to the cabinet to retrieve the Armagnac. I pour us drinks: a generous single for the Bishop and a tiny tot for me. With both my hands full I am unable to push myself back to the settee where His Highness is seated. He acknowledges my dilemma and heaves himself to his feet. He pushes me in my chair towards the mantlepiece. He then reaches for his drink (he knows it's the larger one). The smoke from his cigar licks my face and renders me temporarily incapacitated. I retch, and to cover it up, I gobble up my brandy in one panicky gulp.

'That's the Joseph I know,' Bishop Hillary nods approvingly. 'Have another one.'

The inside of my mouth and my throat are burning. The aftertaste of the brandy is disgusting. 'No, thank you,' I mumble. 'I'd love to but I shouldn't. I'm still on medication for the wretched COVID.'

'Aw, of course you are.' He blows a puff of smoke in my face, looking sympathetic to my plight. Maybe I should also mention that I have become intolerant of tobacco fumes? I decide against that. One small baby step at a time. For now I can at least get away with not getting off my face on the damned brandy.

The Bishop props his cigar on the edge of an ashtray. His hand disappears into the depths of his pocket. He is rummaging for something. I cross my fingers and pray he isn't searching for yet another type of drug. Turkish pipe, anyone? A line of coke?

Fortunately, all he brings to the surface is an envelope folded in half.

'Now, Joseph, my son,' he mutters. He takes out of the envelope what seems to be a letter and waves it at me, 'about your letter of resignation–'

My letter of resignation? My blood chills instantly to a below-zero level and starts draining from my brain all the way down to the tips of my toes where it sets in ten narrow icicles. It is a good thing that I am sitting for I would surely collapse in a heap right in front of him. I am not only shocked, but I am also mortified. Have I resigned my cushy priest's post? Why would I do such a stupid, careless thing? Am I about to lose my home? Alien as it may seem, it is still the only home I know right now. How long have I got before I have to move out? And where will I go? Where are my relatives? Do I have any relatives? I cannot remember! My mind is steeped in fog. I am an invalid, bound to a wheelchair. I definitely fall within the vulnerable category. Where will I go? Is there a homeless colony anywhere nearby? 'Oh my God,' I whisper in horror.

His Excellency doesn't hear my cry. He goes on about the sodding letter, 'You see, my son, your resignation has been a thorn in my side ever since you handed it in. A priest resigning from God's service – it is unthinkable. A travesty! And it's happening on my watch. What have I done to deserve it? I ask myself,' he steeples his fingers and presses them against his lips, 'and I have no answers... Frankly, I don't even know how to process this... this betrayal. It's a sacrilege of the holy vows!'

I sense that my situation is salvageable and that I can avoid joblessness and homelessness if I act now. I speak with keen haste, 'What if I took it back?'

There is a glimmer of hope in the Bishop's sunken eyes. 'Withdraw your resignation?'

'Yes! To be honest with you, I can't even remember what

possessed me in the first place to commit such an... unthinkable sacrilege. What was I on?' I try to take it lightly. I give a nervous chuckle.

'It was Devil's work, my son,' the Bishop gazes at me, deadly serious, 'the Devil was hard at work leading you astray... But yes, I agree, we shall put it behind us and forget this ever happened.'

'Amen,' say I. He frowns, but doesn't chastise me for my flippancy. Instead, he pulls out a lighter from his bottomless pocket and sets fire to my resignation. He drops it into the ashtray where we watch it burn. The flames blacken the side of his cigar.

When the unfortunate letter is nothing but ashes, the Bishop rubs his hands together, pleased. 'So that's that,' he pronounces. He picks up his cigar and relights it.

'Thank you, sir,' I chirp.

'For God's sake, man! What's with the *sir*? Call me bloody Bishop, will you!'

Bloody Bishop, I think in the privacy of my own head, *he's got quite a temper on him. I'd better tread carefully around the old bugger.*

I find Jane in the kitchen, attending to the washing up. She is doing it by hand even though I can see there is a perfectly adequate dishwasher near the sink. Her bare hands are blistered with the white foam of the washing-up liquid. I advise her to use gloves. Or the dishwasher.

'I know what I'm doing,' she tells me unceremoniously. She then shoots me a sharp inquiring look. 'Anything else?'

I pull a mysterious face. 'I've got some news for you,' I announce. 'Come, sit down.'

She wipes her hands on her apron and perches on a stool by the breakfast table. Her back is straight, her chin up in a show of defiance, but I can tell she is a bundle of nerves. She is kind of telling me, *hit me with it, why don't you?* I don't think she is expecting good tidings. All of her anti-missile defences are up: her posture, her arms folded on her chest and her hard gaze.

'And it's good news. You are now on the payroll,' I beam at her, hoping to disarm her. 'The Bishop is happy with your... credentials. I assured him of your good community standing.'

'You did? I never–' Doubt and disbelief sprout on her face in red blotches.

'You are a respectable and decent woman. I wouldn't have engaged your services otherwise. I'm not a fool.'

A nervous chuckle escapes her. She squints at me. 'I wouldn't be so sure, Father.'

'I need you, Jane Cuthbert,' I admit. 'I need you by my side. Especially now that I'm a little... lost.'

She cups her chin in her hands and covers her face with her fingers spread across it like a fan. Her fingertips press into her eyes. After a short ominous silence, she breaks down in tears. Sobs come from deep within her and pulse through her body in waves. I gawp, baffled. I have no idea what I may have said to upset her. 'Didn't you hear me, Jane? It's good news!' I reiterate just in case we misunderstood each other.

'Yes! Yes, I heard you. Thank you. Is that what you want to hear, Father? Thank you!' She wipes her face with the balls of her fists and rises to her feet. She dries her hands in the folds of her apron, then smooths the creases. She sniffles. Her actions are erratic. She is emitting low grunts.

'I'm happy!' She literally shouts.

'You certainly don't look it.' I feel a little disappointed in her. Is this all the gratitude I am going to get for my trouble?

'I don't feel happy, Father.' Tears roll down her cheeks, and now she doesn't even try to stop them. 'I don't mean to be ungrateful, but it's all been for nothing...'

'How do you mean?'

'Matthew – he's not coming back,' she spits out. 'They made him an offer – one of them what you can't refuse. He's staying there, in Boston, with his new girlfriend. A new life... It's great. An opportunity of a lifetime, he tells me. I should be happy for him, but I ain't! I'm not happy, and that's God's honest truth. I'm empty. I have a hole inside my chest the size of a millstone, right here!' She thuds her breast with her fist.

'Matthew? Who is Matthew?' I ask stupidly. I should venture a guess that Matthew must be a boyfriend – after all, Jane is a young woman, in her mid-thirties, there's bound to be a boyfriend lurking somewhere in the wings.

'Come on, Father! My son, Matthew! Don't tell me you forgot that too!'

'I did, I'm afraid. My memory is shot. He's your son, then. I see.' I rub my temples. This helps me to think. So Matthew is her son, and he is not coming back. Now I understand. I can feel her pain. That emptiness. That burning grief. I can feel it too. It's huge. It's unbearable. Your child being snatched away from you – that cuts deep into your guts. It hurts. It leaves a livid scar. I know it so well! It bites into you, and it will gnaw away, eating you alive. I don't know how, but I know this feeling intimately. It crushes you and grinds you to powder. 'I'm so sorry, Jane. There are no words to describe it, but I know how you feel.'

I reach out to her and attempt to pull her into my arms. She steps away.

'How could you possibly know? No disrespect, Father, but you have no idea how I feel. You've never had a child – you don't know the first thing about it. Not a bloody clue! Just stop,' she waves her hands over her head, 'stop trying to understand! Leave me alone! I've got the washing up to finish. The water's getting cold. Go,' she points me to the exit.

As she thrusts her arm out I notice an ugly scar creeping out of her wrist across her forearm. It is ragged and red, probably inflicted in anger, or pain, with a serrated or blunt blade. The rutted skin is stretched to cake over the veins lying beneath it. I stare at her arm. I can't help myself. I ask, 'Is Matthew the reason for that? You tried to take your own life? Oh, Jane… It's not like he's dead.'

'What?' She is confused. Do I really have to spell it out for her? No. She will work it out for herself. The pain is too raw now, but with time she'll realise this is not the end of the world. Her son has just moved to another town, across the pond. He will come to see her. When he is ready he will.

My discovery however leads me to another interesting conclusion. I venture a speculation and run it past her: 'Is that why the Diocese received that anonymous complaint about you? Your attempted suicide… You slit your wrists and the word got out. People love a good gossip. They don't care if they destroy somebody's life in the process. It's such a shame!'

She is genuinely confounded. She turns her hands, palms up and scrutinises her scars. 'What? These?' She shows me her forearms aligned with each other. There are scars on both of them, I note, but the right one is fainter.

I nod.

'You did lose your marbles, Father, didn't you?' She shakes her head. 'It wasn't me. It was that nutter! You saved me, actually. Can't you remember? If you hadn't come when you did, I would've bled to death. You must remember!'

'No. Nothing. Nothing at all,' I confess. 'Why don't you enlighten me?'

And so she does. It's quite a story. It chills me to the bone. I almost find it hard to believe that such sick individuals exist in the real world outside of horror films.

I have finally found my feet, in more ways than one.

First of all, I have no more need for the wheelchair. I can walk unaided. I have regained my strength and, thank God, seem to be unaffected by long COVID. In fact, I am as fit as the butcher's dog. But more importantly, I have also found myself on the spiritual plane.

It took me several weeks of feeling in the dark. I had to rediscover all the tools of the trade related to my vocation. I spent long nights studying the ins and outs of being a priest. I started with re-reading the Holy Book. All I could remember from it was the nativity story – you know, the three wise men, a couple of shepherds washing their socks, and a braying donkey. The rest of the plot was a mystery – a *tabula rasa*. I expected to be bored to my back teeth, but the story took me by surprise. I found it to be a first-rate thriller with a number of tear-jerking moments, some real human drama and well fleshed out characters. It had it all: war and bloodshed, betrayal, political intrigue and clever little anecdotes that made me reflect about the meaning of life and my purpose in it (I believe that in religious circles *anecdotes* are called *parables*. I really ought to start using the correct terminology if I want to stay in the job).

Apart from my Bible bedtime reading, I also dipped my toe into the murky waters of catholic rituals, and – believe you me – there are many of those! There is a whole complex calendar of celebrations and mortifications, fasting, feasting and an abundance of praying in various formats, some involving painful prostration and self-flagellation, while others are as harmless as singing and playing with glass beads. I memorised the order of the Holy Mass, and even ventured into foreign languages by studying some basic Latin mumblings (see above). I explored the sacraments, the virtues as well as the deadly sins, and discovered that there were seven of each, mystically interlinked with each other, a bit like Yin and Yan. I researched the lives of many a

Saint and found soothing consolation in the fact that some of them had started as thieves, murderers and good-for-nothing wastrels before they saw the light. There was hope for me yet, I cried with joy. I now have the Ten Commandments burned into my memory. You could shake me awake in the middle of the night and ask me what the fifth Commandment was, and I would sing it out to you: *Thou shalt not kill!* Praise be to the Lord for I am ready to resume my duties.

It hadn't been easy by any stretch of the imagination. My memory didn't do much to help. It wouldn't co-operate. Sometimes, when I tried to remember, it would send me on a wild goose chase to times and places that couldn't be true. Take this false memory that came to me in the form of a dream: me being a girl, wearing frilly, white socks and pushing a doll in a toy-pram, singing fucking lullabies. Or this one: me giving birth, my waters breaking, midwives urging me to push, blood and sweat galore. Trust me it was such a vivid experience that I woke up screaming in pain – actual pain. Yes, I know what the Bishop would say – the Devil was hard at work, leading me to doubt my sanity. He even superimposed on me this acute and irresistible yearning for my child – a child I do not have! The mind can be so easily manipulated into believing all sorts of fantasies. Only the other day, I woke up in floods of tears crying for my lost son. It could be Jane's fault, I think. She forever whinges about missing Matthew. Her grief has rubbed off on me.

Small setbacks aside, I believe I have triumphed. I have rejected false memories, no-memories, nightmares, temptations and doubts. I am a man, born again, and on my way to reclaim my true self. I am nearly there. I am nearly me.

Tomorrow I am to be reunited with my flock, so this morning I visit a barber. Something has to be done about my disgusting, long hair. So unbecoming of a priest! My idea of a man of the cloth is an elegant short haircut, a clean-shaven chin and most of all, well-manicured nails. Let's face it: who would want to take communion from a hand carrying filth under its fingernails? Especially in this time of pandemic. So, I have my haircut (inclusive of conditioning and styling) and a manicure.

I return to the rectory feeling immeasurably better about myself.

Jane takes one look at me and grasps her chest in horror. 'Father, what happened to your hair?'

'A well overdue haircut happened,' I tell her.

'But you never... I never!' She is still clutching her chest and I am beginning to fear that she may be going into cardiac arrest. With her eyes bulging and her mouth gaping, she certainly resembles a cat with a furball, desperate to cough it out.

'What is the matter? Spit it out!' I encourage her, trying to help her relieve the discomfort.

'Your hair was your... your pride and joy. You were like Samson, you used to say.'

'Samson?'

'Samson and Delilah, Father! Keep up!' She cries. 'You were like Samson with your long hair. It made you invincible, you'd say. What is the matter with *you!*'

'I changed my ways,' I say gently so as not to agitate her any further. 'It was time to do something different with my hair.' As I say that, I hide my hands behind my back. The last thing I want is for her to behold my manicured nails.

'So, no more wind in your hair when you ride your motorbike?' She asks, something bordering on nostalgia rippling in her eyes.

'No more motorbikes for me, full stop,' I declare. 'The bloody thing nearly killed me.'

Today is the big day. Father Jacob is going to hand the reins of running The Sacred Heart back to me. The church is full despite this being an ordinary Sunday on the Church calendar. People have attended out of curiosity to take a look at me and assess the extent of the damage to my body inflicted by the virus. They probably want to steal a glimpse of the incisions on my throat where the ventilator tube went. Alas, they will go home disappointed as my white collar covers the scar. But, to give my flock their due, they have also come here en masse this Sunday morning to welcome me back. They could have stayed in bed watching a cookery programme.

I feel overwhelmed with emotion. So many faces, all of them alien to me, but nonetheless they move me to tears with their genuine enthusiasm and tender, loving care for me. I join Father Jacob in the holy rites (I know them by heart, having watched Jacob deliver Mass on several occasions, and taken diligent notes. I have even practised in front of the mirror in the privacy of my bedroom.). I fancy I'm doing rather well. The congregation keenly responds to my invocations. My voice booms pleasingly under the high vaulted ceiling and echoes against the walls encrusted with the murals of The Stations of the Cross. We say the Lord's Prayer and sing together in harmonious unison.

Praise be! I belong!

At the end, Father Jacob proceeds to the notices and announcements. He says his goodbyes and thanks my parishioners for their warm welcome and hospitality over the last three months.

'And now I am delighted to return The Sacred Heart into

the capable hands of Father Joseph. He is back with us after his long illness. And he's itching to get back into the saddle. I'm sure you'll all join me in welcoming him back.' He steps down from the lectern and gestures towards me.

I get up. The congregation bursts into spontaneous applause. I nearly burst into tears.

'I am incredibly happy to be back,' I begin, 'and I'm thankful for your prayers and positive thoughts. They helped me to pull through. Without them – God knows – I could be dead. So I want to say thank you to all of you, my friends.' I watch with huge satisfaction as at least two elderly ladies take out hankies and wipe their eyes. A man blows his nose loudly. I take credit for that too. I have moved them to tears. 'I'm happy to be alive and to be back here. Back home with you.' More tears are being shed and dabbed with crumpled hankies. 'I want to roll up my sleeves and serve you as best as I can. You and Our Lord, of course.'

'Amen,' I hear a few voices eager to interact.

'But, perhaps, not everything is as it should be, or as you remember. In fact, I have a confession to make.'

Sniffles, coughs and pew creaking all stop in an instant. An expectant silence grips the congregation. They hold their combined breaths, waiting for my revelation and hoping it was worth getting up early this Sunday morning. I can see Jane shift uncomfortably at the far end of the second pew. She is probably worried I've changed my mind and am about to tell them that I am leaving. Wrong!

'Sadly, the evil COVID has robbed me of my memories of you,' I announce. 'I can't remember your faces or your names... It may be only temporary – I pray that it is – and it may all yet come back to me, but for now, my friends, if I don't recognise you, think nothing of it. If I act like I don't know you, don't take it personally. Come to me, let's shake hands and become reacquainted. So, let me start – this is I,' I smile humbly, 'Father Joseph. Tell me your name.'

A collective gasp, closely followed by a collective sigh of relief, answer me. I step down from my podium. A queue forms in the main aisle as my faithful parishioners line up to introduce themselves to me. It probably feels good for some of them, especially those with a lot on their conscience. This is a new beginning for me as well as for them. I used to know all their sins and failings, but as from now everyone gets a second chance. So it's carte blanche for all. Of course, God is bound to be keeping records and will have all our transgressions stored somewhere in heaven on a hard drive, but we will cross that bridge when we die and go to heaven to face him.

First in the line is an enormous woman flanked by two skinny men, the younger one being a replica of the older. The woman's dress could pass for a tent. It starts narrow, tightly circling her double chin and from there it spreads in yards of fabric to cover her bosom and even more widely to encompass her ample hips. Two ankles, deformed by swelling, protrude from under the tent and refuse to be contained by a pair of flat swede Hush Puppies. They are literally spilling out of them. The woman's face is flushed red with the effort of getting up and waddling hurriedly to take her place at the front of the queue. She wipes sweat from her forehead with a tissue she retrieves from a bag with a Gucci buckle (a fake, I can tell at first glance). The older man's face on the other hand is pale, almost grey, as if it has been pickled in vinegar. His complexion matches his wispy grey hair. The younger one is also going bald, but his hair is mousy brown and his skin has a faint pinkish hue. He has youth on his side, but not for much longer. He is in his late thirties.

The woman extends her padded hand towards me. Her eyes

are narrowed with doubt as she peers at me and says, 'I'm Mrs Keating.'

I take her hand in mine. I observe my closed fingers with pleasure – the nails look immaculate. 'Thank you for coming, Mrs Keating. I look forward to learning more about you.'

The doubt in her eyes releases its grip, but only marginally.

'And this is Mr Keating, my husband,' she points to the older man.

'Mr Keating,' I smile. He does too, but rather nervously.

'And Rory, my son.'

'Hello Father,' Rory says. He is grinning at me. His parents may be hesitant but Rory at least is pleased to see me, no questions asked.

'Great to be back, Rory.'

The massive tent of Mrs Keating departs, supported by the two tent rods of her husband and son. I truly hope that the woman considers going on a rapid diet. Otherwise, I predict, she won't live to reach her statutory retirement age.

I am approached by the next person. It is one of the two ladies I saw weep earlier. Her eyes are still moist with tears, which is touching. Her hand is trembling as she reaches out to me, but as soon as our hands meet, I discover that her grip is firm.

'Welcome back, Father,' she says. 'I've been praying for you day and night.'

'Thank you, Mrs...' I wait for her name.

'Miss, Father,' she informs, blushing slightly. 'Miss Pitt. But you always call me Gemma.'

'Thank you, Gemma.'

'Oh bless you, Father!' She rejoices, and starts telling me something else but is gently pushed out of the way by the next person. It is a long queue after all. If we are to finish this introduction ceremony by lunchtime, we'd better get a move on.

The elderly man who dislodges Miss Pitt from the head of the queue and shakes my hand enthusiastically is Joseph McCully. 'Your namesake,' he informs me, 'so you aren't likely to forget my name in a hurry.'

I don't, but he is the last person whose name I commit to memory. The rest of them, I'm afraid, escape me the moment they tell me who they are. Too many of them, but then again, I remind myself, we have time to get to know each other. I'm not going anywhere. I'm here to stay.

It has been three weeks since my return into the lap of my family. I still struggle to truly regard them as my loved ones. My relationship with them seems no more spontaneous or natural than painting by numbers.

Before Yvonne leaves for work (according to my mental notes, she is an assistant headteacher at a secondary school), she suggests I peruse the family photo albums – *to refresh my memory*. Hugh agrees. He is about to lock himself in his study. He works from home (he is a barrister, fancy that!). I decline and insist that I see those court files from Christopher's trial that Hugh promised me last night. I am dying to get to know my son. Somehow, I don't believe photographs will give me the full picture, excuse the unintended pun.

Hugh brings two gigantic lever arch files for me, and I spread their contents on the dining room table. I sit at the table, ready to dig in.

'Coffee?' My husband offers. 'It's no trouble – I'm making, anyway... You may not recall this but I can't start my day without at least two mugs of strong Americano.'

I nod, pleased. There are times, I discover, when he is truly a man after my own heart. 'God, I'd love a strong black coffee, thank you. Two sugars.'

He scratches his temple, an expression of stoic acquiescence in his eyes. He says, 'You don't drink coffee and you definitely don't take sugar, Mills, but I guess you don't recall that either.'

What I clearly recall is that I enjoy coffee, but couldn't drink it without sugar. I sigh, 'Like the good doctor said, it looks like I got my wires crossed in the accident. He did say the head injuries could have affected my personality – changes in habits, likes, dislikes... The extent of it, I do recall him saying this, is yet to be established. I could become a totally new... woman. I could start eating meat, drinking coffee and taking sugar with it.' My voice rises a fraction. I'm bloody frustrated with the mystery of who I have become, and even more so with who I used to be. 'I could, for example, start swearing, which I'm tempted to right now, because – in all fucking honesty – right now I don't know my elbow from my arse!'

'I see,' Hugh gives me an indulgent smile. 'So coffee, is it?'

'Yes, please. With two fucking sugars.'

As soon as Hugh is out of the room and a mug full of fragrant coffee is steaming before me, I begin to study the court documentation from my son's trial. The charges laid against him, and his partner in crime, one Sally Turner, are nowhere near being a mere trifle. They are accused of defrauding a number of their bank clients – thirty-two, to be exact – out of their hard-earned savings over a period of eight months, to the mind-numbing tune of £893,300, take or leave a few pennies. The files read like a second-rate thriller: unsympathetic characters, a convoluted plot with forged statements from a non-existent investment fund in an eco-unfriendly fracking enterprise, unrepentant greed and zero emotional depth, arrogance and denial, victims' lives left in ruin – and all of that just on the part of Christopher Bramley-Jones, my son. Sally Turner, on the other hand, sees the light, confesses, returns her share of their ill-gotten gains, and takes an overdose of sleeping pills. She can do and say no more. Christopher seizes the moment to deflect the blame away from himself and channel it towards the woman who can no longer contradict him. He claims he was only Sally's subordinate who did what she told him to do without realising the extent of her wickedness. He claims he never saw a penny of the loot. The jury don't believe him, mainly because of the glaring gap in the accounts. Sally has repaid £400,000, less some forty-thousand which she spent on simple life pleasures while the scheme was in full swing and thriving. So, where is the other half of the stolen money? There is only one logical conclusion: Christopher has it but he isn't giving it back. The police search for it but the trail goes cold. After all, Christopher Bramley-Jones is a professional banker – he knows how to move funds without leaving any traces. Traces or not, he is found guilty and sentenced to five years in prison.

'Well, fucking, deserved,' I mumble under my breath. I can't believe that I have brought up this sorry excuse for a human being. 'What a bastard!' I add.

I drink my coffee, which is by now cold, but I can't tear myself away from the files to make a fresh cup. I put aside the bank statements of all the victims who have been ripped off by way of monthly "investment" instalments drained away from their accounts. Christopher and Sally were careful not to raise suspicions. They didn't just bluntly empty their customers' accounts altogether but tactically clutched only up to a third of each person's savings. In many cases, no one would be any the wiser about their missing funds. Most victims were old, hapless and definitely not financially savvy. They would take the knowledge of what the actual balance of their life savings was to their graves, or so Christopher and Sally had hoped.

I read the transcripts of the victims' witness statements at the trial, and my heart bleeds for them. An elderly couple, Mr and Mrs Sweeny: he suffering from Alzheimer's, she, his carer, recently diagnosed with cancer – they badly needed every penny of their savings to finance their move to sheltered accommodation... Jenny Chevalier, a widow, living on her pension, saving what her late husband left her to provide for her son, a young man with Down's syndrome... Fiona and Robert Gordon, a couple in their mid-forties, who have been saving all their lives to finally become first-time home owners – all they wanted was a one-bedroom flat that they could call their own; time has run out for them to get a long-term mortgage and they had to accumulate a large deposit. My son Christopher stole not just their money, but also their dreams. It is so unchristian, and I am beginning to despise the bastard.

'Grandma? What you doing?' Joshua is standing in the doorway, peering at the piles of papers scattered on the table. His eyes are still full of sleep. His tiny bare feet look cold on the tiled floor. He is wiggling his toes.

'I'm reading about your father's crimes,' I reply bluntly. I have been caught unawares and simply can't control my anger. I add, 'About how he is a cheating-thieving bastard!'

'That's what Peter says, too,' Joshua informs me without so much as a flinch. 'But you told me not to ever say that again. How come you can and I can't?'

'Well, I... well...' I stumble. I will have to solve this conundrum later. 'What would you like for breakfast? I think there's still some bacon left in the fridge. A bacon bun, then?'

Watching Joshua devour his bacon bun is a feast for my eyes. I don't believe I have made anyone this happy ever before in my life. Juices are dribbling from the corners of his mouth as he bites seemingly more than he can chew and munches each enormous mouthful with impressive proficiency. Not a crumb is left on the plate. He wipes his chin with his hand and licks his fingers. When he is fully satiated I ask what his plan is for the day. He gazes at me with narrowed eyes, calculating something in his little head. I can tell he is contemplating his response carefully. I quickly gather that he isn't used to being asked – he is used to being told. He is probably thinking that I am putting him to a test and that there could be dire consequences for the wrong sort of answer. His face loses its bacon-juice enhanced glow and it crumples. 'Auntie Yvonne left me school work to do,' he admits.

'Oh dear,' I commiserate.

He cocks his head, intrigued. He can detect it in my tone that I'm sympathetic to his plight. He decides to push the boundary and see what happens. He says, 'But it's all on the laptop,' he points to a laptop on the sideboard, 'and I have to do it at the table.'

Since I gape at him without comprehension he elaborates, 'Cos I'm not s'posed to do it on the floor, or in my bedroom, or on my knee... It's not good for my posture. Auntie Yvonne says I must work at the table, as if I was at school. But you've got all your stuff there,' he gestures towards my files.

I get it! This is his escape clause from homework. I am going to go with it – my inner rebel eggs me on. 'Sorry, I can't move *my stuff* just yet.' I throw my arms in the air with theatrical despair. 'I can't let you mess up my papers, I'm afraid. The table is off limits for you, young man.'

He beams. 'It's OK, Grandma, I understand. You'll have to tell Auntie Yvonne.'

'I will. I'll explain it to her.'

'OK.' He is peering at me expectantly. I will now have to fill the void that I've created in his day by letting him off the hook with his homework and instead offer him some viable alternatives.

'We'll do something else, then,' I suggest and go blank.

'I can show you Flip and Flop!'

We are watching two goldfish swimming in a large tank installed under the stairs in the hallway. The tank is lit with artificial light and fitted with a variety of weeds and underwater toy shipwrecks. The two creatures have it all to themselves. Bubbles are fizzing to the surface, relentlessly expelled by a water pump. Joshua tells me which one is Flip and which one is Flop, but I instantly forget who is who. They look the same to me.

'They're so big for goldfish,' I comment, just to say something complimentary.

It is taken as an insult. Josh glares at me. 'They are sharks!'

'Ah! That explains their size.'

'They were this tiny when we bought them,' Josh shows me the space of two inches between the palms of his hands.

'Did we buy them – you and me?'

'Um... you paid for them, but they were for me. They're mine. Don't you remember, Grandma?' He looks at me forcefully.

'To be honest with you, Josh, since my accident I can't remember very much.'

'OK,' he relaxes, and presents a gap in his top teeth as he grins at me, 'but I can tell you what you can't remember. We got them the same day you died.'

A chilly current creeps up my spine. 'I didn't die, Joshua.'

'I know, I can see that, doh!' He rolls his eyes. 'But I thought you did. You looked dead. I talked to you but you didn't answer. I pushed you – just to see what you'd do – and you fell on top of me – and I was scared.' He swallows and thrusts his chin forward defiantly. 'Not scared for me! For the sharks! You nearly squashed Flip and Flop in the bag. I had to save them. We had only just got them!'

'Yeah, I totally get it,' I nod. 'Of course, I forgot – you were there with me. You saw it happen.'

'I know! I told Grandad, but he didn't believe me.'

'Told him what?'

Joshua's eyes are round with the genuine and unquestionable truthfulness of what he is about to share with me, 'That it was the alien what killed you! He had this ginormous black bubble head and he flew at you when you was telling me not to call Dad a cheating-thieving bastard.'

'Ah that...' I mumble.

'You didn't see him coming, but I did 'cos I was looking right at you. His bubble head smashed your window and the window smashed the bubble, and I saw the alien zoom out, and jump into you. And he was gone – inside you, and you was dead. I know 'cos I checked and you didn't answer me. You just dropped dead and nearly squashed the sharks.'

'So you had to save them and carry them away,' I nod, fully convinced.

'Yeah!' He is relieved. He gives me a big satisfied sigh. At long last someone has believed his story.

'Thanks for telling me, Josh. Now I know how it all happened.' I stifle a smirk. I have to give it to him. The boy has an imagination – describing a biker as an alien with a bubble for a head! He can spin a good yarn. That's our English lesson done for the day – story telling.

With the lockdown out of the way, we can visit Christopher in prison. We are sitting at a small table; he comes in and sits facing us. He looks a bit peaky – a far cry from his tanned, toned self in the boat photo. That's what prison does to people, I muse without an ounce of pity for him. He deserves to be here.

He looks at me plaintively. I think he expects sympathy. I avert my eyes. There is a niggle of guilt at the back of my mind – what the hell happened to my unconditional motherly love? Shouldn't I be feeling something – something other than contempt for the conniving rat? Maybe I would if he showed remorse, if he cried out how sorry he was, if he offered to make amends. I will him to confess and atone. That'd be the right thing to do and then, I am sure, I'd be able to love the scoundrel again. But Christopher does nothing of the sort. Instead he whines about the torturous three months of his incarceration: how slowly the hours drag when one has nothing to do, about the lowlifes – *the real criminals in this shithole* – he is forced to rub shoulders with, about the unimaginable dangers a prisoner's life is beset with, about the shitty quality of food and his growing chances of developing scurvy, about his burning indigestion and the lack of proper medical care, and finally about the two inmates who contracted COVID, and died. Not because he is sorry for them, mind, but because it could have happened to him.

'Is there no way, Dad, that you can get me out of here? I don't mind wearing a tracker,' he says hopefully.

Hugh shakes his head. 'We've been there before, son. No can do. Just grit your teeth and bear it. Keep your head down, stay out of trouble. You'll be out by Christmas.'

'Christmas is a lifetime away! In this bloody place, six months can be a lifetime, believe you me,' Christopher pleads. 'Surely a tracker... I don't mind completing my sentence under house arrest. This place is a death trap! Just get me out of here.'

Hugh snorts, amused. 'They don't do trackers for non-violent offenders like you – there's no need to know where you are when you're out. They want you here as a deterrent to other get-rich-quick mastermind-wannabes.'

'Community service?' Christopher squeaks feebly.

Hugh purses his lips and folds his arms on his chest. He strikes me as someone who won't waste his breath repeating himself.

Christopher drops his head into his hands in a gesture of final defeat. I can hear the rattle of his breath as he exhales heavily.

We sit for a while in sombre silence. Although he hasn't asked about Joshua, I feel he might like to know how his child is faring under our care. I break into a rapid-fire monologue about Josh's sharks – Flip and Flop, about the spot of gardening we've been enjoying and the rocking horse he rides on the patio when there is nothing else to do. I tell Christopher that Joshua misses him (which is a big fat whopper because I have no evidence of that at all).

'I'll make it up to him when I'm out. Give him a cuddle from me, will you?' I detect a quiver of tenderness in Christopher's voice. I warm to him, but only by a fraction. At least he seems to love his child.

'I will, son,' I assure him.

'By the way, Mum,' there is a sharp change to his tone – a sudden alertness, almost panic, 'you did manage to get my... my belongings from the house, didn't you?'

'Your belongings?' I blink at him without comprehension.

'Remember? A few... items... the box with my old papers from the garage?' He gives me a furtive glance, urging me to say *yes, all is well, I've got your items.* Only I can't because I have no idea what he is talking about.

'Papers?' I mumble haplessly.

'Oh, you know, Mum – papers, my old school certificates, some photos, bits and bobs, and... all that. Papers! You did get the box? Tell me you did.' His teeth are clenched and the last sentence comes out as a hiss.

'I might've... I can't remember very much. You see, after the accident–'

'Oh, Mother, think!' Christopher loses control over his frustration. His lips curl down as he bangs his fist on the little table that separates us. The thud alerts the prison guard who is standing nearby. He fixes Christopher with a searching glare. Christopher puts up his hands palms out and smiles apologetically. *Sorry*, he mouths.

'There's a box, I recall,' Hugh says, 'a cardboard box – with my plastic archive boxes from work. Only that one looks different. I was wondering if it was mine, or if someone else's had got mixed up with my lot. I had a few boxes packed in the office to work from home.'

'A cardboard box? Brown?'

'Yes, it is as a matter of fact,' Hugh nods.

Christopher exhales with relief. 'That's mine.' He looks at me, all charm and eternal gratitude, 'Thanks, Mum. You're a bloody star!'

The next morning I can't wait for Hugh to depart to his study. I send Joshua to the garden to kick a ball around. I tell him to practice penalty shots. I even set up makeshift goal posts with a net curtain draped between them.

Christopher's box is in the cellar. I drag it towards the bottom step over which hangs a strong 100-watt light bulb that illuminates the treacherously steep stairwell. The rest of the cellar is shrouded in darkness and filled with junk. A few vents allow a small amount of light and air inside. I sit on the bottom step and start sieving through the contents of the box.

Indeed, as indicated by Christopher, I do find a folder with his certificates and diplomas on top of the stash, but I soon realise that it is placed there strategically to mislead a potential burglar. Or a police detective. In fact, all of the documents in that folder appear to be photocopies of the originals. Underneath the folder, I discover another decoy: a photo album. There are photographs sparsely glued to the first four pages, and then nothing. I skim the top layer of the contents of the box and put the folder and the album on the floor. I dig deeper. Something tells me I am about to hit the mother lode.

My instincts were correct. At the bottom of the box are bank statements and share certificates – Christopher's secret loot. I page through them, adding sums in my head roughly, and arrive at the overall figure of £410,000.

'Well, hello there!' I welcome my discovery with open arms. The thing is that all these bank statements and shares are in my name. Cunningly, the greedy-smarmy shit calling himself my son set the whole operation under my name. I gaze at my signature at the bottom of the Terms and Conditions and wonder whether I was in on it. The fact that I can't remember means nothing. I can't imagine I had it in me to conspire with Christopher to defraud all those decent people of their savings. He must have forged my signature, I am sure of that. He must have thought that I would never find out, that I would be too stupid or too trusting to look. He had it all planned: to take the hit and serve his time, then on his release grab the dough and sail over the horizon. Probably on that fancy yacht of his...

I examine *my* signature. It is straightforward and easy to forge. It starts with a large C that links with Bramley via a lowercase B. The second barrel, *Jones*, doesn't form part of it, though there is an intimation of a capital J at the end. I climb the stairs to the hallway to fetch a pen. When I return to the cellar I begin to practise. It takes me some twenty minutes to achieve perfection. My forgery of my signature is indistinguishable from Christopher's. I smile under my breath. 'Change of plans,' I announce to the four empty walls of the cellar. 'We're having a change of plans, ladies and gentlemen.' I know exactly what I need to do.

JOSEPH

At first I was looking forward to confessions. Who wouldn't? I expected them to be like thumbing through the society pages of a tabloid – brimming with juicy revelations, indiscretions, breakups, scandals, adulteries and other harmless, albeit titillating, disclosures. Not a chance! If you choose to become a priest in the hope of living vicariously through other people's deepest secrets via the confessional box, you will have made a grievous mistake. The stuff you will hear in the confessional will bore you into submission. It is like watching paint dry, and it isn't even any vivid prime colour – it is plain, dull magnolia.

This morning I am snoozing through a trickle of tedious transgressions that sweet old ladies share with me in a God-fearing whisper: impure thoughts (alas without elaboration), missing the Sunday Mass, calling the Lord's name in vain, a few instances of minor blasphemy and coveting thy neighbour's new fridge-freezer. Based on my previous experience of severe nether-region discomfort, I have brought a soft cushion to sit on. It is one of those with an inbuilt memory. It shapes itself around my bottom to accommodate and protect its various protrusions and irregularities, including my well-endowed groin area. The cushion is God-sent.

There are long breaks between the penitents. According to my timetable, I am to be boxed in here for two hours solid, whether or not anyone comes to seek absolution. Rules are rules. I've heard four paltry confessions so far, each more boring than the previous one. On the last one, I could hardly stop myself from telling Miss Pitt to go and sin in earnest, and to only come back when she had something to report that was worth wasting God's (and my) time on. The woman is a bloody saint, for crying out loud!

She left twenty minutes ago, and I have another forty minutes left. I shift on my shape-remembering cushion, moving my body from side to side in order to restore my blood circulation. I feel like a hen sitting on eggs, waiting for the damned things to hatch.

A mere shadow of a human form registers behind my curtain as it slinks past. A new, and hopefully my last penitent for the day slides into the confessional. I hear the floor creak as he goes down on his knees.

'Bless me, Father, for I have sinned,' he intones in a whisper so bland and soft that I feel compelled to look through the grid to make sure that someone is indeed there.

I detect a shady figure of a man with an abundance of facial hair: a thick beard almost reaching up to his eyes. Against church etiquette and common sense (this is after all a warm August morning), he is wearing a beanie hat. It's too big for him so it hangs loosely on the bridge of his nose. The slits of his eyes are hardly visible and I can't tell what colour they are. I smell peppermint on his breath.

I mumble my blessing, and lean towards him, my ear pressed to the grid.

'I hear you lost your memory, Father. Do you remember me?'

'I'm afraid not, my son,' I repeat my mantra, 'but whatever sins you confessed to me in the past were and will remain between you and God, whether I remember them or not. I am not that important in the grander scheme of things.'

'I know,' he says, 'you're just a vessel.'

'Indeed.'

'And so am I.' That sounds quite mysterious.

I say nothing and listen.

'So you don't remember anything? Nothing?' I detect frustration in his thin whisper which transforms into a hiss.

'No. But, like I said, you don't need to recite your past transgression–'

'I've no transgressions to recite, Father,' I sense admonishment in his toneless whisper. 'You were my confidante – a messenger between me and the Almighty. And you forgot the message. I'm disappointed.'

'I'm your messenger? I don't understand...'

'You were supposed to take my messages to God. My deeds – everything I've done to please him.'

'Pleasing God is not a sin. You should only bring sins to the confessional stall, my son, not your good deeds. Go in peace.'

'But I do bring sins, Father. I bring other people's sins. And I told you about how I punished them whores. And you were supposed to keep track of it. You forgot! How could you forget? You call yourself God's representative on earth?' Angry hisses filter through his teeth and his thick beard.

I have no idea what to make of his ravings. He has managed to unsettle me. He is full of menace and anger – not quite the penitent type, I presume. He should be remorseful. He isn't.

'Do you seek absolution, my son?' I ask him. 'If so, you need to confess your sins first, and then we'll see what we can do.'

'Are you deaf? Or are you taking the piss, Father?' He sizzles.

'What do you want?' I feel it's time for me to show my claws. The man is a nuisance.

'I want you to remember.'

'Well, I can't. So, if you've got nothing new to add...'

'Oh, I do, Father. But I'll start from the beginning to bring you up to speed.'

'If you insist.' I sigh. It looks like this is going to be a long session and I'll be late for lunch. Jane hates it when I am late. Especially after the last time when I was late for the fish pie dinner. That was when the accident happened. I wish I had my mobile on me to send her a discreet text about the expected delay.

Soon however all my earthly worries and considerations fade into insignificance. What the man says next puts everything into perspective.

'There've been six of them, whores of Babylon, but it should've been seven. It's your fault, Father, that she is still walking this earth, spreading her filth and disease. You stood in the way of God's justice, and you'll answer for it, but not to me. I wash my hands of you.'

I feel I should be relieved and thanking my lucky stars, but I'm increasingly uneasy. My ignorance of the Holy Scriptures may be to blame here. I truly cannot recall the details of the fall of Babylon, or how many whores there were. Six or seven is all the same to me. But I soon learn the man isn't talking about ancient history, and neither is he referring to the real Babylon. He tells me about Cardiff, Gloucester, Bristol, Weston-Super-Mare, Salisbury, Basingstoke and Swindon – our very own, twenty-first century backyard. He speaks in such a faint whisper that I miss some of the details. He isn't keen to elaborate on them either. He just wants to relish each execution and relive how it made him feel. Meantime, I feel sick to the depths of my stomach. Bile comes up to my throat and constricts it, like an invisible hand. I'm beginning to lose oxygen. Breathing becomes an arduous effort, just like it was when COVID took my breath away in hospital. I am gasping for air. I think this is a panic attack.

'...She didn't fight back. She knew she was getting what she deserved – God's justice. The pier was deserted, as it would be out of season. That's normal. I'd clocked the CCTV cameras beforehand when we'd gone to Weston on a day trip in the summer. I'd planned every move well ahead so I knew which way to go to avoid the cameras. My guess is they didn't work anyways, but you can't be too careful, as you well know. I couldn't afford to get caught on my first mission 'cos you and I both know there'd be no one to finish the job. You wouldn't've, Father, would you?'

I'm still dumbstruck, not even able to nod or shake my head. Deep inside, I want to scream for help. I must be rescued from this maniac.

'Yeah, I know you wouldn't. Even though you know damn well them whores spread diseases. No man is safe from them. They eat into your body and soul. Anyhow, you know what they are, but you want to keep your hands clean. Kid gloves, and all that... I don't blame you for that. You have your job. I've got mine. That said, you shouldn't of messed about with the Cuthbert woman. You should of let her die.'

As blood circulation resumes its cycle around my body and reaches my brain, I am beginning to realise he is referring to Jane, and that he is the *nutter* who attacked her.

'She went under like a rock. Nothing. Not a ripple to be

seen. I'm thinking the whore couldn't swim. Do you call that ironic, Father?'

I would call that barbaric and insane. If only I could speak! He pushed a woman off the pier, and let her drown.

'I checked she was dead the next day, just in case she had tricked me. They can be tricky, whores. Nothing on the first day. So I stuck around, and waited. Two days later, bingo! That would have been what? Hm,' he pauses to contemplate the date, 'beginning of March. Two years ago. Two and a half now. Time flies, eh?'

I swallow the bile burning in my windpipe.

'I stood there with the crowd and watched them carry her body off the beach. She'd washed up half a mile up north. They said – a drowning accident. Truth be told it'd been a stormy night. The winds could take your head off if you weren't careful. God was watching over me. He sent that storm to make my job easier. He didn't have to. I would of still done it, but it was good to know I had the Almighty in my corner... So that was that. Job done. Six to go, I said to myself. God willing.

'I done another one the same way, you know, 'cos it'd been so easy... and clean the first time round. You know – without getting my hands dirty. In Cardiff Harbour it was. It wasn't hard to find the harlot. They all crawl out at night and prowl in dark alleys. You just have to know where to look. And the water was there, handy. The bitch guessed what was coming to her. She tried to claw at my sleeve. Maybe she thought, stupid cow, that she could take me with her. I ain't much to look at, but take my word for it, I got muscles of steel, I do. I work out. Not of late 'cos of COVID... You gotta stay at home, protect the NHS, as Boris says. Anyways, I had to prise her claws open and gave her a push. Off she went. Thrashed about for a minute or two, no longer, and joined the other whore at the bottom of the big blue sea.' He chuckles.

I can tell he is getting high on his own words. The more excited he becomes, the less careful he is with his speech. The words are now less sophisticated, less biblical. Foul language creeps in. Traces of accent break though his whisper, but I am still working on what it is. All I can say is it isn't a hundred percent Bristolian.

'...She was pissed as a newt, Father. Couldn't stay on the pavement. I thought she'd get run over before I even got my hands on her. I followed her sorry arse anyways, just to see where she lived, like, and what could be done to rid the world of the filth she was. She got home. It was a long workers' terrace. You know them brick terraces all over Basingstoke? It was just after ten at night, but I could see the windows were dark. No lights, I gathered, nobody else was home. She lived alone was my guess. I took the risk and pushed her inside as soon as she opened the door. It shut behind me with a clank. Gave me an almighty fright, I remember,' he sniggers. 'As I said, God is my witness and he is by my side. It was a risk well taken. There was no one there, just the drunken whore. She fell to the floor when I barged in – must've fallen funny on her head 'cos she passed out. In all honestly, she didn't need much help to drop off her feet. Like I said, she was off her head, couldn't walk straight. My first thought was she was dead, but then she moaned. The job wasn't finished. I dragged her to the kitchen. God was watching over me – she had a gas oven. Just what I needed. I draped her over the oven door and shoved her head inside, turned on the gas and took myself out. Not a soul in the street as I left. And it was a nice summer night – warm and still young. Moon was big as a plate and bright as anything. The street should of been buzzing with folks, on a Friday night like that, in June. But there was no one. You know why, don't ya?'

'God was watching over you,' I hear myself say, my voice coming from some tomb inside my chest.

'Exactly that!' He titters. 'You get it, Father! You didn't get it the first time round I told ya. Good... Your time in hospital, on your deathbed – it made you see the light, I reckon. I'm happy for you, Father. We're on the same side, like I keep telling you, but we have different jobs to do. You be my messenger. I deliver God's will.'

I retch at the mere thought of being on the same side as this psychopath. It would be wonderful if this was just a dream, if I had simply dozed off, listening to some old lady's small trespasses, and had this crazy dream. I wish I could wake up from it. I pinch myself on my thigh, and I can feel the sting of the pain, but I can also hear the man's droning whisper. He is still here. He is still sharing with me his monstrous crimes. He is real.

'...That one, Father, trust me – that was the lowest of them all. I puked my guts out when I was done. You would too if you was there.

'She took me to her room. Over a betting shop it was. Just a single room. A curtain – tatty, see-through gauze, piss-yellow from smoke – was hung between the bed and what was on the other side: a kinda kitchenette. But was it dirty! And full of shit all over! The place stunk to high heaven. Rot, blood, sweat – you name it. She threw herself onto the filthy sheets, on her back, legs wide open, leering at me. God, my Lord, I said to myself, guide my hand. I didn't have a plan, to be truthful with you. I'd been to the betting shop, put a bet on a dog race, and was on my way, minding my own business. She stopped me, clutched my arm. *Hey, lover boy, want some action?* I couldn't say no, could I? It had to be done, but I didn't know how. I like to plan ahead and I don't like to leave any marks, or anything. In the end, it isn't my work – it's God's. I'm just a tool in his hands.

'She was lying there, and I thought I'd have to throttle the bitch. Then God showed me the way. The shit in the kitchenette – there was spoons and syringes, and some skunk. Not like she was arsed to hide it. I gave her a slap to keep her quiet and got the dope ready for her. Stuck it into her arm. A nice and tidy overdose by a pro. Not the first one and not the last one. The world became a better place without the poxy whore.'

Maybe he is a fantasist, I try to reason with my irrational side which by now is in the thralls of white panic. None of that has happened. The man is making it all up – an attention seeker with a seriously screwed up imagination. But something tells me he is telling the truth.

'...To be honest with you, Father, if I didn't know the good Lord had led me to that place for a reason, I'd of said it was a stroke of good luck. But I don't believe in luck. I believe in God, just as you do. He takes me places I wouldn't choose to go myself, but I let myself be guided by him. I know he won't lead me astray, you see.

'It was a back alley in Gloucester town, behind the shop fronts, not far from the Docks. I had been coming back home from a job up north and thought I ought to stop for a prayer at the cathedral. I like praying at the cathedral. I can feel God's presence there much stronger than here.

'I'd been praying there for longer than I planned. It was dark by the time I left. I heard the screams a mile off. The bitch was yelling and squealing like a pig. At first, I thought she was being butchered, or something worse, but as I drew closer, I saw what was up. She and her man, a pimp more likely than not I thought, was having a row. It was her, mostly, cursing and pointing her finger in his face. She had a big gob on her, full of profanities: *Eff off, you effing bastard, son of a bitch, I hate you!* And she wouldn't shut up. I was going to turn a blind eye and be on my way, but then she launches herself at him and starts throwing blows at his chest. He takes it, no problem. I'm thinking *what a poofter*, but I stay out of it. It's not my battle, you know. But then, she slaps him, though it's more like she rakes his face with her nails. I'm not that far away – it's a narrow alley – and I can see blood tracks on his cheek. So, he loses it – grabs her hand and twists her arm behind her until she yelps in pain. And he throws her to the ground, face down, you see. She doesn't see it coming. She doesn't have enough time to thrust her hand out to cushion the fall so it's flat out on her nose. *You broke my effing nose*, she yells, but he just tells her to fuck the hell off – pardon my French, Father, but they are his words, not mine – and he walks away.

'I watch her for a bit. She scrambles onto her all fours. Wobbles and feels her face with her fingers, like she is blind or something like that. Maybe her nose is broken 'cos blood is dripping from it onto the pavement. She's wailing. I look around me. Again, not a soul in sight. I cross the street towards her. It turns out she ain't blind 'cos she sees me coming and says to help her. *Call an ambulance, please*, she tells me.

'I don't carry my mobile on me, Father, so as they can't track my movements. I seen it done on the telly. The cops do it all the time. So, I tell her, *sorry, miss, I ain't got a phone.*

'*Use mine*, she tells me, *In my bag...* She's kinda swaying on her hands and knees. My guess is she's concussed. *Hurry*, she tells me again. I'm sick of the bitch telling me what to do. I look at her – tits hanging out of her low top, skirt too short to cover her arse – she's just asking for it. God has put her in my path for a reason.

'I kick her in the stomach. Her body flies up and she's on her back. I keep kicking – more like stomping down on her, like you do on a filthy cockroach. I grind her face into the pavement with me boot. She stops bleating. Job done.

'I read later in the papers, she was a student and the bloke was her boyfriend, also a student at the Gloucester UWE campus. He was charged with her killing. I followed it up a bit on the telly, out of curiosity. He was found guilty, sentenced to twelve years. He was pleading innocence all along, but truth be told, he'd started it. I only finished what he started.

'They showed her parents on the telly. Tears and all. Serves them right. They should of kept her at home. Not gallivanting in the night in skimpy dresses, inviting trouble. A university student, my arse! Woman's place is at home.'

I vaguely remember that case – a young woman from Cumbria beaten to death by her boyfriend in Gloucester. My stomach lurches. This man isn't a fantasist. I listen with growing horror as he describes yet another murder, *on God's orders* supposedly. This time it is a foreign woman who had the misfortune to catch his eye in Swindon. He tells me he threw her off a pedestrian bridge over a motorway. He tells me he made it look like she jumped.

His whisper turns into a low hiss when he starts telling me about Jane Cuthbert. I already know this story, but not from him. I know Jane's side of it, but it all fits. It happened, and he did it to her. I, apparently, found her and took her to hospital.

'Like I said, Father, God will judge you, not me. But I'd be careful what scum you mix with. If I was you, I would. She is a whore. You ought to be rid of her. Cleanse your soul, Father. Repent. It's never too late. The Lord is merciful.'

I am dumbfounded. Is he telling me to atone? Is he telling me to finish what he started? What is this sick, deluded maniac actually saying to me?

I've no chance to ask him. He crosses himself hurriedly. 'Good to have you back, Father. I'll be in touch. God bless.'

I hear the wooden floorboards creak again as he rises from his knees. The hinges of the door squeak as he leaves the booth. My wide-open eyes see his silhouette slither behind the curtain. Crossing the main aisle on his way to the exit, he pauses.

Reverently, he bows before the altar and makes a sign of The Cross. Then he slinks out of sight.

I force my mind to take charge of my body. My limbs are numb, my jaw slacks and my heart is going berserk inside my ribcage. *Pull yourself together*, I articulate my wishes, and my body reacts. I jerk into action, burst out of the confessional and run after the man.

On the footpath leading to the car park, I crash into Jane. She looks pale and shaken. She grips my forearm. 'Father, I think I saw him... The man who–'

'Which way did he go?'

She points towards the street, her finger trembling.

The car park exits onto the main road where you can take either the right or the left turn. I fix her with my eyes and urge her to think. 'Which way did he turn, left or right?'

'Left,' she nods at me.

'OK, you stay here,' I start, and quickly change my mind, 'Actually no. Go to the priory, lock the door.'

I don't listen when she tries to reason with me about the man being dangerous. So am I! I am going to get this bastard. How on earth did I let him get away with the murders when he first told me about them? What was I thinking?

I run to the top of the car park and scan the pavement to the right. A wiry dark figure is walking away briskly. It's him. I follow. I am taller than him and I have a larger, sturdier frame, but I've just recovered from COVID and I have little strength. My jog gradually slows to a power walk and then to just dragging my feet and gasping for air. He is putting more distance between us.

He spots me following him. He looks over his shoulder once, stops and cocks his head. He shades his eyes with his hand against the glaring sun. It can't be too difficult to notice me. I am a big man and I am running along the street, dressed in my cassock. I stand out from the crowd.

He turns around and quickens his pace. I try to do the same, but I'm failing miserably. At least, I maintain visual contact, but then I lose that too. He takes a turn to the left by a corner shop with fresh produce stalls out on the pavement. Feeling like my lungs are about to explode, and dripping with cold sweat and puffing like I'm giving birth, I finally reach the corner shop and look for him in a narrow alleyway. I am in luck – he has just reached the top of the path and turned right. But I'm conscious of the fact that he has clocked me. He knows I'm following him.

I struggle on, cursing myself for leaving my mobile at the priory. I should be calling the police. Jane was right: he is a psychopath and he is dangerous. Out of caution or simply because I am on my last legs, I slow down. I walk gingerly, fearing what may be waiting for me when I reach the end of this alleyway. Will he be crouched there waiting for me?

I am here on the open road at last, but he isn't.

The street is empty. It's a narrow residential lane lined with rows of terrace houses on both sides, culminating with a dead end. At the back stands a row of single garages or perhaps storage units with a cluster of wheelie bins blocking the entry. Some are overturned, some still upright. They must have been emptied earlier today.

I explore the area around the garages, hoping to find a back alley or a footpath that would allow him to continue on his escape route. There is nothing but a steep slope towards a fairly wide stream – about six feet at least. I can't imagine that he would have jumped over it. On the other side grow thick brambles.

I return to the street. I check the cars parked by the kerb in case he may have hidden in one of them. Again, nothing.

They are empty. There's a van with windows at the back painted over so I can't peep inside. He could be stowed away in there. But it doesn't look like the doors have been forced open.

'Bloody hell,' I curse under my breath. 'Where the fuck is he?'

'Father? Is that you? I'll be damned if it isn't!' I hear a squeaky female voice with twangs of an Irish accent rattling in it. It is Mrs Keating. She is standing in the doorway of one of the houses. She must live here.

'Oh Mrs Keating!' I exclaim. There is still hope, I'm thinking. 'How good to see you. I'm looking for a man. About five-foot-five, slim build, kind of wiry, with a thick beard, though come to think of it, that may be fake. He was wearing a black hoodie, jeans...'

'That'd be what everyone wears around here.' She scowls at me.

'You'd notice him. He moves... um... silently, on soft knees–'

'Whatever are you on about, Father? I've no idea. Never clapped my eyes on anyone looking like that round here.' She shakes her head doubtfully. 'You look out of breath, I say! Would you like to come in for a cuppa? It's no trouble.'

'I can't Mrs Keating. I have to find that man. I followed him all the way here and this is where I lost him. He must be–'

'Why would you follow anyone? Has he taken something from you?'

'Worse than that, Mrs Keating. He's a very dangerous man. A murderer.'

Mrs Keating crosses herself, her mouth gaping open. 'Holy Mary, mother of God, you can't be serious! We don't have that kinda people live in our neighbourhood, God forbid. Here everybody knows everybody. I'd know if there was murderers about. You sure you ain't mistaken, Father?'

'I'm so sorry, Jane – I lost him.'

She had done as I told her and locked herself inside the priory. She opens the door only after I tell her it's me. She is still as white as a sheet.

'It's OK, Father. At least, you're in one piece and he didn't get you. That's what I thought could well happen. He's a nutter! Come inside and catch your breath.'

She clearly doesn't have much confidence in my stamina, but who could blame her. I am a panting wreck. My cassock is drenched in my sweat.

We head for the safety of the kitchen. She puts the kettle on. There is always comfort to be taken from a nice cup of tea.

I tell Jane everything the beastly man has told me. She is speechless, just as I was. She is shaking her head with stubborn, irrational denial. 'It can't be,' she mumbles. 'He can't have done all of that... killing. It's madness...'

'He has, Jane. I'm ninety-nine percent sure. I couldn't believe it either, but when he told me about what he did to you, I knew, beyond any doubt, that he killed all those women just as he said he did.'

'Why?' She is peering at me with her large, tear-swollen eyes. 'Why would anyone do such a thing?'

What am I supposed to say to that? I can't possibly tell her the truth – that he was executing women he considered unclean, the whores of Babylon who to his mind were spreading some mysterious disease of body and soul, whatever that means! I can't throw at her all the insane nonsense he spewed out at me. I can't bring myself to tell her that he thought he acted with God's blessing. What would that do to her faith?

'There was no reason. He is a madman. He didn't need a reason.'

'I still... I don't know... It can't be real.' She is looking lost – a lost sheep I have to do something to save. I have to rescue her again.

'It is real. I'm afraid it is as real as you and me sitting right now in this kitchen, having tea. But we can double-check, if you like – go online and check local news. He gave me places and approximate dates. It shouldn't be hard to verify everything he said.' Deep in my gut I know he didn't make anything up, and I don't need to rake over the news to satisfy myself, but I guess Jane needs that. She needs to be sure. Seeing it (or reading about it online in this day and age) is believing.

We go to my office and embark on the search. We scour the news on the web over the last two years from the time of the first incident he told me about – the drowning of the woman at Weston-Super-Mare. It's all there, correct and accounted for. The dates correspond. We are gazing at her face in an online article. She was indeed a prostitute. She was also a mother of two young children. Her name was Katie Regan. The other cases follow suit. Those women existed. They died in suspicious circumstances, but not suspicious enough for the police to open full-blown inquiries. The only exception is the murder of Amy Vernon, the student found beaten to death in Gloucester. Her boyfriend, Aaron Wilding, is serving a custodial sentence for killing her. His trial has only recently been on the national news. The other deaths passed unnoticed. They were presumed to be accidental deaths or suicide.

'I have to go and report this to the police,' I say. 'Otherwise, he'll get away with it, scot free. They will never put these cases together unless I tell them what he confessed to me.'

She peers at me anxiously. 'But that would be breaking the seal of confession, Father,' she whispers. 'You would be excommunicated.'

That possibility hasn't occurred to me. It is one of those rites, rules and rituals I plainly forgot all about. Thinking about it now, as she reminds me of my holy vows, I begin to understand why I may have decided to leave the priesthood. I must have been planning to report that man to the Authorities. Obviously, I was! Otherwise, I wouldn't be able to look myself in the eye. I may not remember much at all, but I know who I am. I know my standards. I know I couldn't stand by, covering up for a serial killer just because of some ridiculous seal!

'Nevertheless, it has to be done, Jane. There's no other way. We can't let the man run loose in the night, murdering women, can we now? I'll have to break the seal of confession and take the consequences. Resign, if that is what it has to come to.' I must admit I am rather sad. I surprise myself. I was really enjoying being a priest, being useful to people in my little community, listening to their worries, helping them battle their demons, preaching love and hope. All that has been making my life worthwhile. I suppose that's why they call my job a vocation. I give a heavy sigh.

'Oh well, so be it. I have to do it.'

Jane puckers her lips and fixes me with a steady and determined gaze. 'Yes, it has to be done,' says she. 'But it isn't you who has to do it. It's me.'

CAMILLA

In the next couple of days after my discovery of Christopher's villainous conduct, I find myself extremely busy saving his soul from eternal damnation – I am sorting out the return of stolen funds to their rightful owners.

It isn't easy to shift the money about especially because I neither know any of *my* passwords nor am I able to find the nominated email address or mobile number in order to reset them. My temporary amnesia is a good smokescreen however. I can use it to claim utter ignorance of my own affairs, and remain credible. For the digital hurdles to be removed however, I have to present myself at the bank in person and prove my identity.

The branch manager I have an appointment with is a young lady dressed in a beautifully tailored trouser suit and incredibly high heels. Her shoulder-length hair is black and shiny, styled to give it a fashionable crunched effect. She welcomes me with open arms – well, after a fashion.

'Mrs Bramley-Jones, delighted you could make it! I am Jennifer Stiles.' She strides towards me, a pearly-white smile gracing her glistening lips. Those lips scream, *kiss me!* I am tempted, but I know my manners and offer her my hand to shake.

She winces and her bright smile is replaced with an apologetic grimace as she rejects my courtesy, 'Better not shake hands – we have strict rules on social distancing at the moment.'

'Oh that!' I roll my eyes. 'I'm still learning the new normal – I slept through the whole lockdown, you see.'

She tilts her head, intrigued.

'I was in hospital, in a coma, right through the lockdown,' I clarify though she already knows that – I told her on the phone. She clearly didn't take it in.

'I'm so sorry to hear that,' she commiserates, her glittering lips pouting with sympathy. 'Was it COVID?'

'No, thank God, it wasn't! I had been in an accident.'

'Oh... Nothing too serious, I hope.'

'Other than losing my memory, no, nothing too bad.'

'Great!' She beams, back in character. Young people these days, I muse, know only how to handle good news.

'If you'll follow me, please, Mrs Bramley-Jones.'

She leads me into her office. There is just about the space of two metres between us as I sit in the chair she offers me whilst she takes a seat behind her desk. It is a rather humid July afternoon. Despite the wide-open window, the room is hot and stuffy with palpable additional heat being pumped by her computer and a large printer. She extricates herself from her suit jacket. Underneath she is wearing an incredibly tight white shirt. The button sitting on the level of her bra is just about holding it all together. Beneath, her breasts are screaming to be let out. I am strangely attracted to her and can't take my eyes off her cleavage.

'So... Mrs Bramley-Jones,' she forces my eyes up to her face, 'you have lost your PIN?'

'I've lost my memory, to be exact.' I correct her.

'So, you can't remember your PIN?'

'Or much else, for that matter. But I need to make a few payments rather urgently... You asked me to bring two photo IDs and a utility statement. I've got my driving licence, passport and our council tax bill,' I shove the documents in front of her. 'Is this sufficient?'

'Perfect!' She puts on a performance of examining my passport. She peers attentively at my photo and then fleetingly looks at me. She beams again. Clearly, I have passed the test. I am who I say I am, which is a relief.

'I'll need to take photocopies of your documents, if you don't mind.'

'Go right ahead.'

She gets up and leans over the photocopier machine. Her breasts are now positively jumping out at me. I'm doing my best to show restraint. I am dumbfounded. I don't know what to make of my strange new impulses. Have I always been attracted to women? Am I a closet lesbian? I find that thought rather exciting. I feel blood rush to my face. I am hyperventilating. Oh, the deep buried secrets I am yet to uncover about myself!

'Are you alright, Mrs Bramley-Jones?'

'Yes... It's the heat. Very hot in here,' I wave my hand over my burning cheeks.

'I must apologise. Our air-conditioning needs servicing, but with the lockdown restrictions we couldn't get anyone.'

'Don't worry. I'll get over it.'

'Great!' she beams yet again. She is well-practised at customer-friendly beaming. She passes my documents back to me and tidies the photocopies into a neat pile which she slides into a manila folder. I am surprised that they still deal with real paper in the business world. I thought it was all digital these days.

'So, shall we set you up with a new PIN and password? I'll need your email address and–'

'That won't be necessary,' I stop her half-sentence, 'I want to organise a number of banker's drafts and they will dispose of the entire balance. Then I'll be closing this account.'

'I see,' she is still smiling, happy to oblige.

'Here is a list of payees.' I pass her a handwritten list of Christopher's victims with the amounts due to them. I worked them out on a pro-rata basis, without favouring anyone.

Jennifer Stiles casts her eyes over the list and her jaw tangibly drops. 'Thirty-two banker's drafts?'

'I'm sorry, it's quite a few of them. I hate owing people money. I thought I'd do it in one go and be done with it.'

'Yes, of course... This will involve a bit of paperwork... I wish I had known in advance what your intentions were. We normally ask for at least twenty-four-hours prior notice.' There is a note of admonishment in her tone. 'Would you like to come back tomorrow?'

'No. I'll wait.'

I am dispatched to the main foyer and seated there with a cup of coffee (which is incredibly nice of Jennifer Stiles. I do realise I've messed up her day and I fully appreciate her professionalism). Looking at her puzzled, if not altogether suspicious expression, I begin to worry that she may be calling the police while I wait. I am a sitting duck. Any minute now, I fear, the cops will arrive in a fanfare of flashing blue lights and wailing sirens, cuff me and take me to the station. Will I be able to call upon Hugh to represent me? Then again, I tell myself, Jennifer Stiles has no grounds to report any crime as no crime has been committed. I have just proven my identity to her and I am legitimately disposing of my funds in a way I deem fit. My business is mine alone, and her business is to act on my instructions. There is nothing illegal about that. I hope.

Nearly two long hours later, I leave the bank, clutching a batch of thirty-two white envelopes, each containing a fat-juicy banker's draft. I head for a quiet café in a secluded arcade. There, over another cup of strong coffee (double Americano with three sugars), I meticulously check each draft and address each envelope to the correct recipient. I attempt to disguise my handwriting so that it cannot be traced back to me, though in all honestly, what does my handwriting actually look like? I don't know, but just in case, I print the names in awkward capital letters – *awkward* because I'm writing with my left hand. I have already established that I am right-handed based on the hand I use to hold my toothbrush and to stir my coffee.

I conclude that I can't risk using the Royal Mail to send the letters by recorded delivery. To do that I'd have to state the sender's address – *my* address. I wish to remain anonymous and therefore I will have to deliver each letter myself.

I finish my coffee, pay at the counter, and head for my car which I parked at the top level of the Rupert Street car park. There, I enter the first address into the SATNAV. As soon as my navigator plans my route, I start the engine and drive off to make my personal delivery.

Weaving my way in and out of Bristol's backstreets, I feel strangely at home. Everything seems familiar and that bizarre sense of déjà vu follows me around. I am very pleased with myself. I whistle under my breath a jolly, lively tune. I realise, to my amusement, that it is *Jingle Bells*. It is the middle of July but it does feel like the season of goodwill has come early.

It is a bright and sunny Saturday morning. It's been ten days since I compensated Christopher's victims on his behalf. He doesn't know it yet, but I will have to tell him soon so that he can brace himself for the real world out there, one where people have to work for a living. There will be no proceeds of crime to fall back on. It may sound cruel. I realise he has already lost his freedom, not to mention his home and his fancy yacht, but then again – were they truly, honestly his in the first place? How much of his house deposit was stolen money? He will be angry with me, I've no illusions about that, but I will make no apologies. I did him a favour. When he learns the difference between right and wrong, he will thank me. I will, of course, have to carry out serious remedial work on his soul. I look forward to the challenge.

In the past ten days, I have been looking over my shoulder, half-expecting plain-clothes detectives to knock on the door and interrogate me about my hefty *donations* to my son's victims. I have made up my answers – they cross-reference my acute and disorienting amnesia with a compelling sense of restorative justice. The combination of the two played on my conscience and forced me to act. I will have to explain how I came across the funds and that could incriminate Christopher. Then again, he is already in prison for this particular crime so it's water off a duck's back as far as he is concerned. I've given it a lot of thought. So far, however, I have attracted no interest from any law-enforcement agencies. May this obscurity last!

After a hearty breakfast, I take a break from my anxieties. I go out into the garden where Josh is already waiting for me by the shed. We are building a boat which we intend to launch today on the canal. It's only a model boat, but it's crafted to perfection, if I say so myself. I'm proud of my engineering skills no end. All that's left to do is to attach the sail to the mast. Josh is jumping out of his skin with excitement. I am more stable, working on the stitching. It's one area I'm not very good at, which is surprising for a lady. I had no problem with sawing, sanding or drilling, but stitching is something else. I work in focussed silence.

A cloud of tobacco smoke whiffs past the shed. I inhale it with relish. I have accepted that I'm a keen second-hand smoker without remorse. I peep out of the window to find Hugh on the patio, puffing on his pipe. Yvonne joins him, bringing two mugs of coffee to the party. The coffee smells almost as good as the tobacco and I wish in passing that I was up there with them. But I can't let Josh down. He is watching me intently, dead keen to float the boat asap.

'I don't recognise her at all,' I hear Hugh say, his voice distant but clear. 'It's like Mills disappeared three months ago, and this total stranger turned up in her place. It's Mills by the look of her, but it's like she is possessed... Everything's different about her. I mean -everything! Her habits, how she speaks, what she says. I don't know this woman from Adam...'

'I know what you mean,' Yvonne's voice is hollow. She is not even trying to defend me.

'I could understand the memory loss, but it's so much more... Have you noticed she chews her fingernails? Mills would never do that to her nails.'

'Blimey!'

'She fucking scares me.'

'Let's hope it passes. We were told to expect mood swings and–'

'Mood swings – yes! But not a comprehensive personality makeover!'

'Give her time and space, Hugh. That's all you can do.'

'Oh, I have! I've been sleeping in the spare room for a month. It's a crappy soft bed, and it's doing my back in. How much more time must I give the woman? What if she stays this way for good? I can't take it!' Resentment, anger and despair resonate violently in Hugh's voice. It's like a whole marching brass band is beating away in white fury.

Yvonne seems to have no answers since she doesn't reply.

They sit in gloomy silence for a while. I am nearly finished with the sail. The boat will soon be ready. I would hate to come out of the shed now. They would know I was listening. But Josh won't lie low. He is raring to go. I begin to deploy delaying tactics and pretend to be considering the benefits of varnishing the main body of the boat. Josh asks if that's something to do with waterproofing it. It could be, I tell him, more than keen to cling on to this new lifeline he has thrown my way.

'Another coffee?' I am horrified to hear Yvonne ask. Will they ever leave?

'Nah. Let's do the sodding shopping early, and be done with it.' Hugh, mercifully, gets up. He empties his pipe, taps it on the table to loosen any trapped tobacco, and slips the pipe into his pocket. Yvonne picks up the mugs, and they both disappear inside.

'Ta-da!' I present the completed boat to Joshua. 'She doesn't need waterproofing after all. Let's see if this baby can float.'

'I'll show you a shortcut,' Joshua refuses to climb into the car so that I can drive us to the canal. He wants to walk. 'It's quicker my way!'

He leads me to the raspberry bush, behind which I discover a sizeable hole in the wall. We crawl through it on our knees, carefully passing the boat between us so it doesn't get damaged. The slope beyond our garden boundary is steep. I nearly lose my footing and roll down the hill. Josh catches my hand, 'Careful, Grandma!' He steadies me. 'One step at a time...'

We negotiate the slope, holding hands. Above our heads, the stone walls of our house loom like the fortifications of some medieval castle. Soon, they vanish behind the thick and leafy canopy of trees. We emerge onto a flat area inhabited by a family of four majestic yew trees. Their trunks snake across the forest floor and interlace with one another. It's like walking into a nest of giant pythons.

'This way, Grandma,' Josh calls out to me. 'You must be super careful here,' he points towards a mesh of brambles. 'Last time, I got stung and I did a roly poly into the river, and drowned... Remember, I told you.'

I seem to remember something to that effect. I thought he was making it up. One never knows with kids – when they're telling the truth and when they're lying through their teeth.

'I see what you mean...' The brambles are really thick and thorny, and they're flanked by a thriving colony of stinging nettles. I can now believe Josh is telling the truth. 'Let's go around them.'

There is no way around them unless we want to go back home and drive. I find another solution: I resource two sturdy branches. We prep them for our purposes, which is to use them as machetes. Josh is fascinated and makes several references to Indiana Jones. I am pleased to learn that we have a few interests in common. I am a big Indiana Jones fan, I can feel it in my bones.

We tear through the undergrowth, wielding our machetes, smashing the nettles to pulp. It's good fun, actually. We pop out onto a field where docile-looking cows are grazing idly. One of the herd has separated and is standing just by the line of brambles. We nearly bump into her.

Josh clutches my hand, but it isn't because he is frightened. In fact, he is offering me assurances of the cow's harmlessness, 'Don't be scared, Grandma. I know this cow. She's OK.'

'That's good to know.'

Josh points down the slope towards a waterway glimmering at the foot of the hill. 'It's deep,' he warns me. 'You mustn't trip and drown.'

'OK. I'll be super careful.'

'And don't drop the boat.' He peers anxiously at our model vessel. 'Maybe I should carry it... Can I?'

'I've got it in hand.' I don't trust a seven-year-old to safely transport my masterpiece down the steep gradient of a bumpy grazing paddock. Too much sweat and too many long hours have gone into it.

At the foot of the hill, Josh points towards a lock. 'We can cross over that bridge,' he instructs me and leads the way.

As we approach, I go soft in my knees. I need to stop to recover my breath. And my wits. I know this lock! I realise it is like hundreds of other similar locks scattered on canals all over the county, but somehow this very lock is more than familiar – it feels like home. We cross it to the mooring side. Narrowboats bob up and down in an orderly line. I am experiencing the same sense of déjà vu as I did when I navigated around the backstreets of Bristol, delivering letters. I have been here before! And I don't mean as a passer-by. I live in the area – of course, I would've come here before. But this is different. I know these boats. I know what they look like inside: what pictures hang on the walls, the patterns on the upholstery, the scents of weed, cooked cabbage and smoked fish embedded in the curtains and bedding onboard these boats. I know the names of these boats' owners!

The first boat belongs to Ruthie and her father. Opposite across the canal I recognise Jeremiah's rusty vessel. It sits camouflaged under the overhanging branches of a weeping willow. Then—

'Why, if it isn't young Joshua!' A male voice interrupts my contemplations. Joshua lets go of my hand and takes off towards the man. He is tall and athletic, his hair a bundle of blonde dreadlocks, his eyes—

'Loki!' Josh and I shout in unison.

Josh throws himself trustingly into Loki's strong arms and they scoop him from the ground effortlessly, and spin him around. I have the irresistible urge to join my grandson – to charge at Loki and squeeze him in a huge, manly bearhug.

'Loki, you sodding bastard!' I bawl, ecstatic. 'Long time, no see!'

Both Loki and Joshua gawp at me, ever so slightly taken aback by my overfamiliarity and possibly by the foul language that rolls off my tongue with such ease.

'It's OK, Loki,' Joshua explains, 'It's my Grandma. She's weird, but she's OK. She's been in an accident and lost her marbles. That's what Grandad says anyways.'

'That's all right, then,' Loki grins at me. 'Nice to meet you, ma'am.' He extends the spade of his large hand towards me. I touch it with trembling fingers. He scoops up my hand. It disappears into his as he shakes it. 'A fine young grandson you've got here, ma'am.'

I'm no ma'am, I want to scream, *I'm Noah! Remember Noah? It's me! I don't know what I'm doing in a woman's skin and I haven't got a clue how I got here, but it's still me! Same old Noah. The priest. Father Joseph. My name is Joseph Steedman. I am a priest. My parish is The Sacred Heart in Bristol. I live there. That dark-green narrowboat over there, just beside yours, the one that is freshly painted and doesn't yet have a name – it's mine! I keep the key in the Tupperware box inside the gumboot. When I bought that boat, it was a wreck. I've spent years refurbishing it, playing drums with you and Jeremiah, smoking pot and sometimes the fish we caught, talking to God and letting Ruthie do my Tarot card readings. It is I, Joe, but you lot – you call me Noah...*

I don't say any of that. I realise I would sound nuts, and if Hugh found out, he'd have me certified, no questions asked. But there isn't a shred of doubt in my mind about who I am and who I am not. I'm definitely not Camilla Bramley-Jones, whose skin I seem to currently occupy. This is something I will have to explore and understand later. Maybe I will never understand it. After all, as the Bard tells us, *there are more things in heaven and earth, Horatio, than are dreamt of in your philosophy...*

One thing is for certain. I must go home and check on my flock.

It is a Saturday morning. The church of The Sacred Heart seems deserted. It is so peaceful and quiet. It's just how I remember it.

I enter the narrow, paved path leading to the church through the cemetery. I've brought Josh with me. Hugh was too busy to look after him. Josh takes off at the first opportunity. He's racing amongst the graves as if it was an obstacle course.

The canopies of mature trees distributed amongst the graves create a dense screen. It blocks out the sunlight and gives an ambience of reflective serenity. Two squirrels chase each other in the branches and scare off a bunch of noisy blue tits. The birds skid and whizz overhead, none too pleased. The squirrels are nowhere to be seen to answer for their untimely intrusion.

Wreaths and bouquets of flowers are withering in the August heat on a freshly dug grave. One of my parishioners has died recently. I wonder who it is. I approach the headstone. Mrs Cornelia Rendell, 97. May the Lord have mercy on her soul. I remember the old lady, her fur-trimmed hat and a fur coat which I am sure was the real article. There just isn't telling old ladies that wearing real fur is a disgrace. They remember the war and its barbarity. Cruelty to little furry animals isn't high on their list of worldly concerns. I pause over Mrs Rendell's grave and say a prayer.

I am standing in the church doorway and my knees go weak with emotion. I have to lean against the wall to steady myself. My God, I am back...

I dip my fingers in the holy water, fall on one knee before the Body of Christ, and cross myself. Josh runs on ahead. I follow him nervously and admonish him for running.

'Slow down! Walk!'

He doesn't listen. He is excited and bursting with energy – a little explorer. He circles behind the pews, swooping and pretending to be a Spitfire. He stops suddenly to behold the organ overhead. He is awestruck.

'What's that?'

'It's a church organ – like a gigantic piano.'

He loses interest and runs off.

At last he finds some entertainment at the back of the church in the play area. I leave him to play with rubber dinosaurs. I am home. I have returned into the fold.

I take a seat in a pew behind the thick round pillar separating the transepts. It's right at the back, so I'm not too far away from Josh. I want to keep an eye on him, but soon I am lost in my own thoughts – in my past. Emotions rage inside me. Questions crowd my head.

How has it come to this? How did my soul land within the body of this woman, Camilla Bramley-Jones of all people? I never even knew of her existence. There was an accident, I know this much. Her car collided with my motorbike. I remember it vividly now. What they say is true: seconds before you die, your soul departs your body. And so did mine. But it didn't go very far. It shot off like a bullet and struck Camilla's eyes. I remember those eyes – rounded in shock, with the black of her pupils spilling over her irises. And then, nothing... So, here I am, inside her carnal persona, haplessly living her life and now, at last, reliving my own memories. But how did it happen?

How was it possible? This isn't a possession. I am not a demon. I didn't take on this woman's form to corrupt her. I am just me – Joseph Steedman, a priest. Why is my soul not my own anymore? Why is it trapped inside Camilla? More and more questions crowd into my head, questions to which I have no answers. Am I dead? I must be... Has my earthly body expired? It must have since my soul has left it, but... What happened to Camilla's soul? It isn't here, with me. Has she gone off into the afterlife, leaving her mortal shell for me to take over, like a snail?

My musings are disrupted by the creaky sound of the sacristy door opening behind the altar. I know that sound. Those hinges have been crying out to be oiled for years. I never got round to doing that. I crane my neck to see who it is. Before I do, there is another sound – that of a metal bucket being dropped onto the tiled stone floor. I know it is Jane Cuthbert before I even cast my eyes upon her. There she is, pressing a mop into the funnel of the bucket, her back to me. I recognise those firm round buttocks that I have been resisting since I employed her as a cleaner. God sent that woman to lead me to temptation – to test my chastity. If I am not mistaken, I passed that test with flying colours. But it took some serious self-denial.

I clasp my hand on my mouth to prevent a gasp of joy from escaping and alarming poor Jane. I just sit there and watch her work. I will have to speak to her to explain as best I can that I am back, only in... an altered form.

The descending afternoon sun penetrates the stained-glass windows and the whole interior of the church is filled with the phantasmagoria of dancing lights and colours. I go down on my knees, convinced that God is about to speak to me and make it all clear at last. I feel that unbearable lightness of being, that only a soul, free of its material shell, can feel. I want to sing and cry, both at the same time. I am happy. I am at peace, until-

I didn't hear him arrive. He walks past my pew, softly and without a sound. It is more a slither than a walk. I look up just to catch his profile. I recognise him in an instant. My heart sinks to the bottom of my gut. It's the Prophet.

JOSEPH

The police station appears to be as deserted a place as the church. We are the only two people waiting in the reception (if *reception* is the correct word for it. It is a waiting parlour after a fashion). Shady characters, some drunk, some raving mad, some subdued and bewildered, are occasionally led by uniformed officers through the entrance and taken down to the cells behind a locked gate. They vanish there as quickly as they appear, followed by a faint whiff of alcohol fumes and disagreeable language.

Armed with a portfolio of newspaper articles we have printed off the internet, we remain steadfast in our resolve to see a police detective. Two hours later one is delivered into our clutches.

'I'm Detective Constable Heron.' A man in his thirties with thinning red hair and a long chin is peering at us from the height of his 6ft"2. He indeed resembles a long-legged heron with the strong beak of his chin and, fleetingly, I wonder if *heron* may in fact be his nickname.

I crane my neck to look behind him, half-expecting to see someone older and of higher rank. DCI Barnaby is who I have in mind. After all, we are to report a serial killer and a mere constable seems a little light-weight. Alas, Barnaby or Morse do not join us.

'I understand you have a serious crime to report. Multiple murders?' He is gazing at us doubtfully.

'Indeed,' I say, and Jane nods her agreement.

'OK. I will take your statement. If you can follow me, please.'

We tread behind Heron who takes us to a minimalist interview room featuring furniture dating probably to the early eighties. We sit around a foldable table, in foldable chairs. I suspect a picnic basket may be on its way when DC Heron asks if we would like any beverages, mentioning tea, coffee or water.

We decline all of the above. We have waited long enough. Our respective bladders are bursting as it is, and neither of us is keen on using the police station facilities.

'I hope you don't mind me recording this interview,' DC Heron asks.

'Not at all.' I am impressed with the idea of speaking for the tape in an interrogation room. It's one of the things on my bucket list. This also means that we are being taken seriously.

He switches on the machine and makes the necessary introductions, instructing us to state our names clearly for the tape (even though there is no tape anywhere in sight. Still, it's the thought that matters). I am beginning to feel slightly hot under the collar, but Jane looks as cool as a cucumber.

'So, who would like to start?' DC Heron asks as if it is a game of snakes and ladders.

'It'd be me,' Jane begins. 'I was attacked at the beginning of March by a man. He put me in hospital. He cut my wrists and made it look like suicide. I'd have bled to death but for Father Joseph. He found me in the nick of time and called an ambulance. You should have it all on record 'cos your colleagues came to the hospital and took my statement. I never heard from them again, mind. My guess is they didn't believe that I was attacked by a psychopath. Your people thought that I had a bad day and did it myself. But it's all there in my statement if you care to check.'

'I will, of course,' DC Heron nods meekly.

'OK. You do that.' Jane rounds on him with a critical eye. She is a tough cookie, that Jane Cuthbert, I muse admiringly.

'So, truth be told, you didn't have much to go on 'cos I couldn't remember much about the man and what happened exactly. But this afternoon I saw him. And I recognised him. I told Father Joseph,' her voice wobbles a bit at this point. She is not a seasoned liar, 'and he followed him. I was too scared to go with the Father. I still have nightmares... But I was sure it was the man who tried to kill me.'

Her voice is tremulous and emotions break through the surface of her cool demeanour when she says she was scared. I take over. It's my turn anyway. 'Yes, as Jane said – I did follow him from the church to Milne Way. That's where I lost him, I'm afraid. It's a cul-de-sac. I have no idea where he went from there. Perhaps that's where he lives.'

'You say you followed him from the church,' Heron says. 'So, Miss Cuthbert, you spotted the man physically present in the vicinity of the church, is that right? He came to the church?'

Jane nods, her jaw visibly tightening.

'That's why we're concerned,' I point out, 'that he came to finish the job. Jane's life may be in danger.'

Heron shifts in his foldable chair which creaks with alarm. He rises to his feet, his long torso extending like a monocular telescope. 'I'll have to leave you for a few minutes. I need to ask my senior officer to join us.'

That's better, I am thinking while we're waiting. I squeeze Jane's hand to offer her reassurance. I can feel it is very cold and still trembling, but she doesn't withdraw it from me. In fact, she reciprocates and tries to smile. 'We're doing alright, Father.'

DC Heron returns with DI Edwards, a thickset man in his fifties, closely resembling DCI Barnaby from the golden era of Midsomer Murders. Introductions are made and we are asked to repeat everything with more details added in response to DI Edwards's incisive questioning. Jane agrees to help their sketch artist to put together a portrait of the culprit for release to the public. I don't hold much hope for that to be of particular use due to the bushy beard and oversized beanie featuring prominently in the whole image. Mrs Keating certainly didn't recognise the man from my description of him.

The detectives thank us for doing our citizen's duty and it looks like the interview may be at an end. However, we haven't yet arrived at the heart of the matter. I catch Jane's eye and gesture towards our portfolio lying in her lap.

'That's not all,' she says.

The officers settle back in their chairs.

'When I saw him – the man,' she is lying again so her volume is low and her voice tremors, 'I remembered what happened the night he attacked me. He talked to me about the other women he... he killed. I wasn't the only one.'

The air thickens with expectancy. DCI Edwards bites his upper lip and DC Heron's eyes widen under his intensely furrowed forehead.

'He stayed with me while I was lying there, dying. I mean, after he slit my veins, he stayed to boast about his other... victims. He was... very proud of himself. It all came back to me when I saw him, you see?'

The officers nod in unison. I join them, crossing my fingers behind my back. I should be telling them this, but I can't. The damned seal of confession! I just hope Jane doesn't slip up. I'm rooting for her. I will definitely grant her absolution for bearing false witness.

'I remembered the places, the timings and when he said it happened. He told me how he did it. He gave me names, but... I forgot them.'

At this point I want to kick her ankle under the table. She is going too far. He can't have known the names of most of his victims. They were randomly selected in what were opportunistic attacks. I don't do the kicking, but I jump in.

'Well, when Jane told me about them, we – the two of us – researched the internet archives for the news of those poor souls. We found most of them, names and all. Here,' I pick up the folder containing the printouts from Jane's lap, and slide it across the table to DCI Edwards, 'we printed all the cases Jane remembered and we were lucky to find mentions of them in the news. You can have it.'

DCI Edwards picks up the folder and starts paging through the articles and announcements we have printed. He is totally absorbed in this activity.

I am not good at sitting still and idle so I fill the silence with speculation: 'You can probably see it for yourself, detectives – it is staring you in the face, really: the man is a serial killer. But he's also very careful. He never strikes twice in the same place or using the same method. We're so lucky – in a way – that he... um... confided in Jane. He, of course, thought she'd die and his secret would die with her. But, well, we got him!

'We... I mean, you – you really have to act quickly to find him. Before he kills again. I don't think he's going to stop of his own volition. The man is a fanatic. Religious fanatic, you see–'

I'm interrupted by DCI Edwards before I reveal more than I would be reasonably expected to know. When he speaks, I realise it doesn't matter. He doesn't believe us anyway.

'So... Miss Jane Cuthbert,' he pronounces her name

pointedly, 'you're telling us that this serial killer who attacked you in March was somehow able to tell you about the murder he committed three months later – in June? The young lady who jumped off the bridge in Swindon, I mean. He predicted that... Or was it some form of forward planning on his part?'

Jane and I gaze at each other hopelessly. We have no answers unless we hit a reverse button and revert to the truth about the man's confession – to me. I don't know what stops me. It may be the fact that I feel utterly stupid and I know that no matter what I tell them now, they won't believe a word I say.

'You do realise that wasting police time is an offence?' DCI Edwards stands up and leaves the room.

What occurs afterwards uncoils like an overwound clock spring. We don't have time to regroup or to think of our next step. It is the nutter who takes charge of the situation. All we can do is react.

Our misfired trip to the police station is a fresh memory from which we're still smarting. This is Saturday – the morning after. Jane and I haven't spoken a word to each other. After breakfast I retreat to my office to work on my homily for tomorrow. Jane proceeds to the church, mop in hand, to get on with her Saturday cleaning.

The day is luxuriously warm and calm. I open my window overlooking the cemetery. Birds are singing in the treetops. Leaves are rustling faintly like gently handled tissue paper. I am halfway through my sermon and briefly peer out of the window, searching the sky for a word that seems to have escaped me. It happens to me sometimes that I lose words. This one is right there on the tip of my tongue. I just need to focus and be still for a few seconds, and it will come to me.

That's when I see him.

It is unmistakably the psychotic nutter: the same woolly beanie, black hoodie and false beard. I now have no doubt that it is false – it has come loose under his temple it sits lopsided on his face. He is snaking across the graveyard, stealthily, on his bent knees, his shoulders hunched. He seems to have come from the north-east corner of the cemetery where the compost heaps are. He reaches the path leading to the church's main entrance.

Jane is there, alone.

She is in lethal danger.

Panicked, I look around my study, but I don't know – or can't remember – what exactly I am looking for. I abandon the idea of finding it. I drop everything, and run.

In the hallway I now remember that what I was trying to find was my mobile. Too late now to go back and fetch it, I decide. The landline phone is also in my office. I ought to call the police. I waste precious time, hesitating. Calling 999 may cost me more time that I don't have. How long will it take him to kill Jane? Seconds?

I run.

I cross the churchyard between the priory and the church, go through the door and burst into the nave.

What I am confronted with is an apocalyptic scene. Jane is sprawled on the floor awkwardly. She is not moving. But there is more than enough commotion. A middle-aged woman is leaping in long strides towards the man and jumps onto his back. She wraps her legs around his waist and is punching the living daylights out of him. He struggles to dislodge her, spinning on the spot and trying to protect his head with his hands. His beard is flapping, holding on to his left ear for dear life. His beanie has departed from his head. It's always been too big for him. He has limp, mousy-brown hair. I still can't see his face.

I am momentarily spellbound and paralysed with

indecision. Should I perhaps run back to the priory and call the cops, or should I intervene—

'Grandma!!!' A young boy – maybe seven years of age – emerges from the play area and springs towards the battleground by the altar.

As I watch his tiny frame, I have a moment of instant recognition. A flash of bright light blinds me, and then I can see. I can see it all. The whole world spins around me.

...

This is Joshua, my grandson. I am Camilla Bramley-Jones. Mills to those who know me well. I am her, but at the same time I'm standing fifty yards away from her, watching as she grips the nutter's back with her thighs, doing her best to scratch his eyes out.

Josh is running away from me (the passive me, the me standing at the back of the church and watching everything in slow motion). He is running straight into the mouth of danger.

...

'Joshua, stop!' I scream and launch after him. I grab him mid-flight and push him firmly into the pews. I put my finger to my lips, 'Shhh,' I say, 'Climb under that bench and don't come out until I tell you.'

He stares at me bamboozled, but does as he is told. That must be a first!

I leave him there safe and hurry towards the carnage by the altar. For a split second, I fear I am too late. The nutter has displaced Mills from his back. She falls to the floor, on her back and I can see her eyes flash with terror as he presses his knee into her chest and reaches for her throat with his clawed hands.

I am upon them. In my mind I'm no longer the big and manly Father Joseph – I am again a small, frail female in her mid-fifties. I am Mills. *You cannot tackle this man, logic tells me.* Frantically, I search the altar for a reliable weapon.

I find it. It is a large silver crucifix encrusted with jewels. I grab it and take a swing at the man's head. I whack it with all my might. He slumps onto Mills. Hers and my eyes meet for a split second and we blink out stupefaction at each other. She recovers her wits faster than me.

'Call the cops,' she wheezes.

I whack the assailant again, for good measure, before I dash back to the priory to finally dial the bloody 999.

The church hasn't been this busy since I arrived in the parish. It's teeming with police and forensic officers, as well as paramedics in their green uniforms. They carry Jane out on a stretcher. She is conscious, praise be, but suffered cuts to her chest and neck area that will require stitching. The bastard came armed with a kitchen knife. The knife is being packed into an evidence bag by a man in a blue boiler suit. Jane gives me a faint smile and lets her eyelids drop. The smile lingers on her lips. It's unusual, I note, because she is not a smiley person. Ever since I've known her she has either wept or scowled. This is her first beatific manifestation. I'm pleased for her. She is no longer afraid. She is at peace.

Jane's stretcher is followed closely by another one. This one carries the nutter. He, too, is alive though unconscious. In the privacy of my own head, I congratulate myself on the blows I dealt him. I knocked the bastard for six.

I look at his calm, pale face. It is hard to believe that I know this individual. I know him as an ordinary, God-fearing young man from a decent family well established in the community. His mother is my most ardent parishioner – a woman possessed of strong Christian principles. It is unfathomable that she would raise a serial killer. Because that's exactly what her son is – Rory Keating is a serial killer.

His mother will never accept it. Never.

I can't imagine, not for one second, that Mrs Keating was aware of what Rory was getting up to in the night. Maybe she had some suspicions but she'd have banished them from her mind, just like any loving mother would. I am a mother. I can understand that. I stood by my prodigal son despite the evidence of his guilt staring me in the face. I'll always stand by him, I suppose. To my mind Christopher will always be an innocent little boy with big blue eyes and golden locks, riding his rocking horse and shouting, 'Giddy-up! Giddy-up!'. I remember being appalled when he was convicted and sentenced to prison. I was angry with the judge, the jury, the whole justice system. I was furious with Hugh for abandoning Christopher to the wolves. I was convinced they were all wrong, stupid and malicious. And I believed in my son even when I suspected that he may be lying. Because a mother has to keep faith in her child. And I do – to this day, I do. Mrs Keating will be no different. I briefly ponder whether I should be the one to tell her about Rory. She may find it easier if the news comes from her priest.

The two stretchers, one carrying Rory and the other Jane, leave the church building together. Their proximity to each other makes me feel uncomfortable. It occurs to me that I can't let that man – conscious or unconscious – be near Jane. I am suddenly panic-stricken. I call out to DCI Edwards. 'Don't put them in the same ambulance! The man is a nutter,' I tell him.

He smiles ruefully. 'Of course not, Father. Rest assured, Miss Cuthbert will be safe.'

He has already taken my statement, and apologised for not taking us seriously when we came to the station.

I wouldn't have believed myself, I said to him, *such things only happen in bad films.*

And in life, he added.

I peer towards Mills. I still find it extraordinarily unsettling to be looking at myself with somebody else's eyes. It's like an out-of-body experience. And me talking about myself in the third person is even more bizarre. I wonder if this state of affairs is only temporary or if I will have to get used to being someone else.

She gazes back at me, equally shell-shocked. I wonder if she knows that she isn't quite herself – that I am her. She may well do. Otherwise, how would she have found her way here, to The Sacred Heart? Was she guided by the real Father Joseph? Has he brought her here?

I'm glad she isn't badly hurt. The medics decided she didn't require a trip to the hospital.

DC Heron is talking to her – asking her questions about what happened. She is economic with descriptions (I wouldn't be) and limits herself to nodding and shaking her head, with a few monosyllabic grunts in between. Her eyes leave me and stray over to the back of the church, and that's where they freeze in horror.

'Joshua!' she screams. 'Where's Josh?'

DC Heron looks baffled. 'Who's Joshua, ma'am?' he asks.

She jumps to her feet. 'A little boy, my grandson. He was in the play area. Where is he!'

'Joshua!' I too jump to my feet. I totally forgot. How could I? What sort of grandmother am I!

I leap in long strides towards the pew where I told Joshua to hide, hoping to God Almighty that he is still there. I kneel on the floor and crane my head to search under the benches. A small face with wide eyes is peering back at me.

'Can I come out now?' he asks me.

'Yes! It's all over now. Out you come, young man.'

I can't help pulling him into my arms and kissing him all over his little ginger head. I feel every copper's alert eyes on my back. They're thinking, *What is that mad priest doing to the little boy? Pervert!*

Mills darts towards us and joins in with the group hug. She doesn't push me away. We must be suffocating poor Joshua for he begins to wriggle under our vice-like embrace and frees himself. DC Heron asks him if he is OK, who he is and if he knows either of us.

'My name is Joshua Bramley-Jones,' he replies eloquently, and points to Mills, 'and that's my grandma.' Then he gestures towards me and says matter-of-factly, 'And he gave me some of his chips, in the shop, the other day. So I know him too.'

'We're all old friends,' I add, holding back tears of joy.

Later in the afternoon, when the emergency services finally leave the scene, Joseph and I, stranded in each other's carnal form, sit on a bench under the chestnut tree regally rooted in the centre of the graveyard. From here, we can keep an eye on Joshua who is trampling over the graves, flapping his arms and claiming to be a vampire. At some point, I have to chastise him for trying to dig up the dead from one of the freshest graves.

'Vampires don't do that, Joshua. Stop the digging now.'

'I saw a film and they dug graves there. I saw it!' He is obstinate, like his grandad.

'They were necromancers, not vampires.'

'What are micromans?'

'They're bad people, worse than vampires.'

'That's what I am – a microman!'

Joseph steps in. He is quite protective over the people he buried here in his many years. 'I wouldn't do it if I were you.'

'Why?'

'If you dig up a dead person, they'll haunt you for the rest of your life. They don't like their sleep disturbed.'

'I'm not scared of ghosts,' Joshua puffs up his cheeks.

'And they will smell and have maggots crawling out of their eyeholes,' Joseph's voice drops to an ominous whisper.

Joshua wrinkles his nose. He is looking a little hesitant.

'Just stick with being a vampire,' I suggest helpfully.

'OK.' He opens his arms and flies away.

We have promised him a trip to McDonald's for burgers and French fries, provided he gives us a few minutes to talk in private. Now is our chance to compare notes.

The chestnut tree offers welcome shade. The day has been hot, in more ways than one. Dappled specks of light dance on what used to be *my* face. I keep staring at the woman sat next to me, searching her eyes for traces of Joseph – for some distortion of light in them, for something alien and masculine. I can't see anything. The knowledge that it is I who belong in that body could not be proved if proof was asked for.

'How long have you known?' I ask him.

'I've only realised this morning. We went down to the canal to float a boat Josh and I made, and that's when I bumped into my old pals: Loki, Jeremiah – the old brigade from my previous life... That was it. I knew who I was. Everything came back to me in a flash. It was some sort of ... rapture. If I ever witnessed a miracle, that was it. And you?'

'When I ran into the church, Joshua popped out of the play area. I saw him, and I knew. I thought my heart would break out of my ribcage.'

'Yes, it was quite a shock. I still can't figure out how it happened.'

'The accident, I suppose.'

'The accident, yes...' he furrows his forehead pensively. 'We collided with each other on the road, my motorbike slammed into your car door; glass shattered... That was the accident, yes, but how did we... how did we jump ship?'

'I don't know,' I say truthfully. 'You should know – you're the priest!'

He chuckles and throws his arms in the air. 'It beats me, I'm afraid. Strange forces have been at work, and here we are – in each other's skins, as it were.'

I scrutinise my old body with a critical eye. That man is in charge of it now and I don't like what he's done to it. 'I can't believe what you did to my nails!' I can't stop myself from saying that. I used to take such great pride in my nails. Joseph desecrated them – he's hacked them down to the skin. I can see dirt compressed under his thumb nails as if he used them to scratch tar out of tarmac. Judging by the torn cuticles I suspect he is partial to chewing his – my – nails. I am disgusted, and oddly bereaved.

'And you had a haircut,' he points out, his lips twisted with dismay. 'I liked my hair long. It was the rebel in me. I loved the wind in my hair when I rode my bike on country roads – the sense of unbridled freedom.'

'I don't like motorbikes. I got rid of yours. It was a write-off anyway. I have a nice and practical Fiat Uno now,' I inform him, wickedly pleased with myself.

'Fiat bloody Uno?' He scowls, dismayed.

'That's what I prefer, and let's face it, it's my life now.'

'As yours is mine,' he retorts with a devilish smile.

'Is there a way we can reclaim our rightful bodies?' A priest should know, I am hoping, how to restore the natural order. A reversed miracle, perhaps? What should happen now is me returning to myself, taking my grandson's hand and driving us home to Middle Norton to be reunited with Hugh.

But Joseph doesn't know how to make that happen. He scratches his head doubtfully. 'Not a clue,' he says with resignation, 'I fear we may be sentenced to each other for life.

Maybe after death, there'll be some kind of soul exchange at Heaven's door.'

'You're joking, right?'

'No, I truly don't know how we can back out of this absurd situation.'

I nod, sad but not entirely despondent. I look around me and relish my new home: the priory where, in my study, I can read the Bible and prepare sermons. I have to confess (but only to myself) that I enjoy preaching. People come every Sunday to listen to me – to Camilla Bramley-Jones, a housewife, who has never done a day of real work – instructing them about life, love, good and evil, and how to tell the difference. Now I have a chance to prove myself, to earn a living and be of use to my flock. I love it. I wouldn't swap it for my old meaningless existence.

'In that case I'm happy to stay here and carry on with your work,' I say.

He laughs. 'That's more than I was prepared to do. You don't know this but I was planning to leave the priesthood. I gave my notice to the Bishop.'

'Yes, I know. I took it back.'

His laughter reminds me briefly of the old Mills, of how I used to be before I married Hugh and became his mainstay. Before I lost myself in his needs and demands. Before he absorbed me into the fabric of his ever so important career. Come to think of it, I realise, by being here without him I have found the old Mills. I consider myself lucky.

I ask Joseph, 'And you? Are you happy being...me?'

'No,' says he. 'Middle-class housewifery isn't my style. Poor Hugh isn't too pleased either. He's been sleeping in the spare room for weeks now. He's getting cranky.'

It's my turn to chortle. I can just see Hugh's face as he is being denied his conjugal rights night in and night out. 'He'll have to find solace in his pipe,' I comment. 'I bet he hasn't given up?'

'Smokes like a chimney – the pipe, cigars, cigarettes. No one tells him to stop. I have an occasional one myself.'

I am not happy about that. 'Please don't do that to my body,' I plead.

'Only if you let my hair grow.'

We shake on it, and sit silently for a few minutes watching Joshua play amongst the headstones.

'So, how's everything at home? Have you seen Christopher?'

'Yes,' he nods, 'and there's something I must tell you, about Christopher.'

I bite my lip. I fear the news isn't good. It never is around Christopher.

'I found bank accounts he opened in your name. Do you know anything about them?'

I shake my head.

'I suspected as much. He kept his spoils in those accounts, nearly half a million quid. It wasn't his money, you know that, don't you?'

I sit, stiff and tight-lipped. I don't want to hear it.

'Well, anyway, I gave it all back. To his victims. It had to be done.'

'I know,' I manage to say. This feels like the final nail in the coffin of my maternal faith in my son. But it is also a second chance, for Christopher. I look into Joseph's eyes (he is somewhere there behind the narrow pupils), and say, 'Thank you, Joseph.'

'Glad to be of service. Can I ask for something in return?'

'As long as it's legal,' I try to sound glib and cool. 'Fire away.'

'My narrowboat... I have a narrowboat on the canal. The papers are in your name. I spent years restoring it and I'd love it back. I don't think you'd have much use for it. Would you mind selling it to me, at a discount?'

'It's yours.'

'Thanks,' says he. 'Is there anything you'd like me to get you from home?'

'No,' I say, after a short reflection. 'I have no use for my old wardrobe, and I can get a new anti-wrinkle cream on my priestly stipend. Your face does need intense moisturising. Try to take better care of mine, will you?'

He nods. I notice his fingers are crossed.

'Of course, I'd like to be able to see Joshua,' I say, something catching in my throat.

'Yes, we'll make a plan for regular visits. I'll tell Hugh I found God and need a priest close by to guide me.'

'Thank you, Joseph.'

'Joe. Call me Joe.'

'I'm Mills to friends and family. You're a friend, aren't you?'

'There you are, then.' He smiles pleasantly at me. 'I guess we could go further and say we're soulmates.'

'Very unlikely ones,' I feel compelled to point out.

Joshua shouts to us from behind a moss-draped stone angel. 'I'm hungry! You promised we'd have McDonalds!'

We head for the nearest outlet. I suppose I can always have a salad and tea.

PART 5

THE END IS NIGH

JOSEPH
(CAMILLA, ACTUALLY)

I'm driving my small but perfectly formed Fiat Uno along the winding country roads of North-East Wiltshire. They can be quite treacherous, and these days I am extra cautious. The last thing I want is another accident. This lane is narrow, strangulated by thick, overhanging foliage of roadside hedging and trees. These roads date back to the era of the Anglo-Saxons. Not far from here an epic battle took place some eight hundred years ago. I am not surprised – the hilly and unpredictable terrain would make a perfect battle ground.

I am heading for the village of Erlestoke, and more to the point, to Her Majesty's correctional facility located there. I have recently secured the position of Prison Chaplain. So far I have two inmates who have accepted my support. There are others who are considering it. I am working on them. My firm belief is that nobody is entirely evil, that deep down, inside every man lingers goodness, care and even love, and those qualities can be teased out of people with the right approach and a lot of patience. I think most crimes are the result of a misunderstanding. Some people misunderstand what is good for them – and what is good for them, I think, is being good to others, or as the Bible has it: doing unto others as you would have them do unto you.

One of my two Erlestoke parishioners is Rory Keating. He and I have been working our guts out to correct his misconceptions about God's will. We have already covered Mary Magdalene and how she was given a chance to transform from a harlot to a saint, and lived to become one of Christ's greatest successes. Letting fallen women live to give them that chance is an objective Rory is slowly adopting as his own. There have been hiccups along the way – two steps forward, one step back, as the saying goes – but I'm not a quitter. I will have Rory Keating converted to the bright side of life by the time he's out. Admittedly, time is on my side. Rory has received a life sentence with the minimum term of twenty years without parole.

Today we will celebrate the life of Selina Cortés, the last of his victims. She was the young woman he tracked down in Swindon, kidnapped and threw off the bridge onto the carriageway below. A car drove over her body in the early hours of the following morning before the driver realised that there was something lying in the road. She was dead by then.

As with the other victims, I have compiled as much deeply personal information as I was allowed access to. I want Rory to get to know them – really get to know them.

I show him a photograph of a young man in a wheelchair, a tube taped to his cheek. The tube leads to an oxygen bottle attached at the back of the chair. You can tell that the young man's eyes are smiling because wrinkles shoot out of the corners of this eyes. Because of the tube, you can't see his lips. Above his head hangs a HAPPY BIRTHDAY banner, light twinkling in the silver foil. Next to the young man stands a beaming Selina.

'That night,' I tell Rory, who is staring at the photo mulishly, 'James Cross was celebrating his twenty-first birthday. He suffers from motor-neurone disease. It's a degenerative condition – he will never get better. Selina was his carer – his favourite carer, his parents tell me. He wept when he was told she had killed herself. And he wept again at your trial, when it turned out that it was you. She wouldn't have done it – she wouldn't have abandoned James. He couldn't understand why anyone would do something so evil to that girl. She was his angel.

'So it follows, Rory, that she wasn't a harlot. Can you see that? You made a mistake – a grievous mistake.'

Rory takes his eyes off the photo and nails them to the floor. A stubborn scowl sits on his face. I am familiar with it. It comes out when Rory believes there are mitigating circumstances. It is usually an assertion that he had been *led on*, as it is in this case.

'It's her fault. She was barely covered – low top, short skirt, like a slut. I've proof. I took photos of her.'

'I know, Rory. The police found them. Your mother was devastated when they showed her what you did to that girl.'

'What was I s'posed to make of her? Flaunting herself, she was. Led me on,' he mutters grudgingly.

'She was dressed for a party, Rory. Remember? I told you it was James's twenty-first. She left later than she intended, became confused in the dark and got off at the wrong stop. She wasn't soliciting – she was lost.'

Rory mutters an apology under his breath.

'That's good, Rory,' I rejoice. 'That's a good start. Are you going to write to James?'

'Maybe I will,' he mumbles.

I leave him to it. Next month, when I return, we will be talking about Jane Cuthbert. I left her till last because she is still alive and Rory will have a chance to address his letter to her. If he chooses to write it.

My second Erlestoke parishioner is a harder nut to crack. He is a non-believer, by which I mean he doesn't believe in anything but himself. It is difficult to point out the errors of their ways to people who have no convictions other than their own self-interest.

He is ungrateful and cunning. I can tell that he entertains me only because he thinks there is something in it for him, and that something isn't his salvation. He is charming and polite, but, when I raised the subject of his victims with him, I felt like I was banging my head against a brick wall. It was the brick wall of his indifference.

He is bitter too. He was supposed to be out by last Christmas but he failed to persuade the Parole Board that he was a man rehabilitated. They saw through him. I remember his rage when he told me about it. He frightened me.

This man is hard work but I won't give up on him. I will save his soul if it kills me.

There is a knock on the door of my small room.

'Come in, Christopher,' I invite him.

CAMILLA
(JOSEPH, ACTUALLY)

Morning has just broken. Dew sits undisturbed on the grass, shimmering mischievously in the rising sun. Ducks have emerged from the reeds, quacking and calling out to each other to spread the word that the humans are out and about – crumbs of bread from breakfast tables may be on offer. A squadron of ducks swoop to the mooring area. Two swans are paddling from the direction of the bridge, eager to partake in the feast.

We are walking from the car park area – Hugh, Yvonne, Josh and I. Hugh is kind enough to carry my heaviest suitcase. I have to accept that a woman's body has its limitations when it comes to weight lifting, so I carry Joshua's rucksack. Joshua carries his lunch box. Yvonne, her canvas bag.

My old mates are gathered on the bank: Loki, Jeremiah, Ruthie and even her father leaning on his Zimmer frame. They know who I am – who I really am under the skin of a middle-aged woman with fading highlights. It didn't surprise me at all that they weren't shocked in the least when I told them the truth. They are the only people, apart from me and Mills of course, who know. They took the news in their stride as if a man's soul stranded inside another person's body was the most ordinary, commonplace occurrence. I guess it was the way I played the drums – that was what convinced them. We played drums – Loki, Jeremiah and I – through the night, like we used to. Ruthie and Trudy danced. We were pissed as newts. That was last Saturday, a week ago. That Saturday when everything started to make sense again.

We approach my boat. Before Hugh steps onboard with my bags, he pauses and fixes me with a semi-plaintive and semi-apologetic gaze. He has been beating himself up over this – blaming his inattention and selfishness – since I told him I was leaving.

'Are you really sure?' he asks for the millionth time.

'I am, Hugh, I truly am.' I speak for myself, but also for Camilla. She too has made a choice to leave him.

'Look,' he is muttering, clearly embarrassed to be begging, 'we could change a few things... I could change – give you more... What is it that you want, Mills? More independence? More holidays?' He has begun to speculate, again. 'We could book a cruise to the Tropics. A five-star cruise ship, three gourmet meals a day, entertainment, sightseeing on the open seas–'

'I'm happy with my narrowboat. It's my home,' I inform him.

'Your home is... at home,' he reminds me, a twitch of frustration pulling at his lip. 'Keep the boat, I don't mind. We can have it refurbished, and all that. Just take a short break, sail away but – please, Mills, come back home.'

I am sorry for him. This has nothing to do with him. My decision was made all those years ago when I first bought the wreck of this narrowboat and began to dream. Poor Hugh Bramley-Jones has been pulled into something beyond his control, and beyond his imagination. I can't tell him the truth. He couldn't handle it. He would probably have me committed.

He threatened that behind my back, to Yvonne, when I went out of the room, but I heard him. I'm not taking chances against the best barrister in the whole of the South West.

I touch his shoulder. That's all I can bring myself to do in terms of intimacy between us. Anything more would feel queer, in all possible ways. 'We'll stay in touch, Hugh. This is my world and it's where I belong. But I'll always come back here, to this spot. Every time, I swear, I'll pop over for a beer.'

He frowns at the idea. Of course, once again, I am acting out of character – out of his wife's character.

'...or for a cup of tea,' I modify my earlier statement. 'And I'll be back in September to drop off Josh and Yvonne.'

'Yeah, Grandad. Don't worry. We'll be back,' Josh assures Hugh from his end. Josh is beside himself with excitement. He is going on a boat trip. I suspect he is looking forward to swimming with sharks at some point of this voyage even though I explained to him that English canals are not sharks' natural habitat. *There was a shark lost in The Thames,* he countered me. There was no arguing with him. He will see for himself. He may yet prove me wrong.

Hugh is defeated. The undefeatable barrister is overcome by events beyond logic and reason. He expels a heavy sigh and heaves my suitcase onto the deck. He helps all three of us onboard over the gangplank. He hugs his sister and Josh, and gives me a curt nod.

We wave to him, and he waves back, haltingly. I go into the cabin and start the engine. I manoeuvre my beautiful narrowboat out into the canal. Did I mention that I named her *The Soulmate?* A fitting title, I reckon. *The Soulmate* is followed by three other boats. Loki, Jeremiah and Ruth are joining me on this adventure. Loki said I would need all the help I can get, *considering my current state.* I think he meant my frailty as a woman. I don't feel weak or fragile. I guess I've got used to being a woman. Nevertheless, I will enjoy their company.

We travel in single file, a bit like a mother duck with her ducklings in tow. I look up towards the far bank where a lone cow is grazing on top of the hill. The mysteries that cow has witnessed! I chuckle under my breath. I show the cow to Josh.

'See there,' I say, pointing to the beast.

'Yeah,' he nods, 'it's the same cow. It's got titties. Bulls don't have them.'

'Right you are!'

Our flotilla of three narrowboats and one battered and rusty motorboat glides into the rising sun.

THE END

ABOUT THE AUTHOR

Best known for her crime fiction, Anna Legat is the author of cosy mysteries *The Shires*, the flint-sharp *DI Gillian Marsh* detective series, and *Goode's Law*, a trilogy of legal thrillers set on the international stage.

Murder isn't the only thing on Anna's mind. She also writes historical fiction and her ideal genre would be where history and crime converge. She is currently working on a historical crime series, *A Case for Copernicus*, set in Renaissance Europe at the turn of the XV century.

Anna read law with European political history at university. Apart from writing, she has been making a living as a lawyer, a teacher, a silver-service waitress and a librarian (not all at the same time). She has lived in far-flung places but has now settled in a small town near the beautiful city of Bath.

A NOTE FROM THE PUBLISHER

Thank you for reading this book. If you enjoyed it please do consider leaving a review on Amazon to help others find it too.

We hate typos. All of our books have been rigorously edited and proofread, but sometimes mistakes do slip through. If you have spotted a typo, please do let us know and we can get it amended within hours.

info@bloodhoundbooks.com